Fairy Tale Murders

BY **Kelly Money**

PUBLISHED BY FIDELI PUBLISHING INC.

ISBN: 978-1-60414-804-6

Special Dedication goes out to my friend, mentor and inspiration, Marilyn Little, who passed away in February of 2013. Thank you for bringing Jill into my life and always sitting on the patio listening to my ideas. Your inspiration and strength has touched me in so many ways and I miss you dearly. As you would say, "Life is fun...if you don't weaken." Thanks for helping me stay strong.

I appreciate all who have helped me through this process. Special thanks to Faby for all the exhausting re-reads and sleeping with one eye open. ;) Evelyn thanks for keeping it real and being honest. I also want to give special thanks to Janelle & Jim (Mom and Dad) for always encouraging me to keep working at it, as you have with everything in my life. Audra, if it wasn't for you I would never have such a great cover for the book. Much Appreciated!

Finally...sorry boys, you can't read this book for quite a while. Just know you are loved.

Chapter 1

S tan lived in his father's basement. He was surrounded by his personal collection of books that provided him escapes from a world that didn't even know he existed.

This morning was no different from any other. He waited for his father to call his name, as it was time to leave for work, and they always rode to Country Haven Mortuary together. His father owned and ran it, just as his grandfather had done before him. Stan helped out around the mortuary, setting up the fixation forceps, bleeding jar and embalming fluid. He always felt that he should be in college, in the middle of his second year. Instead, he was stuck working in the family business with dead people.

Half asleep, he heard his father call down the stairs, signaling that they would leave in twenty minutes. They always arrived at work about twenty minutes before seven.

Getting out of bed every morning meant the same routine as every other day. Stan felt as if he had no pride in getting himself ready only to be ridiculed by his father. Each day after putting his clothes on he washed his face, sometimes shaved, and went upstairs for breakfast. The ride to work was always the same as it was this day. His father berated him about how he looked. "Take pride in your appearance, Son. This is how people see you." Stan simply nodded his head and stared down at his shoelaces. "Hair in your eyes, unshaven, shirt hanging out, it is pretty obvious why you don't have a girlfriend. Don't you want a girlfriend, Son?" Stan avoided answering as he counted the minutes until they arrived at work. "Answer me! Don't you care how you look?"

Stan realized that he had to answer for this to go away. "I understand," he replied. "I will try better tomorrow." He knew his reply wouldn't be enough.

"And to think, you wanted to be a doctor. You can't even take care of yourself, let alone other people."

I would be a great doctor, he thought to himself, but was afraid to say aloud. I have read every book I can get my hands on to learn. People would look up to me and respect me. Even you, Father, would be proud. That would scare you, though. Wouldn't it, Father? You couldn't handle your son being better than you, respected, and rich enough to take care of himself.

They pulled up in the mortuary's back driveway. Luckily, he knew that his father would lose all interest in talking, and instead start focusing on the work at hand.

Opening the mortuary was not a difficult thing to do. His father expected him to be close by to help but it always came with the price of Stan losing a little more self-esteem every day. After going through his normal routine, Stan went into the basement to prep the embalming room. They were normally the only ones working until midmorning — unless there was an appointment or a viewing. This morning their first viewing wasn't until eleven, so they had plenty of time to prep. He worked through his normal routine without incident, and continued going through his own fantasies of a different life. A new life filled with him being a doctor, a lawyer or even someone with even more power. More than anything Stan desired a power not only over him but someday others.

He smelled her before he saw her. He wanted to run away as fast as he could but as he turned the corner to head out, he almost ran directly into her.

"Excuse me, can you help me?" she asked. It took a few seconds for him to respond.

Stan's throat closed up as he attempted to speak, after a moment he said "Umm...yeah, do you want something?" He just wanted to get away as fast as he could. Before she could respond, he said, "Let me go get my father. He can help you. He will come right up." Stan started heading away as quickly as he could, but the woman stopped him again just as he started to turn the corner.

"Good grief! I am not going to bite. My name is Kristen Jackson and you are holding the viewing for my mother, Pauline Jackson, tomorrow afternoon. I am really hoping to see the room before the viewing. Will that be possible?"

It wasn't until he turned around that he noticed she had walked up right behind him while firing her questions. Trying not to sound irritated, he replied, "Once again, if you could just wait here, I am getting someone who can help you." He practically ran away without turning back, without knowing whether she tried to respond or not. Once he knew he was out of sight, he moved quickly, but remained careful not to run; his father could hear his footsteps from below, and he absolutely hated running. "Walk with purpose, Son, but don't run," he would say. "It makes you look weak."

Practically running through the embalming door, but careful not to slam it, Stan called for his father. "There is a woman who needs your help upstairs. She wants to talk to you."

"Well, what does she want?" his father replied from the back room.

After hesitating and thinking before he spoke he replied "She wants to see the room for the Jackson viewing tomorrow."

"Well, did you show it to her?"

"No, I told her I would get you. The room isn't ready and I don't know what to tell her." He prayed in his head that his father would just take care of this and not make him go back and talk to her. *Please... Please... Please....* He could feel the sweat running down his sides while he waited for his answer.

"Show her the room, don't be such a coward," his father said. "It's just showing a room, for god's sake. I am too busy getting things ready for when her mother arrives. I will meet with her later, after her mother has been prepped."

The walk back to the lobby was a much more labored walk; his strides were shorter as he tried to buy time. As he walked up to the client, he meekly tried to explain what his father told him to say.

"Follow me," he said, without making eye contact. "I will show you the room, but it isn't ready yet, so it may not even be worth your while." He turned and started walking, feeling her follow behind him. He could smell her as she walked behind him, and he could feel her tiny footsteps as she followed too closely.

"Here it is," he said as they entered the room. "I will just leave you to look around, and I am going to go back to work. I am sure you know the way out now." He turned to leave, knowing she would pester him with another question.

Sure enough, she couldn't resist. "Is there any way I can see the body sooner than tomorrow morning? I have my mother's favorite outfit for the viewing and I have brought you a photo so you know how she looked at her best."

"I will have to have someone contact you about that, but I don't see it happening," he hastily replied. "We won't get the body until today. Then she will get embalmed either later today or tonight, and then we will get her cleaned and made up."

She grimaced at his words. "I understand," she said. "I just want to make sure everything is in order."

This was when he caught a quick glimpse of her. Her eyes were all puffy from crying, and she just stood there like she had nowhere else to be. He took this as an opportunity to sneak away and get to his own work.

The day progressed very nicely, without any further interference from Kristen Jackson. Her mother arrived, but not until much later than expected. When this happened, Stan's father usually waited until after dinner to go back and embalm. Sometimes he made Stan come with him. He dreaded those nights.

"Okay, it is after six," his father eventually said. "Let's lock up, go home, and eat. We can come back later to finish."

Once his father made up his mind to do something, there was no changing it. Stan knew better than to tell him that what he really wanted was to go home and finish his book. So, resigned to what his father wanted, he just nodded his head in agreement.

The aroma of the meat cooking in the crock pot greeted him as he walked in the door. It wasn't until then that he realized how hungry he was. Going through his normal routine, he set the table and poured them both a glass of milk. Stan was hoping this would be one of those nights when his father decided to watch TV and eat, which meant Stan could eat downstairs, if he wanted.

"Sit down, Son," his said, as he continued moving around behind him. "I want to talk to you about some things."

Stan felt his whole body slump at the thought of hearing his lecture again. His mind started to wander as he struggled to drown out his speech.

"When I was a boy, my father would have never let me look so disheveled. You have no friends, no girlfriend, and no pride. Don't you want pride for yourself, Son?"

He could hear the pause, waiting to hear more about how he was a disappointment. Calculating how he wanted to respond to this, he waited for a second prompt, knowing it was on its way. He waited and waited, but all he could hear was silence. The next thing he heard was a big gasp coming from behind him. It startled him, because it felt like someone was breathing down his neck. Thinking it was one of his tactics to get him to talk, he just sat and waited. Suddenly, he felt his father grab the back of his chair. Before he could even turn around, his father's shoulder grazed his back as he fell down. Stan sat there frozen, unsure of what to do, but then he looked around to see his father writhing on the floor.

Begrudgingly Stan laid his fork down and forced his chair back just enough to slide out and kneel down beside his father. He couldn't help but to wonder if his father was playing another mind game.

"Help, call 911!..." His father said in a raspy, weak voice.

Stan stared down at his father, who looked so helpless. That's when Stan realized he could take advantage of practicing CPR, after studying it from one of his books. He bent over, prepared to begin when his father sputtered, "I said help, you piece-of-shit son, you're not helping." "I swear you are the stupidest boy ever."

In obedience, Stan got off his knees and ran to make the call. He picked up the avocado green phone from what had to have been there since he was born. But then hearing his father gasping for air an eerie calm came over Stan, and he placed the phone back into the cradle. He walked over to the table, having to step over his father's writhing body, and sat down. He heard gurgling sounds behind him while he reached over and took his plate of food and glass of milk and placed it in front of himself at his father's chair this time. He took a bite of food and savored the taste of the meat. He felt a small glimmer of excitement and his heartbeat picked up. He couldn't remember food tasting so good and, as he watched his father with his outstretched arm begging for help, he started to feel redemption for the first time in his life. Stan took a hearty drink of milk, but couldn't take his eyes off his father. He was feeling powerful. He could see how weak his father was, Stan was the one with the power now. The longer he sat there looking at his father the more he felt empowered and he realized what he needed to do next to gain real freedom. This was Stan's chance and he could see more clearly now than ever what he needed and, even more importantly, what he wanted to do.

After he'd finished his meal, Stan stood and looked once again down at his father on the floor. His eyes were as big as saucers, pleading with his son to help him. He was so immobilized that he couldn't speak. Stan thought "ha, no lectures, no words" just silence as his father laid there, clutching his chest and begging his son for help.

Stan said, "Ah, who is the pathetic one now?"

His father's expression turned from panic to fear in the span of a heartbeat. The color slowly drained from his body as Stan stood there and watched. The longer he watched, the better he felt. He crouched down and took a long, hard look at his father. The fear in his eyes made Stan feel more powerful than he had ever felt before.

"You should really take better care of yourself, Father. You look terrible," Stan said. He laughed, something he hadn't done in years.

"Shh, shh, it will be all right, Father. I will call 911, in just a minute." He reached down, put his hand over his father's mouth, and squeezed his nose between his index finger and thumb. Surprisingly, his father didn't struggle. Stan couldn't remember the last time he looked his father in the eyes, but now he couldn't stop looking at them. As Stan watched in bewilderment, his heart raced and he felt alive. Stan wasn't even sure how long he had been doing this, but his father's body suddenly went limp, and his eyes turned to stone. After removing his hand, Stan stood up and just stared at him. Was it really over? Was he really dead? He kept waiting for him to start lecturing him or give him his condescending stare. All he heard was his own heartbeat slowing down and his breathing return to normal.

He sat back down at the table, careful not to move the body. He finished his milk, and then got up and walked to the sink. He washed and dried the dishes and then put the dishes back on the table, empty and clean.

That's when he did what his father had wanted him to do earlier and called 911.

"Operator, please state your emergency."

He tried to sound as panicked as possible and said, "My father is lying on the kitchen floor. I just came upstairs to see if dinner was ready and I found him like this."

"Ok, who am I speaking with?"

"I am his son," Stan replied, thinking the less he said the better.

"I have dispatched an ambulance to you. Do you know if he is breathing?"

"I don't know. He looks really bad, though. His eyes are open and not blinking."

"He may be in shock, so I am going to need you to…"

7

He pretended to go through the motions of what the operator told him to do. Within a short amount of time, paramedics arrived at the house. They proceeded to work on his father, but stopped once they realized what Stan already knew — the bastard was dead. And he was glad for it!

It didn't take long for the paramedics to get rid of the body. Stan's father still had to go through the whole process of going to the hospital, then to the morgue, only to come back to the mortuary. Stan knew his father wanted to be cremated and that he had made it very clear to everyone that he didn't want anyone looking at his dead body. Stan knew his father had a reputation as the best mortician in town and he would never want anyone making a big deal out of his death. Stan was more than happy to oblige his father with cremation, he wanted him gone as soon as possible and he didn't want a body to look at giving him memories of unsavory times. Stan relished at the thought of firing up the crematorium and burning his father to ash.

Chapter 2

K ate's feet hit the pavement with a rhythm much slower than her heartbeat. She steadied her breathing as she tried to gain speed. Turning the corner, she maneuvered around her partner, Harper, and heard him slowing behind her. Her mind wandered, as she looked at all the people around her, their wide eyes full of both fear and excitement. She knew without even looking at her watch that she was going to be late to Kristen's mom's viewing. She winced in pain, not knowing if it was from the hot pursuit she was engaged in, or the fact that she was letting down her best friend since childhood. The thought of Kristen's face helped her regain her focus and reality came flooding back in.

Twilight was setting in, and she lost her target as the shadows of the buildings darkened the street. She slowed just enough to survey her surroundings, and noticed a young boy leaning on his bicycle, cautiously pointing down an alley.

"This is Officer Kingsley," she called to dispatch. "I am in foot pursuit, turning down the alley off of Sixth and Van Buren."

She could hear a response from the radio, but her mind was already preparing as she slowed and turned down the alley. As nightfall took over, the street lamps started flickering on as they slowly lighted the streets, but not the alley. Kate drew her gun and crept through the alley. She pounced around trashcans and old boxes — many of which were homes for the homeless. She could only hope that they were not home as she walked through moving boxes, with her hand steady and gun loaded.

She moved toward the back of the alley where she could see a chain-link fence separating the alley from what looked like the back of a restaurant. She could hear faint music growing louder as she moved toward the only way the suspect could have gone. Since her location was already obvious, she raised her voice and decided to call out and identify herself.

"This is Detective Kingsley with the Topeka Police Department. Just come out with your hands up. There is no reason for anyone to get hurt. Just come out, nice and slow."

She heard a noise that was just a slight shuffle of feet. She turned and looked up, spotting someone in full flight heading right toward her from the fire escape landing. She steadied herself for the inevitable crash and held tight to her gun.

Within seconds, she was wrestling with him, and at a clear disadvantage. His fist ran right through her jaw and the sound of the impact resonated throughout her head. Her gun made a loud clang on the asphalt, she brought her right knee up with all her force and rammed it right into his groin. Kate pushed him off her and scrambled to find her gun. She couldn't imagine it was very far from her, she patted her hand around but couldn't find it. She felt like she was in one of those movies where you were on the edge of your seat, watching and willing the person on screen to make it to their gun or bat, or whatever it was that would help them take down the bad guy.

Her luck wasn't quite as good as in the movies. Just when she found her gun and tried to pick it up, a steel-toed boot slammed into her side, knocking the breath out of her and forcing her to drop the gun. Lying there, Kate tried to catch her breath as she looked for him, and wondered where the hell her backup was. While she called dispatch, she heard the perp get up, stumble and then break into a run. Willing herself up to all fours, she was determined to once again find her gun. She looked up and could see the suspect had stopped running, he was cut off by Harper who stood at the only way out. He made a break toward the chain-link fence, his steel toes clanging on the chain links.

Running on pure adrenaline and feeling no pain, she was up and over the fence with much less effort than it took him. Gaining in yet another footrace, she followed him through the back doors of a restaurant called Little Italy. Once inside, she leaped onto a chair, then a linen-covered table. She jumped from table to table before she took him down, crashing into another table covered with plates of fresh pasta.

After she pinned the suspect, she looked around and saw a full audience of diners, and a band that had stopped playing to stare at them. Harper caught up to her and helped her with the cuffs. Within seconds, the whole place was filled with police. The band started playing again, and the restaurant erupted in applause. Turning her head to look at Harper, she could feel a spaghetti noodle slap her across the face, and she realize she was covered in spaghetti.

She turned to everyone and, with a wry smile, politely said, "Dinner is on me!"

Harper handed the gun to her. "You need to keep better track of this," he said. He was grinning.

Kate took the gun and handed the suspect over to the officers. She then checked the time.

"Shit, Harper, I missed the viewing." Her shoulders slumped as she felt Harper's hand on her back.

"I am sure she'll understand," Harper said. "You go. I'll finish up all the paperwork."

"I can't go like this, look at me," she said, pointing to her noodle-covered head.

"Well, then go clean yourself up and call her. Kate, she will understand."

"All right, I'm out of here. Thanks for everything, Harper. How much do I owe you now?"

"Bunches and bunches, Kate, bunches and bunches," Harper said.

She returned his smile and started out the front door but realized she was quite far away from her car. What had started out as routine follow up on a lukewarm investigation ended up as a fifteen-block chase. She begrudgingly walked as a patrol car slowed down beside her. "Can I give you a ride, Detective?"

"You are a life saver. The thought of the walk back doesn't really seem appealing in the state I am in," Kate said. She ran her fingers through her hair and pulled out more pasta.

After getting dropped off at her car, she fumbled for her keys, grabbed her phone, and dialed Kristen's number. "Hey Kristen, I am so sorry. You will not believe the foot chase I was just in. This guy ran across practically all of Topeka. You should see me now; I am covered in spaghetti…" she stopped herself, realizing that she was making this about her. "Look, Kristen, I know I have let you down, and I can't tell you how sorry I am. I really wanted to be there for you, and I know this is a big deal for me to miss. Please call me." She was silenced by the long beep that let her know she had exceeded her time.

Heading for home, she almost turned around and headed for Kristen's instead. But, after seeing herself in the rearview mirror, she decided to wait for Kristen to call back before she headed over. Driving the familiar drive home, she thought of Kristen and how bad she felt for her losing her mother. She felt thankful that she was off work when the accident happened. Otherwise, she would have been tempted to show up at the scene and have memories burned into her mind that didn't need to be there.

After walking through the door, she laid her cell phone on the counter, and headed straight for the shower. As the water ran over her, she was relieved to know that the red was from the pasta sauce and not from injuries.

Once out of the shower, she immediately checked her phone, and felt sad that Kristen hadn't called back. She tried her one more time before crawling into bed and turning on the TV. Within minutes, her cell phone fell out of her hand, sleep took over and everything went black.

Chapter 3

There was something calming about knowing he was alone in the house where he grew up. No more berating, just peace and quiet. It didn't take long for him to start thinking about what needed to be done. Without his father, the mortuary could not run by itself. Stan would have to step up and make it work, until he knew what he wanted to do.

The first thing that needed to be done was the embalming of Mrs. Jackson. It was too late to call in the backup embalmer. There was no reason why he couldn't do it himself; he had watched his father do it all his life. Stan knew the process by heart. He should be able to do it and stay under the radar despite being unlicensed, he would just say his father did it before he died, if anyone even asked.

He washed up and combed his hair before he headed to the car. The drive to the mortuary was the best drive he had ever had. He listened to the radio and laughed with the disc jockeys.

After unlocking the door and bolting it behind him, he proceeded to the basement. Everything was in perfect order. Mrs. Jackson was on the table, waiting. He walked over and stared down at her realizing that he was going to have some work to do to make her presentable. He noticed many swollen areas from what appeared to be a broken cheekbone along with a large gash on her forehead. Even with all the injuries she suffered she still looked too young to have died so suddenly. He was sure her daughter Kristen was very sad when she received the phone call telling her that her mother had died. The thought made him smile slyly to himself. After all, she was a very pushy woman who practically ordered him to talk to her. She was lucky he didn't make her mom look like a clown. He could do it. He had that power over Mrs. Jackson now.

The embalming process was actually rather simple, and he was amazed at how easily it came to him. He started by assembling all his necessary tools, and he felt like he had done this his whole life, rather than this one time.

He had to move Mrs. Jackson's limbs around because the poor thing had some rigor setting in, and he wanted her to look best for her pictures. He could hear a cricket singing in the distance, and felt soothed. He started by shaving any peach fuzz from her face; the makeup would apply better without it. His father used to say that even women had facial hair, and he believed it after seeing many women with more hair than some men. Without even looking, he reached behind himself and grabbed the disinfecting spray. He could smell the strong stench as he applied it to the body. He used a special device to hold her hands across her chest. It seemed so natural to be doing this, and he wondered if his father had felt as much satisfaction as he did.

He positioned Mrs. Jackson's body and turned her head about fifteen degrees for the viewing. He placed some eye caps on her eyeballs, and dabbed a little glue on the lids to keep them closed. Grabbing the injector gun, he closed and positioned her mouth.

His mind started to wander with thoughts of selling the mortuary, which was full of bad memories, and going to school. He continued working as he daydreamed, finding the artery and the vein in her neck. After setting them both up in tubes, he began the process of draining the blood and filling the body with the embalming fluid.

He hadn't ever been this close to the procedure, so he took extra time making sure he had the details down. He was amazed that he could smell the difference between the embalming fluid and her blood, and he wondered if his father could smell that distinction as well. He noticed the blood seemed to be draining too slowly, and he reached down to adjust it. As he tried adjusting the tube, his glove slipped, and blood squirted out all over the table and sprayed him. He gasped and when he opened his mouth the blood found its way onto his tongue. Stan felt faint as the blood continued to run and, rather than stopping the flow, he watched it. Mesmerized by the flow of the blood, he savored the taste in his mouth, and ran his fingers through the spray.

Not knowing what was happening, he took his other hand and laid it up against his groin. Upon touching himself, he released a soft moan at the pleasure and pain swelling up beneath his pants. Squeezing himself harder, he moaned again. He massaged himself with one hand and with the other he felt the stream of blood running from her body onto his. Her lifeless body laid there while he filled himself with all the hope and excitement his life had been missing.

Unable to release all the pressure in his groin, he savored the moment, and prayed that it would never end. Eventually, the blood flow slowed and stopped, but his body was still responding to the jolt of electricity shooting through him. He stood there in amazement, and he wanted to cry from happiness as he now knew that his life did have purpose. He was living for the first time.

He looked at his watch and realized that three hours had passed since he started the process. After looking around, he noticed that Mrs. Jackson was all cleaned up and ready to go. He was proud of the fact that he was able to make her look close to the picture given by her daughter. Normally the mortuary had someone who would come in to do the makeup before the viewings. This time he wanted to create the masterpiece, Ms. Jackson was special to him and she even looked like she was smiling and he thought to himself how happy her daughter would be in the morning. He called it a night, locked up, and headed back home.

Morning came, and Stan awoke wondering if the whole evening before had just been a dream. He was so happy to see that he really was alone in the house. He took a long, hot shower, and shaved because he wanted to - not because he was being told. He looked through his clothes until he found a simple button-down shirt with the tags still on it; a shirt that his late Aunt Celia gave him years ago. He made himself breakfast and headed to work. He listened to music on the way, and even started to hum along with some songs. It was seven when he arrived, and he immediately got a start on the day. Kristen was expected at nine, and she would have to deal with Stan now. He didn't feel scared or anxious to talk to her; he was almost eager to. He laughed to himself, thinking of the intimacy her mother and he had the night before.

He knew first on his agenda was to tell the staff what had happened to his father the night before. Ruth would be expecting to see his father and he needed to make sure she understood his wishes and that Stan would be the man in charge now. This was important for everyone to know. Stan was important and he expected respect that he had never received before.

Chapter 4

Kristen felt like today was going to be the worst day of her life. The reality of her mom dying sank into every crevice of her being. No morning phone call asking her what she had to do today. She felt ashamed that she had been bothered by all those morning calls, and today she wished her mother would call, more than any other day in her life.

She felt like a zombie while getting ready to see her mother laid to rest. She picked an outfit her mother would like on her, because her mother liked her in blue and would never want Kristen to wear depressing black. As she headed out the door, her cell phone rang, and she quickly sent the call to voicemail. Her best friend Kate was calling and, as much as she needed to talk to her, she just couldn't. Just hearing her voice would immediately make her cry, and right now she just needed some time away from crying. Kate had been her best friend since second grade, when they lived across the street from each other. Kate would be at the funeral tomorrow, and just knowing she would be there made her feel better.

She headed to Country Haven Mortuary, dreading having to view her mother's body. She just hoped they had done a nice job. Her mind started to drift back to the encounter the day before with that very strange boy. He seemed socially retarded, like he was scared of her. She hoped he was not there; she just didn't feel like being patient.

The parking lot was almost empty. She checked herself in the mirror and headed for the door. The chimes on the door sounded and, before she knew it, she was standing in the lobby. She looked up and noticed a young man who looked very familiar. It dawned on her that he was the same socially awkward boy from the day before. However, something was different, his clothes matched, he was cleanly shaven, his hair was combed, and he had the most piercing blue eyes she had ever seen. This seemed strange, because before he never even looked up at her.

"Good morning, Miss Jackson," he said. "How are you?"

"I'm okay. I had an appointment at nine," she said. "Are you the man I spoke with yesterday?"

"Yes, I am," he said in a very calming voice.

Feeling bewildered, she just stood there as he walked up to her and extended his hand. She shook it, and almost jumped back from the icy cold feel. It sent chills down her spine but, at the same time, she couldn't help herself from staring into those beautiful eyes.

"I am having a really hard time with my mom's death, so I would like to get through this as quickly as possible," she said.

"I understand, and am sorry for your loss," he said with a half-apologetic smile, but a hint of sarcasm. "Why don't we just get right to it and go see your mom? Would that be okay?" He said it with an even unemotional, but very professional, tone. It was like he was reading a script.

"Yes, I suppose I can't put off the inevitable. How does she look?"

"She looks like Sleeping Beauty. We treated her as if she was our own mother." As he spoke, a half smile emerged on his face.

Heading to view her mother was the longest short walk she had ever made. Once she saw her, she immediately started to cry.

"Miss Jackson? He asked. "Doesn't she look beautiful?"

She wanted to tell him not to say that. That she wasn't his mother, and he couldn't call her beautiful in such a creepy, condescending way.

"Yes, she does look very nice," she said instead.

"We want to make sure that everything goes just as you want it to. We work hard here to treat everyone with respect and dignity."

They continued their conversation until she had all the information she needed for that afternoon. Leaving the mortuary gave her a certain peace she couldn't understand. She was anxious to get through the day and never talk to the creepy kid again. He seemed so charming, but somehow sarcastic at the same time.

Kristen headed home to catch some sleep before the day really started, at two, when all her family and friends would bombard her with their sympathies. Oh, she wished this were all over and done with. Before long, she drifted off into a mindless sleep, only to be awoken by her phone.

Irritated by the interruption, she sent the call directly to voicemail. She reminded herself that she needed to call Kate back; she would be worried sick. After hearing that she had a message, she checked her voicemail.

"Hi, this is Stan from the mortuary. Please call if you need anything. Everything is ready, and your mother looks beautiful."

That man was so abrasive. If he said her mom was beautiful one more time, she would scream.

Chapter 5

He heard the chimes on the door as Kristen Jackson left, and immediately decided what he needed to do next. He knew without a doubt that he had to have and devour her. If his life was filled with so much happiness from her mother's blood, he could only imagine what it would feel like when he had the daughter's warm blood covering his cold hands. A new day would start tomorrow. He was so excited he could hardly wait to see her again in a couple hours.

The day seemed to go by so slowly, and he thought that this place was much easier to take care of than his father had made it sound. "Son, it takes serious responsibility to run a place like this and be well respected," he used to always say. Stan smiled to himself as he thought of his father's last desperate moments.

By quarter of two, the door chimes started going constantly. Mrs. Jackson's room started filling up very quickly. Stan ran down to the basement to get some more chairs. Upon returning, he was delighted to see Mrs. Jackson's daughter.

"Nice to see you again, Kristen," he said as he tried looking deep into her soul through her eyes. He couldn't help but wonder what kind of girl she really was. There was no question that she was a looker with her shoulder-length blond hair and hazel eyes. Or were they green? He made a note to find out.

"Good afternoon. Is it Stan?" she said, as if it took every muscle in her body to get the words out. He could tell she wasn't much into pleasantries.

Toying with her, he made a point to again ask, "Doesn't she look absolutely beautiful? Just like Sleeping Beauty." He gave her a smile, knowing that it really bothered her when he'd called her mother beautiful earlier. If she only knew how much he would always remember her mother.

During the viewing, he stood off in the corner of the room, watching her every move. He loved the way she mingled through the crowd, dispensing pleasantries as needed. After a couple hours, the crowd was down to a lonely few, including Kristen. He approached her and asked, "Is there anything else you need?"

"No, I think that is enough for now, Stan," she replied. "I am going to head home and prepare for the service tomorrow. Can you please make sure she is ready to come to the church tomorrow morning?"

"She will be ready and as beautiful as ever for tomorrow," he said, smiling as he walked away. It wasn't long before he heard the last of the door chimes, and he knew he was alone again.

Later, he signed the necessary documents to accept his father. He still remembered the shocked faces when the staff learned that his father had passed. Ruth, the secretary who had been with his father for over 30 years was the first to start with the questions.

"Oh Stan, I am so sorry. What can I do? Do you want me to make you some dinners and bring them over? What about your father? What are his wishes? Do you want me to make arrangements for a viewing? Should I start…"

Stan stopped her with his hand and said, "Ruth, Father's wishes were to be cremated and I am making the arrangements for this. As for a service, you know he never wanted any big deal to be made over his passing. I think it's best to just move forward and let him rest in peace."

Ruth piped in, as she often does "No services, absolutely not Stan! We have to show respect and have some kind of funeral. I think it is appropriate to just do it here. Don't you worry I will make all the arrangements. When do you think he will be ready for viewing?"

Stan knew he wasn't getting away from Ruth and he wanted this to be done as soon as possible; however, he also knew he couldn't bear looking at that man any more than he had to. So, he decided a compromise was in order.

"Ruth, the body will be cremated, no viewing! End of that discussion so let's just move on from it. If you want to put something together then that would be nice. I just don't think I can make those kinds of arrangements for my own father. It is just too difficult emotionally," Stan said, while he tried to show sorrow.

"Oh, of course you poor boy, I will take care of everything. It is not uncommon to have services without a body. We can get a nice urn and put it on display with some flowers and maybe pictures of him. Can you come up with some pictures for the service?" Ruth said in a maternal voice, but it didn't stop there. She continued, "You know, my husband's sister-in-law had the most beautiful service without a viewing, I am telling you Stan it was really nice and tasteful. She even had a band playing her favorite music in the background as everyone gathered and paid their respects. I remember telling my husband that's how I want my services to be."

Stan couldn't take it anymore. He told her to go ahead and write up the obituary and put it in the paper, telling her whatever time she decided for the service is fine. He also assured her that he would find some pictures, (although he would rather burn them). Stan knew Ruth needed to believe that she had a task and that she was helping; otherwise she would be even more unbearable than she already was.

"Thank you Ruth. Now I have to get to work. Now that father is gone I really need to step up. Just let me know what you decide and I will help in any way I can."

"Ok Sweetie, don't you worry about a thing I will take care of everything. Do you want me to make the arrangements with the company we use for cremations? Let me know if you want help picking out an urn, you know we have some really nice ones here," she said, gazing at him in anticipation.

"How about you pick out whatever one you think is appropriate and we can plan on the service in a couple days. I'll take care of the arrangements for cremation. Can you send out the announcements?" Stan said.

Ruth turned towards her office to undoubtedly start making the arrangements. Stan was relieved that she had a task to do, knowing this would keep her occupied so he could get back to enjoying his new found freedom.

It didn't seem surprising to anyone that he would follow in his father's footsteps; everyone seemed to expect it, since he had been groomed to take over. No one even asked about the embalming of Mrs. Jackson. After dealing with his father's arrangements with Ruth it was strangely, business as usual.

After he locked up and made sure that everyone was gone, he proceeded to the basement and started up the old crematorium. His father hadn't used it for years, but that was where he was going. After waiting a while for it to reach the appropriate temperature, he put his father in the burning oven. He would collect the ashes in the morning and find out which urn Ruth had decided on to dump them in. His burden now lifted, he walked out of the room and headed to his car.

Feeling exhilarated, he decided to stop and get something to eat at a restaurant. His father never wanted to eat out because it was a waste of money. The weather was in the twenties, but he felt so warm and happy inside that he barely noticed how cold it was. This late at night, he decided to drive extra carefully, knowing how icy the roads get.

Little Smokey's was a little barbecue restaurant close to the state capital. Stan had driven by it many times when his father took a different route for one reason or another. Stan was able to find a parking spot very close, since it was almost closing time. Stan walked in the door and was greeted right away by a cute little blond.

"Hi, how many people are in your party?" she said.

"Oh, it will be just me. Is it too late to order?" he asked, trying to sound apologetic for arriving so late.

"I am sure we can squeeze you in, no problem."

He thought about how ironic it was that he was eating barbecue while his father was being turned to ash in the oven. It made his food taste so much better. He sat there and started to come up with a plan. He couldn't wait to meet Kristen again. This time, it would be on his terms — and at her home.

Chapter 6

The first thing Stan needed to do was find the book he had with instructions for making a homemade form of chloroform. He thought it should be quite simple, but he needed it to be exact. He couldn't take any chance of it not working.

The ingredients were actually much simpler than he had thought. All he needed was bleach, acetone, and ice. The process didn't take near as long as he thought it would. He would be in bed much earlier than anticipated.

Morning came, and he awoke refreshed and excited. Stan was all ready and out the door in time to be to work by seven. Upon arriving, he went straight down to the basement to make sure his father was nothing but ashes. He collected all his ashes and put them in a bag. On his way up the stairs, he heard the chime of the door opening. He turned the corner from the stairs and walked into the lobby.

"Hello, how can I help you?" he said, before realizing that it was Ruth.

"Oh, hello Stan, how are you doing?" Ruth said. Before he could respond, she continued on, as she always did. "I put the most beautiful urn on your father's desk. Well, I mean your desk now. I hope you like it."

He could tell she was waiting to see if he'd already seen it. He hadn't, but said, "Yes, Ruth, it is perfect. Thank you for paying such close attention to detail. Have you taken care of the obituary and the service?"

"Oh, you know I have! My husband always said I had a keen eye for detail. I am very happy you like it, Stan. The arrangements are for tomorrow afternoon. I hope that is ok with you? I thought the sooner the better. That father of yours needs his respects paid to him, don't you think?" she said with such a proud demeanor.

The thought of paying respects to his father made Stan feel sick to his stomach and with every bit of strength he replied, "That is very true, Ruth. Respect is important and we need to make sure it is given. Thank you for being so helpful. If there isn't anything else, I'd better get started on getting caught up on the day." He started to do what would become a habit of walking away from Ruth's rambling.

That, of course, didn't stop Ruth from continuing on with another turn in the conversation. "The weather man on Channel Three, you know who I mean? The man with the nice tan and the mustache, you know? What was his name? Rob or Tom… Oh, I don't know. Anyway, he said that the snow was coming and to put our snow shoes on. So, Stan, you know your dad always let me go early when the snow came…"

As Stan walked away he was in his own world, planning his big evening. He had everything he needed at work. He needed a janitor jumper, a large garbage can with a lid and wheels, gloves…oh, and a hat. Father absolutely hated when he wore one, which only made doing so that much more appropriate. Lastly, he needed the dreaded station wagon. The car he had always been embarrassed to ride in, but now appreciated for its practicality. Continuing to plan the day, he decided he would stop on his way home and pick up the ingredients to make the chloroform.

"…and John better not plan on me doing any fancy dinner. I am not stopping at the store on the way home with this blizzard coming through town. So, is that okay? Stan? Stan? Have you even heard anything I said?"

"Yes, of course, Ruth," he said from a distance as he waved his hand and said, "Leave whenever you think you need to. Today is looking to be really slow right now."

"Thanks Stan," she said. "You seem different. Have you gotten taller?"

He smiled at her and headed back to the basement. As the day went on rather unproductively, Stan couldn't help but think about his upcoming big date.

It was barely three when Ruth came to find him, and anxiously gave him an update on the weather. "Stan, have you seen the crazy snow out there? It is getting really bad. I think we should just close up and get home. What do you think? Should we lock up?"

"That's fine, Ruth. Just bundle up and head home. Be sure to drive safe. See you in the morning."

"Oh, yes, tomorrow is the big day. We finally get to celebrate your father," she said as she started walking away and putting her coat on. He doubted she even heard him tell her to have a safe drive home.

It wasn't hard finding things to do as he bided his time before his date with Kristen. Before he knew it, night had fallen and the snow was coming down in sheets. He was not worried about driving in the snow, just as long as he didn't get stuck. Kristen only lived about twenty minutes away. He had already driven by of her place so he would be familiar with the layout. He took the elevator up to her apartment. It reminded him of a Motel 6, the way the front doors all faced an inside courtyard. He doubted many people would be up and about at eleven at night.

He parked by the exit door closest to the elevator, put on his gloves and opened the door that he had put some tape on during his visit earlier in the day to keep it from latching. He had everything he needed, including the chloroform and the rolling trashcan. So far he had gone completely unnoticed. He pulled his cap down and zipped up his gray overalls. He pushed the trashcan to the service elevator and pushed the button for the third floor. Lucky number three, he thought.

He knocked on the door just loud enough for her to hear, but not so loud as to wake the neighbors. Finally, he heard her behind the door.

"Who is it?"

"Sorry Miss, this is maintenance," Stan said with the best Southern accent he could muster. "There has been a gas leak, and I have to check all apartments to make sure they are safe. I promise it will only take a minute. I am so sorry it is so late."

The moment of truth was there as he waited to see if she would buy it. He heard the latch unlock and the chain move to open the door. She started walking away from the door just as he stepped in. Without hesitation, he grabbed her from behind, and covered her mouth and nose with a towel saturated with chloroform.

Kristen struggled and screamed through the towel. The chloroform took much longer to take effect than he had thought it would. His arms started to burn from the constant struggle but, just when he thought he couldn't hold her any more, she went limp in his arms and he dominated her. He could feel the power surge through every fiber of his body. He couldn't help but smile at the pure satisfaction of his plan working.

Stan stepped outside her door long enough to pull his trashcan inside. He picked her up in one swoop and dumped her into the can. Good thing she didn't weigh any more than some of the garbage they throw out. He then took out his duct tape and taped the trashcan lid closed. Wheeling her out proved easier than he thought it would. After taking the elevator down, he removed the tape from the exit door, and headed straight for the car. He opened the car's back door, hoisted the can inside, and laid it on its side.

Driving away, he couldn't help but think about how perfectly the plan had worked. The only thing he wished he could have done better was not leaving her front door unlocked as they exited. Other than that, it was perfect. A grieving daughter who left her door unlocked and left in the middle of the night: There were so many ways that scenario could be interpreted, and only one of them involved the truth — kidnapping and, ultimately, murder.

The streets were getting much worse, and he had to really concentrate to stay on the road. When he finally arrived back at the mortuary, he was glad to have made it safely. The advantage was that the roads were practically deserted and, with everyone concentrating on driving so much, he doubted anyone took notice of him at all, and, since it was snowing so hard, his tracks would be covered long before anyone noticed the girl was missing.

Stan pulled up to the loading dock and opened the garage. Before closing the garage door, he quickly looked to make sure no one was around. Maneuvering Kristen through the garage, down the service elevator, and to the special room was a piece of cake, especially in the garbage can. He couldn't hear anything coming from the can, and he assumed she was still knocked out.

He soon realized that getting her out of the can and onto the metal table was harder than he had thought it would be. He could feel her starting to stir as she woke up. Luckily, he had her on the table and completely restrained before she came to.

He relished watching her slowly wake up and realize what was happening. She still couldn't see him, but he could hear her start to scream. He was positive no one could hear her, but it still made him nervous. He grabbed the duct tape and slapped a piece over her mouth. Stan could feel himself getting hard again as he imagined what he was about to do. He had been thinking about it for a while. "Well, hello, Sleeping Beauty," he said.

Kristen's eyes were like daggers staring at him. He started getting all his tools together as he kept talking to her. He reached over and grabbed the tweezers from the table. He leaned down close to her, and moved the tweezers toward her eyes. She started to squirm, and he could hear a muffled scream come from behind the tape. He could only imagine what she must be thinking. Did she think he was going to take her eyeball? Now that would be icky, he thought to himself as he smiled.

"Shh, darling, just a couple souvenirs to remember you by," he said soothingly. "This won't hurt much. Just a little pinch and it will be done."

Stan saw just one tiny tear fall from the corner of her eye as he pulled some of her eyelashes out.

"It's as simple as one, two, three," he said, pulling an eyelash out for each number. "See, that wasn't so bad now, was it?"

Quietly and efficiently, he carefully placed the eyelashes in one of the tiny envelopes usually used for a deceased person's personal effects. He then folded the envelope and placed it in his back pocket for safekeeping.

"You know? You and your mom will at least experience the same thing together. You are much closer to her now, because of me. I will never forget the life you both have given me, and I promise to always keep you dear to my heart."

Her eyes continued to follow him throughout the room as he gathered his things.

"I am going to go start up the cooker. I will be right back. Stay put, okay?" he said, as he saw the fear in her eyes. He couldn't help but feel inner joy as he watch her lie there, powerless.

It was at this point that fear replaced anger in her eyes and, the more fear she showed him, the harder and more excited he got. He hurriedly went and started the incinerator. After coming back to her, he was no longer in a talking mood. He quickly put on his rubber apron, walked up to her, and slit her jugular. She winced in pain. The blood started spewing out everywhere, uncontrollably. It wasn't quite as he had imagined, but the warmth of the blood on his cold hands made him scream with ecstasy. His groin felt like it was going to explode. With one hand, he went under the apron and unzipped his pants. He shot out of his pants and closed his eyes, as he felt her blood run through his fingers. Occasionally, he touched his fingers to his tongue. He finally finished as the blood started to slow; he took his hand saturated in blood and masturbated to his very first orgasm. All those years of almost getting there were gone. He had finally found a way to release the beast within.

When it was over, he looked down at her; her eyes stone dead, just like his father's. He zipped his pants back up, upset at the fact that blood was all over his clothes. He was going to have to perfect this process. He undid the tape, picked her up, and walked over to the oven. Without hesitation, he opened the door and slid her in.

"Good night, my Sleeping Beauty."

Chapter 7

Kate started her day off on the wrong side of the bed. She was out of coffee, which always made her grumpy. And she was out of hairspray. Both of which had been part of an ongoing grocery list, which only got longer. It was freezing outside and, more irritating, was the fact that her car doors were frozen shut. The de-icing spray worked great — when it was not inside the frozen car. So she did the next best thing and used her car keys to run along the door jam in the hopes of loosening the ice. She guessed she would worry about the damage later. After a few minutes, the jam finally released and allowed her to climb inside.

She pulled through the Starbucks drive-through, which had become a routine since she had been out of coffee the last three mornings. It wasn't until she was halfway through her large coffee that she started to feel human again. By the time she got to the precinct, her car was warm and she was happily sipping her coffee.

Once inside the precinct, she could hear the hum of the people, which long ago became a part of her morning routine. After looking through all her messages and checking her phone again, she began getting irritated with her best friend. Kristen had been so depressed since her mother had died a couple days ago that she hadn't been returning Kate's calls. Kate couldn't help but be hurt that Kristen had been avoiding her, not taking into consideration that her mom was like a second mom to Kate. She could still remember Mrs. Jackson making them chocolate-chip cookie dough that they would devour before she had a chance to bake more than a couple cookies. Once they were ready, they were so full from the dough they couldn't even eat any of the cookies.

Kate decided to send her another text message, pleading for her to call her back, or at least text her if she didn't want to talk.

"Detective Kingsley, I need you and Detective Harper to go check out the death of a homeless man under the bridge." Chief, AJ Broxterman, came over and handed her a file. "He is down with the medical examiner now. It seems pretty cut and dry, but it does look like he has some signs of struggle. Boomer is checking the cause of death out now."

"Sure chief, we will head down right now."

Kate started to head for the stairs, and yelled across the room for Harper to join her. "Come on, slowpoke, we may have a case. You will thank me later for not letting you eat another donut." She laughed.

John Harper was a very thin, straight-arrow guy who spent a good portion of his time making sure he was neat and tidy. His desk was always perfect and organized — unless some of Kate's papers poured onto it. Kate couldn't help but love messing up his desk knowing that it made him absolutely crazy. He was the best partner she could ask for, and she had spent many nights eating dinner with his family. He'd been very loyal and protective of her ever since they became partners.

"So, what do we have this bitter morning?" he said, as they headed down the stairs, two at a time.

"Looks like a homeless man died, most likely from the cold weather. Apparently, he had been living in the cardboard houses under the bridge. He was called in on an anonymous tip, probably another homeless person. No one likes a dead man around their home."

As they arrived at the ME's office, she started asking questions, trying to put this case to bed as soon as she could.

"So, what do we have, Boomer?" she asked the ME. "Did he die of the cold?"

When Boomer started to respond, Kate felt her phone vibrate in her pocket and she scrambled to answer it. She realized that she had received a text message rather than a call. She felt relieved, sure it was Kristen finally responding to her. She then felt all the air deflate out of her as she realized that it was just her cell phone carrier offering her discounts on ring tones.

Focusing her attention back to the task at hand, she tried to pick up on the conversation.

"...like a wick. His blood alcohol was way off the charts," Boomer said.

Kate chimed in, "So, was he drunk?" Knowing that would be him and every other homeless person out there. She couldn't really blame them for drinking, knowing that it was one way to endure the cold.

Boomer continued, "That's the funny thing. Normally the alcohol or the cold would seem plausible as cause of death, but on the inside, he tells a different story. This man died as if he was smothered. The bruising on his chest suggests that he struggled with something very heavy on top of him. Where was he found?"

"Um, I think the chief said not far from where he slept. Why?"

"Were there any signs of strangulation?" Harper asked.

"No, there was no bruising anywhere on the neck that would suggest strangulation," Boomer replied. "Saddest part is that the only possession he had on him was a wrinkled old picture of a family that looked very happy at one time."

She hated seeing the homeless living in such poverty, out of the reach of helping hands. Many people would like to act like they didn't even exist, but it broke her heart to see such sad cases. She also hated the fact that this case meant that they had to go out in this bitter cold and interview all the homeless who lived under the bridge.

"Guess we should dress warm today, Harper," she said, not at all pleased about it. "We're heading out to talk with the tenants around his home."

"Could be worse," Harper said reassuringly.

They headed out toward downtown, stopping at 7-11 on their way to pick up two carriers of four coffees each. Kate figured that eight coffees would at least get some cold people to talk to them. Maneuvering the beverages on their laps was a little tricky, but manageable, and they were able to pull up to the Kansas Avenue Bridge without spilling a drop.

Before getting out of the car, she checked her voicemail again; still no Kristen. Kate tried to call her, but the call went straight to voicemail. So, she settled for a quick text saying no more than, "Call me." Irritated, she got out of the car and caught up to Harper, who was already heading down under the bridge.

The coffee was a big hit, but no one gave them any information that would provide closure on the homeless man's death. The most they were able to learn was that his name was Carl. No one knew his last name or where he was from. He had been living under the bridge for about a year and a half, and kept pretty much to himself. Most of the homeless there seemed to be loners, and the only time they got together was to huddle around a fire. Knowing that there was probably much more information about Carl than anyone wanted to admit, they decided to leave and come back at night. The plan was to see if they could get some talkers, if they handed out blankets and warm clothing.

The morning was pretty much gone and lunchtime was nearing. They headed back to the precinct and started making some callbacks. Harper had to meet his wife for an ultrasound on their third baby. Kate decided to take this opportunity to head over and check on Kristen.

"Now, Harper, don't cry if you are having another girl," she teased. "You should be so lucky!" Everyone around started to chime in. Harper just shook his head and started smiling, as they collected their things and headed out.

Kate hated how cold the car was when she first got in. The fog from her breath surrounded her like she was smoking incessantly. She started the car and waited a few minutes for it to warm up. She decided to call Kristen again and let her know she was coming.

"Hey, girl, I know you don't want to talk, but I am on my way with our favorite Thai food, and I won't take no for an answer." She hung up the phone and pulled out of her parking spot.

The streets were still icy, so things took much longer than normal. She had no patience for slow driving, and it made her crazy when cars drove even slower than they needed to. She pulled up to the Thai restaurant and left her car running. She unhooked her key remote from the keychain and headed in to order, locking the doors with the clicker as she walked.

"Oh, hi, Miss Kate. Is it going to be just one today?"

Kate had been coming to this place for years and she knew all the people there. Laila, the owner, was always the greeter, and her husband was always in the back cooking. Sometimes their daughter was there to help, but less often now that she was in college.

"Not today. I am going to order some food to go," she said as she sat herself down at the bar. "I have a friend who could use some cheering up."

Once in the car, she checked her phone again and headed over to Kristen's. She found the best parking she could, headed into the lobby, and went up the elevator to her floor. With lunch in hand, she walked up to her door and began to knock. After a few attempts, she found herself extremely irritated that Kristen was not answering. If Kate had her house key with her, she would have opened the door and sat there until Kristen returned. Or, worse yet, she would pull her out of bed and make her face some reality.

Kate headed back down the elevator and got to her car. She threw the food in the car and looked down the parking lot, noticing Kristen's red Explorer sitting under its cover. Kate slammed her car door, ran back to the elevator, and went back up to Kristen's door. This time, Kate was banging on the door loudly enough that one of the neighbors came out with her baby in her arms.

"Is everything alright?" the neighbor said.

"Yes, everything is fine. I just can't get Kristen to open her door and I've been worried about her since she lost her mother."

"Well, I haven't seen her since she came home from the funeral," her neighbor said. "I felt really bad for her, losing her mom so suddenly. Could you send her my best, please?"

Kate nodded, and then tried the doorknob, and was surprised when it gave her access to the apartment. Why had Kristen left it unlocked? "Kristen, are you home? It's just me, Kate. I'm worried about you, honey."

Silence, just dead silence, came from the apartment. Kate felt a sickness move from her stomach, up her throat, and into her mouth. She thought she was going to throw up. What had Kristen done? Could Kate have missed so much grief that Kristen would take her own life? She continued calling her name as she walked from room to room. No answer. Kate headed for the bedroom, and noticed the bed was not made and all the covers were moved to one side, as if someone had just gotten up after throwing the covers off. She continued into the bathroom. Still sick to her stomach, she moved the shower curtain. To her relief, there was no sign of her at all. However, the sickness still haunted her insides. Something was wrong, really wrong. Where was her best friend? What had happened to her?

Kate started looking for any sign of an explanation, but couldn't find anything that made her feel better. She found Kristen's purse untouched on the kitchen table and her cell phone charging on the counter. Kate listened to the messages, mostly from her, and wrote down the names of all the other people who had left messages. She could feel it in her gut that something bad had happened. The door was unlocked, her purse was there, her car was there, and her cell phone was there. Where could she have gone?

She got her phone and called the precinct. "Yeah, this is Detective Kingsley. I need to file a missing persons report. I understand it has to be a certain amount of time, but I know this is something bad because I know my friend."

After going through all the formalities, she decided to start calling Kristen's family and friends. She either left a message or talked with everyone in Kate's phone. She also wrote down phone numbers for all her missed calls.

She needed to canvass the area and check Kristen's credit cards, but that would take manpower and time. She called Harper and left a message explaining the situation, asking him to help after the ultrasound.

Careful not to touch too much, she closed the door behind her, and started canvassing the area and talking to the neighbors.

Chapter 8

Stan replayed that night endlessly and savored every moment he'd had with Sleeping Beauty. She was everything he could have ever hoped for. The minutes since his new life flowed through his veins eventually turned into hours, which were replaced by days. Although it all still felt fresh in his mind, he started to feel a hunger that he had never known. Stan had to feed this hunger in order to complete his transformation into a new life. He had to find someone to follow Sleeping Beauty, someone to release his inner beast yearning to be free.

Stan had to pick wisely which princess would give him the ultimate satisfaction. Sleeping Beauty was only the beginning and the memories it brought back flooded him with comfort. He remembered his mother reading the fairy tales to him even days before she died. He knew that those memories were the fuel to help him find his next victim. The next memory he thought of was how he begged his mother for one more book, even in her weak state. She only smiled and obliged him by stroking his hair and pulling out Rapunzel.

As Stan sat there and recalled this memory he knew his next victim would be Rapunzel, and he had to make sure that he picked correctly or the fairy tale would not come true. He thought to himself, 'Rapunzel, Rapunzel, come let your hair down'. Feeling inspired, he came back to reality and mentally went over all the crucial steps of perfecting his art.

He knew it had to be better. He couldn't take any chances on sloppiness. Sleeping Beauty was a triumph, indeed, but the process needed to be perfected. He couldn't hunt where he worked and draw any attention to himself. Stan the funeral director had to be much different from the Stan who fed his beast. This meant changes, many changes.

He started off the morning with the normal routine of running the mortuary. He felt mixed emotions knowing his father's service was in a few hours. On one hand he wanted it to be over, but the thought of it made his stomach turn. Going through what few pictures he could find was tasking as he hated seeing his father's image. He continued to schedule appointments and answer the never stopping questions from Ruth. She seemed almost excited to be important in planning the service and kept asking him about detail after exhausting boring detail. He wasn't sure how much more he could take before he exploded.

Everyone seemed to be adjusting, for the most part to the change in management. However, there were crucial things he needed to take quick control of. One of the first things he needed to do was make sure he used Morten, the now full-time embalmer, to work with the clients. He couldn't be doing it anymore, or he would draw attention to himself. He also needed to work on getting his own set of tools, so he wouldn't bring any attention to the fact that he was borrowing Morten's. Morten started working for his father about fifteen years ago, and he was very meticulous and clean. He couldn't take a chance that Morton noticed anything missing or put back wrong.

Stan headed downstairs to meet with Morten and clarify a few things. When he got down there, Morten had a woman on the table that was well into the embalming process. Stan could smell the disinfectant heavy in the air, but, even through the stench, he could smell the sweet blood draining from the body on the table. He could feel the hardness climbing its way into his groin, and it took every muscle he had to control himself. The urge to touch her was so strong he could barely stand it.

"Hey, Stan, what brings you down here? Everything set for the service this afternoon?" Morten said without even looking up from his work.

"You know Ruth, she has total control of everything," Stan said, lightly. "I want to talk to you since we haven't had much of a chance to catch up since my father died."

Morten looked up and smiled at Stan. "Yeah, I know, Ruth can be quite the control freak, but she does get things done. I haven't had a chance to give my condolences. It is a real tragedy about your Dad. We are really going to miss him around here."

"Thanks, I appreciate that," Stan said.

Stan's head started filling with images of his father begging for his life. The power he had over him in the end was priceless.

"I wanted to ask you something, Morten. I was trying to get everything organized in my head about how this place runs. Part of that includes the inventory. Are all the tools you use in here your own, or do they belong to the mortuary? I ask because these look pretty old. I know how difficult my father could be about spending money, and I just want to know if you need anything." Stan said. "Stan, I am glad you asked. This has been needing attention for some time. Ah, where do I start?"

"Well, let's start with these tools. What do you need, Morten?"

Morten looked like a kid at Christmas. He said how much he hated these tools because they were practically antiques, and that he had needed some state-of-the-art stuff for some time. He continued on with the size of the room and how it needed renovating. Stan agreed with most of what he said, until he proceeded to tell him that mortuaries no longer needed incinerators and that they were more of a burden than anything. He went on to say that, if it were removed, they could expand the room and do more than one embalming at a time.

"The incinerator stays, Morten," Stan said, cutting him off. "That is final."

Morten looked up at Stan in disbelief.

Stan realized his newfound confidence probably caught Morten off guard. Carefully he said, "What I mean, Morten, is that this place has been handed down, generation after generation, through my family, and there are some things that I want to keep just for nostalgia. I am sure you can appreciate that, right?"

"Sure, kid, no problem, I sure do appreciate all your help with getting things updated. I couldn't wait to throw out the old and bring in the new."

While Stan could certainly appreciate that same sentiment, he needed those tools for his own purposes.

"Morten, just make sure you talk to me before you throw anything out. I may want to keep some stuff, just because it has been in my family."

Lunchtime came, and Stan was starving. He could feel a difference between hunger for food and hunger from the beast within. He never packed a lunch anymore, even though Ruth had offered to make him one many times. He enjoyed his chance to get out and spend money on something his father would have hated.

On his way to lunch, Stan decided to stop and see if the barber could give him a haircut. He felt rather certain he was available because as he walked up Stan could see him reading a newspaper in his chair.

"Hello, sir, do you have time for a cut?" Stan asked.

"You sure do look like you are in need of one. What can I do you for?"

Stan noticed the barber's license on the wall behind him, which stated that a Tim Horn was licensed to cut hair. "Well, Tim, I think I want to get a little more style, I am ready to go short and have enough in the front to flip up, like his." He pointed to a teenager walking by the window.

"Sure enough," Tim said. "Have a seat."

After the haircut, Stan decided to walk down the street to Taco Tico and eat some lunch. He felt disappointed that he had been looking for Rapunzel for days but had not found her. He tried to calm himself by remembering how his mother used to say that patience was a virtue. However, he wasn't sure how much longer the beast was going to wait before the pangs of hunger set in. He felt both the hunger for the beast and the hunger for the taco burger calling to him.

Walking in to the restaurant Stan headed straight for the counter, already knowing what he wanted. It was at that moment he saw Rapunzel. He thought to himself. SHE IS THE ONE! THE NEXT CHAPTER OF HIS FAIRY TALE!

"Sir, can I take your order?" she said.

He noticed that she was wearing a nametag. Her name was Lauren. She had perfect, long, golden hair braided and wrapped in a barrette. She was exquisite.

"Well, Lauren, I would like to order two taco burgers and a soda." He purposely made eye contact. "You sure are a pretty one, Lauren. I suppose you get that a lot, don't you?"

"Not as much as you think," she said. "Your total will be $4.79."

"Aw, now that is a shame, Lauren. I bet you have them lining up down the block for you."

Stan smiled and handed her a five. He realized that Lauren was not someone to embarrass easily. While she made change, he closed his eyes and envisioned things she could never imagine. He could feel his groin growing tighter, and he knew that he had to learn to control the beast within. He took a deep breath and willed himself to settle down. It helped, but he knew he needed to get moving.

"Will that be to go, sir?" she asked with a forced smile, clearly in a zone.

"Yes, Lauren, please." He walked on down the counter and waited for his food to be ready. He didn't look back at her, but he envisioned her looking at him, and he daydreamed of meeting up with her again. He was happy to have his food and, when he walked back by her, he was relieved that she was already helping another customer. He pretended as he walked away that she was still watching. Rather than turning and being disappointed that she wasn't watching he just kept heading for the door, ever so slowly. He smiled to himself as the resonating words of '*Rapunzel, Rapunzel, let down your hair, so that I may climb the golden stairs* 'echoed through his head. He had much to do to prepare.

Stan was elated as he drove back to the mortuary, excited to meet Lauren, but anxious to get this service over with. It would be starting soon and Stan really wished he could just skip it. When he returned to his office, he found a list of items that Morten had requested to help facilitate his work. Most of it seemed very reasonable, and Stan figured the happier he was the more Stan could get away with. He started making the necessary calls to have the items expedited, especially the tools that Stan needed. He also had Ruth schedule a meeting with all the help at the mortuary. He wanted to enforce new standards at the workplace, and he would tell everyone to abide by them. First on the list were the hours of operation. He would tell the staff that it was imperative that they had social lives too, and that he didn't expect any of them to work late unless otherwise approved by him, which most likely meant when there was a viewing. There would be times he needed the building to himself after hours.

He could hear Ruth working her way through the mortuary looking for him and he knew the time had come. The service was starting. Deciding to get this over with, he started in the direction of Ruth's calls. He turned a corner and almost ran her over.

"Oh, there you are, it's time. Are you ok? I know this has to be hard for you. The room is at full capacity. Your father was very well known and respected, many have shown up. I hope we have enough space." She turned around and started walking towards the service, as if she knew Stan was right behind her.

He willed himself to walk to the service, listening to Ruth talk incessantly about how many people were there. Stan couldn't understand how such a horrible man could be respected by so many. If they only knew the depth of his father's mean streak they would never be here celebrating his life. The closer he got to the service the sicker his stomach felt; his hopes were that his sickness would come across as a mourning son who just lost the greatest man in the world.

The service seemed like eternity even though he kept telling himself that it was a necessity. Stan let Ruth take the lead for the service, there were pictures of his father and the urn as the center of attention. It made Ruth happy and made Stan look like the good son. As he looked out through the crowd of people moving in and out of the room, he tried to give the look of the grieving son, but it was exhausting. When the crowd started to dissipate he found himself feeling better and better, and when the last person left the mortuary Stan felt calm, relaxed and finally at peace. It was over, his father was finally gone and happiness ran through him. He had to restrain himself from whistling in excitement.

After the service, he went in his office, and looked up Taco Tico in the phonebook. Once he found the number, he called.

"Hello, Taco Tico, may I help you?" He recognized the voice. Lauren sounded like she was singing him a lullaby.

"What time do you work until?" Stan said, as he tried to disguise his voice.

"Until eight," she said, sounding confused. "Oh, you must mean the restaurant hours."

"Yes, of course. What time does the restaurant close?" He pretended to sound annoyed that she would misunderstand what he asked for. He smiled to himself.

"Oh, it closes at eleven," she said. He hung up immediately and decided that he would try to follow her after work and see how discreet he could be. By her lack of interest in him at the restaurant he felt confident that she wouldn't notice him.

He made a call to a locksmith and asked him to change the mortuary's locks right after closing time tonight. There was only one viewing and it would be over by five. He needed the locksmith done by eight so he didn't miss his hot date.

Chapter 9

The clock took forever to move, but finally the sun set and darkness covered the night. Lauren had all her tasks done so that she could be on her way at eight. She hated the way the smell of grease permeated all her clothing. She sometimes felt sad that she was too busy for friends and she was also disappointed that her workplace couldn't offer up any friendships to make the hours go by faster. She just had nothing in common with any of the other employees; unlike her, they had no ambition in life. They worked for money to party and Lauren worked for money to go to college. She juggled college and work in the hopes of someday not having to work as hard as her mom did, always having to take double shifts to make ends meet.

As she got older her relationship with her mother changed, instead of a caregiver her mom had become a good friend. Even though they never had much of a chance to see each other they usually left each other notes on the counter in passing. Her mom worked the nightshift as a nurse at Stormont Vail Hospital and they would sometimes go days without seeing each other. Since her mom was sleeping while she was at work and school, and Lauren was sleeping when her mom was at work, they would often take time off to see each other at least once a month. Lauren remembered the previous week when her mom called in sick to work and Lauren skipped school. They started the day with breakfast and then went to the mall for girl-time shopping, followed by manicures and pedicures, then to the movies, dinner and home. They sat on the couch catching up until midnight, telling each other all the things that had happened since the last time they caught up. Lauren knew that someday they would have the chance to talk more and spend more time together. However, her mom agreed that it was important for Lauren to finish school.

After punching her timecard, Lauren headed outside. The wind felt like tiny little pins running across her face as she opened the door and stepped outside. She pulled her hood up, and started walking home. She had to have a job close to home, and one that would work with her school hours. She went to college at Washburn, working on a degree in accounting. It wasn't the most exciting field to work in, but it would pay the bills.

As she walked down the street, she got a weird feeling, and she kept waiting for one of her friends to come out from some bushes and scare her. The wind was so cold that she couldn't even take off her hood to look around. She thought to herself, if they are crazy enough to be out in this weather to scare her, then they deserve the cold.

Luckily, home was only three blocks away, and she made it in record time even with the cold. After walking in the front door, she heard Pepe start barking so fiercely that she might have been scared, if she hadn't known how loveable he was. "Quiet, Pepe, it's only me," she said, and the barking stopped.

Chapter 10

A jolt of electricity ran through Stan. He wanted her right then, so badly that he could hardly stand it. He worked hard to control the beast within and, after driving away from her house, he started to formulate his plan. He needed to check and see who she lived with. A girl that young couldn't afford a house like that. It was a moderate home in a nice family neighborhood, but this girl was not living there alone. He knew that this was going to take some time to prepare. He needed his tools and, more importantly, he needed to know her schedule. After he got home, he called Taco Tico again.

"Taco Tico." No "hello" or "can I help you" followed. He knew this was someone who hardly cared about his job.

"Hi, I go to school with Lauren, and we are working on a group project," Stan said. "Can I speak with her? I don't have her number. I just remembered that she works there."

"She's already gone home."

"Oh, shoot. I really need to talk to her. When will she be back?"

"She works from two to eight tomorrow."

"Oh, great, does she work that shift every day?" Stan asked, hoping he was not becoming too pushy.

"Yeah, most days, but I don't know her days off."

"Great," Stan said. "Oh, one more thing, do you have a number maybe for her roommate?" He bit his tongue, hoping he hadn't crossed a line.

"Dude, I don't know her mom's number. I can leave a message for her if you want, but that is it." He was clearly annoyed with Stan now, and Stan knew that he was very lucky to get the kind of information that he got.

"Sorry, I'll just wait for tomorrow. Thanks dude!"

After hanging up, he gloated about his accomplishment, finding out so much information and being so sly about it. Who would ever suspect anything? He knew that he needed to be very careful with this information and find out the mom's work schedule. The garage of the house didn't look used, so he hoped that her mother was not home. Maybe she worked nights. He thought to himself, could he be so lucky?

He went home and started reading. Before long, he was writing on a pad of paper as he started to formulate his plan. It would be so simple this time. He wouldn't have to wear the janitor costume, but he would keep the rolling trashcan; it seemed to work well. He would park in the alley and be there when she got home. He would make his dry run tomorrow night and see how it would work. He drifted off to sleep, and dreamt of releasing the beast within.

Chapter 11

Kate talked to herself as she went through her best friend's personal belongings, hoping to find a shred of information that would help find her.

"Your friend here was very organized. How did you guys ever become friends?" Harper said with the reluctant start of a smile.

"We've been friends since grade school. We are complete opposites, which is why we got along so well. We never wanted the same things, so we never got into fights. She is like a sister to me, and I share everything with her. That is why it is so frustrating not knowing what is going on with her. She has never alienated me like this before. My best friend is in trouble, and I can't help her. Now she is gone, and I could have stopped this."

"Well, you know as well as I do that you can't blame yourself for this," Harper said. "We will find her, Kate. That's what we do."

"Yeah, but Harper, how will we find her?" The tears started welling in her eyes as she made a modest attempt to hold them back. "Plus, we have nothing! An unlocked door is not enough to lead us in the right direction. None of the neighbors seem to know anything. I just keep hoping that someone will call with information. I have posted fliers everywhere asking for information."

"Something will come up, Kate. We just have to keep looking. We haven't turned up every rock yet, have we? There has to be something here that will help lead us in the right direction. What did you get from the cell phone?"

"I'm still working on it. I have checked the messages, but haven't really found anything useful yet other than condolences from friends, family, and co-workers. There is a call from the mortuary for her mom's viewing, a call from a florist, and a call from her hair stylist confirming her appointment. Nothing really unusual," Kate said in a deflated tone.

"Did you check all the outgoing calls and the incoming calls?" he continued. "We should get the phone to the lab, and they can check any deleted messages as well."

As Harper talked, Kate got lost in her own world as she went through the phone and wrote down all Kristen's outgoing phone numbers on a piece of paper. She didn't recognize all the numbers, and had to call them one by one. As she started writing them down, there were two numbers that came up many times. One was Kate's, but she didn't recognize the other. That second one called a total of nine times in a three-hour period. That seemed unusual, so she started dialing the number.

"Country Haven Mortuary, this is Ruth. How can I help you?"

Kate was deflated for a moment when she realized that the mortuary calling made sense. However, after the moment passed she was curious as to why the mortuary would call her so often in such a short amount of time.

"Hi, this is Detective Kate Kingsley with the Topeka Police Department, and I am investigating a missing person. I am wondering why this mortuary would call someone nine times in a three-hour period, considering that, when they finally left a message, it sounded like a courtesy call."

"Well, I am not sure. Who here left the message?"

"The message was by a man named Stan."

"Oh, Stan, he is the owner of the place. He is kind of new at running things on his own. His father just passed recently. He is probably trying to be thorough. Do you mind me asking who he was calling for?"

"He was calling Kristen Jackson. Her mother just passed, and I know your mortuary facilitated her viewing."

"Oh, I remember her, such a sad story, and her mother getting killed in that car accident. I am sure Stan was just trying to make sure she was taken care of. She was very particular. Poor thing was so sad."

"Could you have Stan give me a call? I just want to follow up with him on her state of mind." She gave Ruth her number and hung up the phone.

Kate continued going through the phone, calling every number she could find. When she finally exhausted her list, she bagged the phone and sent it to the lab. Hopefully, they could find more information than she could.

She put on her coat and decided to head out to start canvassing again. Hopefully, someone saw something, anything that could help them. The weather was as dreary as ever and the ice rained down, making the bitter cold that much more unbearable.

"Wait up for me," Harper said, following her out.

It felt good to have company at such a trying time, and Kate knew that Harper would do whatever it took to support her. She also knew that it was going to be a cold night as they headed out and started knocking on doors again.

Hours passed, and the winds were so bitter that Harper and Kate could barely feel their extremities. They knocked on what seem like hundreds of doors, asking the same questions in different ways. All the doors to the apartments were outside. Kate used to tell Kristen it looked like a Motel 6. It became a joke between them, and Kristen used to always say that she would leave the light on for her. Kate remembered when she bought this place, she had narrowed the search down to three places that they painstakingly looked at. Kristen was not happy with Kate's reluctance about her purchasing a home that had been converted from an apartment to a condo. It pained Kate to remember how she had told Kristen she was buying a glorified apartment. Kristen was so hurt by her comment that she replied, "Not all of us live off a trust fund. Some of us have to budget to have anything. You are so pampered, with your fancy car and nice clothes and paid for "historic" home."

At the time, Kate was so upset that she had said such things; she had never wanted to make Kristen feel bad about having money. She would have been happy to always pay for everything, but Kristen would never have it. She always paid her own way, right down the middle. Kate remembered her response to Kristen was, "At least you have parents who love you. I would trade it all to have had a normal family growing up instead of a drug addict mom and a deadbeat dad. I loved my grandfather, who raised me for most of my childhood, but he was never around. I never even knew how wealthy he was until he left it all to me."

Kate was so upset, and she felt bad for having enough money to live comfortably. However, like most of their disagreements, it ended almost as soon as it started. They really were family.

All the memories Kate had of Kristen kept flowing in and out of her. She felt so helpless, not being able to make any progress in finding her. All she could do was investigate, and she would do everything she could to find out what happened to Kristen. For now, it was time to call it a night. They couldn't knock on doors this late without upsetting the owners and, if they did that, they would get even less information.

"All right Harper, I think it's time to call it a night, don't you think?" Kate said, biting her lip. She knew that Harper would never have given up until she said it was time to go.

"There's always tomorrow," he said with a reassuring smile.

They parted ways and Kate headed home. She always did her best thinking there. Once inside, she sat in her pajamas with a cup of tea and the sound of CNN in the background. With pad and pen at the ready, she tried to create a brainstorming session. She started writing anything that came to mind, in the hopes of looking back on it later and finding something she may have missed.

She awoke hours later, sprawled out between the chair and the ottoman. Her pad of paper sat next to her, filled with words and names in no particular order. She stared at the pad until her eyes got heavy again, and all she could think about was just a few more minutes of sleep.

Chapter 12

Stan woke up, frustrated to have had his dream of Rapunzel interrupted by the sound of his neighbor starting up the snow blower. Indeed, they had lots of snow yesterday, but it was not even daylight out yet and he was already at it. The same thing happened in the summer with the lawn mower. Ron was one of those retired guys who had nothing better to do than annoy his neighbors. He used a riding lawn mower when it would be much more efficient to use a push one. His yard was not big enough to require such a mower. That didn't change the fact that Stan had to listen to him roll his equipment out from the garage on the side of his house. It also didn't help that the window to his room looked out at his driveway.

After wallowing in his irritation over being woken up so early, Stan got up and got ready. He decided that the best way to get back at Ron for waking him up was to keep Ron up that night. Stan thought he could start the generator in the garage and run it for a couple of hours to make his point. Ron was just lucky that Stan didn't decide to turn him to ash; that seemed to quiet everyone down rather quickly. Stan smiled and laughed as he walked to the shower and turned on the water. He knew that Ron wasn't worthy of his time to follow through with any attempts to irritate him, it was always just fun to fantasize.

Even after waiting for the water to get hot, showering and eating breakfast, he was still up earlier than if Ron hadn't woken him. He decided to head to work early and to take a little detour to check on his golden beauty.

The sky looked much clearer today, and the streets traveled nicely since the ice was all but gone. Stan drove past Lauren's house in the morning at a moderate speed, so as not to be noticed. As he passed the house, he noticed a small red pickup truck in the driveway. He thought that mama must be home. He continued to the end of the street and turned the corner to wrap around back through the alley. The closer he got to her house, the faster his heart started to beat. Just as he passed her house, he noticed the huge pile of wood and boxes the neighbors had sitting behind their house. This would be the perfect cover to park behind, because it would give him some shielding from cars in the street passing the alley.

He continued on to work, singing to himself and daydreaming of the events to come. He arrived at work and opened the newly keyed door. He went through his normal routine and headed downstairs to make sure the room would be ready for his new arrival at nine. He unlocked the newly keyed basement door and left it open. Morten was sure to have tons of questions about why he didn't have a key, and Stan needed to come up with an acceptable explanation.

After getting all the crappy busy work done, he headed to his office and worked on the schedule and checked on the arrival of the new tools. By the time he sat at his desk, it was exactly eight. The chimes started singing, and he knew Ruth had arrived.

"Good morning, Ruth," he yelled, as he stayed seated at his desk.

"Oh, hi Stan, how is your morning?"

"Very good, and how has your morning been?" Right after Stan said it, he realized how crazy it was to engage in small talk with Ruth. She never had a simple answer or story. He knew he was in for quite the earful.

"Oh, that silly husband of mine had the nerve to ask me why his favorite dress pants were not ironed. I wanted to reach across the room and smack him. You know, just hard enough to get his attention, but not enough to really hurt him. You know what I mean? Don't you?"

Realizing that this was not a question she expected an answer for, Stan just sat and daydreamed again. He remembered his date with Sleeping Beauty, and how he loved those eyelashes. He loved the way women could tell you so much about themselves through their eyes. They could show mental anguish, or physical pain, fear, elation, and just the pure wonder of what was happening around them. As he continued to daydream, he picked up the pile of messages on his desk, a pile of all the people waiting for a return call from him. The second-to-last one simply said to call Detective Kingsley with the police department. No explanation, just a phone number.

He interrupted Ruth, who had started talking about how she cooked the dinner and cleaned up, and how unfair that was. "Ruth, when did this detective call?"

Ruth kept talking as if he never said a word. She continued on with her story as if it was part of a routine she went through every so often.

"Ruth!" He raised his voice and changed his tone to bring her back to him.

"Huh, what did you say?"

"I said when did this message come in? What did the detective want?"

"Oh, she was asking about Kristen Jackson. You know, the girl whose mother —"

"Yes, yes, Ruth, I know who she is," he interrupted. "What did she want?"

"She wanted to talk to you about Kristen Jackson and her state of mind, something about a missing person. I told her that Kristen was very emotional while making the funeral arrangements and that it was difficult for her to talk to you about it. This was just what I saw with the interactions she had with you and I wasn't even around during much of it. I told the detective that she must have been taken off guard by losing her mother without any warning. The detective still insists on talking with you. Something about why you called her a bunch of times. By the way, why did you call so much? Was there something wrong with the viewing?" Ruth finally stopped to catch a breath.

"She seemed so worried about her mother, and I just wanted to make sure she was okay."

Stan wondered to himself, who the hell was this detective, and why she was so interested in talking to him? He could give her something to think about. Stan wished he knew what she looked like, so he could see if she fit into the fairy tale. The thought made him smile to himself, and only reinforced what he needed to do. Rapunzel needed to go as soon as possible, so the detective would have more to worry about.

"Ok, Ruth. I will take care of it," Stan said as indifferently as he could.

"I'm going to go make some coffee, do you want some?"

"Sure, that sounds lovely," Stan said, as he thought, *whatever it takes to get you out of my hair.*

The rest of the day went by rather uneventfully. He sent Ruth home early at four. To his surprise, Morten didn't have any problem with the locks.

Chapter 13

auren heard the horn outside, and she knew her ride to school had arrived. Her first class was calculus, which she felt she was doing well in, unlike everyone else in class. Numbers seemed to come easy to her.

She grabbed her backpack and some cereal in a baggy and headed out to the car. The snow was so deep it got down between her socks and sneakers. She thought, oh great, now my feet will be wet all day. She hated that!

"Hey, girl, how is your morning?" Lauren said to her friend Dana, thankful that her car was always warm by the time she picked her up.

"Oh, I hate calculus. I wish you could just take my test for me. It is so easy for you," she said as she stuck her tongue out at Lauren.

"You just have to study and you will get it," Lauren said. "Stop partying so much and do the homework, silly."

"I hate homework. Anyway, it is your fault that we're all struggling. You have to show off to the teacher and raise the curve for all of us. Butt kisser!" The formation of a smile emerged around the edges of her mouth.

"Oh, that is so not fair," Lauren said, She laughed, but knew Dana was kind of right. Lauren believed that people like her had to work hard for an education. Daddy wasn't paying for it. She needed every advantage she could get to make sure that she graduated and made enough money to support herself.

Before long, they found a parking spot and headed off to the first of three classes of the day.

Chapter 14

Daylight started shining through the top windows in Kate's living room. Disoriented, she opened her eyes and waited for them to adjust. Within a few seconds, she realized that she was still in that blasted chair. She couldn't help but to think to herself that she was going to pay for not sleeping in her bed.

She strolled over to the thermostat, turned the heat up, and headed straight to the kitchen to start brewing some coffee. She looked through the cupboards and couldn't find a clean coffee cup. She remembered the tea from the night before, grabbed the cup and swapped it with the carafe already dispensing the coffee. She remembered how she used to sit up with Kristen and drink tea. She learned to drink tea at night and coffee in the morning. Kate missed those times. So, she had coffee in the morning — and many times throughout the day — and tea at night.

The shower felt like just what the doctor ordered, hot and steamy. She started to coordinate what she would do to find Kristen that day, and still be able to manage her caseload. Thank God for dry cleaning; otherwise, she would never have had clean clothes. Abbey came in twice a week and picked up, including cleaning the coffee cups. She did what laundry Kate had and made the place look nice and tidy. She loved being organized. She was just very bad at doing it, and it was much easier for Abbey to handle the house.

She headed out the door, dressed in her usual outfit of dress pants, a button-down shirt, and a t-shirt underneath because it was damn cold out there. Shoes were the most important. They had to be comfortable so that she could walk in them or run, if needed. However, they also had to be durable, because she hated shopping and shoes were hard to come by. At least ones she liked.

She loved her BMW utility vehicle. She used the automatic starting timer in the home so her car would be nice and toasty when she was ready to leave. After leaving she flipped through the radio stations until she found a song she liked, and then felt her phone vibrate. Anxiously, she grabbed her phone and answered with an urgent, "This is Kingsley."

"Detective Kingsley, I need you to follow up on the homeless man's death," the chief said. "The mayor wants to know what's going on, and I don't know what to tell him. What do you have?"

"We are working on it sir," Kate said, trying not to sound deflated. "I will put this to bed as soon as possible. We're planning on going back tonight, when more people will be around. We should be able to wrap this up by tomorrow, Chief." She hadn't planned to go back that night, but it wouldn't be a lie if she did it.

"Music to my ears, Kingsley, oh and I wanted to say that I am sorry to hear about your friend going missing. Let me know if there is anything I can do." He hung up the phone before she had a chance to respond.

She dialed Harper and told him the bad news about the commitments she made in solving the homeless case. She knew that he would support her no matter what, and she also knew he understood why she did it. Once they cleared their outstanding case, they would have more time to look for Kristen.

Arriving at the office, she checked the hotline messages for the number she distributed on Kristen's fliers. Most of them were from whack jobs wanting to feel important, but there was always a chance that someone might know something. She started reviewing all the calls and tried to find one worth calling back.

As she stared at her disheveled desk, she tried to remember her last conversation with Kristen. Feeling the blood rise and her stomach start to turn, she tried to remember the call as close to verbatim as she could. It was late morning, on the day of the viewing. She was telling Kate that she was exhausted from making all the arrangements for her mother. She was driving home after leaving the funeral home, and she was very upset about having to view her mother. Kate remembered telling her not to go in the morning, because she was afraid it would be too much for one day. Of course, Kristen couldn't leave it in the hands of the professionals; she had to manage it herself. Kate supposed it gave her the peace of mind she needed, knowing her mother looked good under the circumstances. She remembers asking how she looked, because Kate knew how important it was to Kristen that everything be perfect.

"She looks good, Kate, but I can't quite associate her as Mom," she said. "Even when I was talking to the funeral director, it didn't seem quite real. Kate, he was so proud of the way she turned out, and he even said she looked like Sleeping Beauty. I know he was trying to be nice and make me feel like everything was going to be okay. I just can't look at her and see anything but that she was dead, even when he called her beautiful. All I could see, Kate, was that she was dead and gone and… and… I just miss her so much." Kate could hear her heavy breathing, and she mentally saw the tears rolling down her face.

She sounded so tired on the phone that Kate encouraged her to lie down and said she would call her back in the afternoon to make sure she didn't oversleep. That was the last time Kate talked to Kristen, except the next day at the funeral. And that day, she was obviously somewhere else. She couldn't even manage to talk without the tears pouring down her face. Kate talked to her briefly, and told her that she would talk to her later. Her aunt and uncle drove her home, and that was the last time Kate saw her best friend.

The tears welled up again in Kate's eyes, and she tried drinking some water to push the tightness in her throat down. She thought to herself, what happened to you, Kristen? People don't just disappear.

Chapter 15

Evening came faster than he expected. Stan thought the day was going to be slow, especially with all the planning he wanted to do for the upcoming night. Luckily, he ended up getting busy and completely lost track of time. Ruth came in to say goodbye, and Morten finished and left hours before. The cleaning crew would come at six in the morning to tidy up; another thing his father was too cheap to have done. Stan hated doing all the cleaning. The viewings where there were large numbers of people were the worst, because the floors got so trashed. He smiled to himself as he thought about how happy he was to hire people to do the stuff he hated. His Father saved up a substantial nest egg by being so frugal, and Stan was happy to spend it.

He organized his desk before he left. He noticed the pink Post-it note, and felt the hairs on his neck rise. He wondered what this curious detective wanted. Why him? He had left no trace of anything. He even disposed of her ashes in a dumpster across town. Nobody would find Sleeping Beauty. She was gone, and he knew he was too good to get caught. He needed to give the detective something else to worry about. He grabbed his things and headed to the door, the note flapping in the breeze as he hurried past the desk.

He first drove by the taco place where Lauren worked. Luckily, he was able to see her through the windows at the register as he passed. He took the same route she took home and made sure there wasn't a better place to grab her. Within a couple minutes, he drove by the house and saw that the little red truck wasn't there. He was happy to see that her Mom was not home. He looked in the mirror and tried to give the most sinister smile he could come up with before he burst into tears laughing.

He drove around the back, parked in the alley, and carefully approached the house. He felt very confident that no one was home, since it was almost dark, and there were no lights on. He crept up to the back door and tried to peer into the window on the door. He looked inside and saw a dog running up and barking fiercely.

The dog caught him by surprise; he thought that he really should have factored that into the equation. He couldn't forget this in the future. He ran back to the car, remembering he just screamed like a girl for the whole neighborhood to hear. He got into the car, started it up, and drove as quickly and quietly as he could out of the alley, taking various back streets away from her home.

Once he felt safe, he stopped and looked at himself in the mirror. He tried to smile, but even Stan could see that it was strained and not real. His heart finally started to slow to its normal beat, and he began to think with more clarity. Once he felt completely in control again, he decided to go get something to eat. He stopped at the first place he could see and pulled in the parking lot. As he walked up the sidewalk, he saw a newspaper in the window displaying the headline, "Best Thai food in town." Unsure of what Thai food was, he decided to try it.

The restaurant was modestly full, but luckily there was a table for one available. He scanned the room as he followed the hostess to his table. Mostly couples, a few families, and two different groups of people. One was a bunch of middle-aged men — hiding from their wives, he supposed. The other group he found fascinating. He could see a badge on one of the guys and, for a few long seconds, he couldn't take his eyes off the badge. As he looked up, everyone in the group was engaged in a serious conversation. Everyone but one woman, she looked directly in his eyes and followed him until he gave up the stare first. He appreciated her display of dominance, and wondered if she was a copper or one of the little wives meeting her hubby for dinner. He knew it would be a cold day in hell if she was just a wife. She was a copper. He wanted to look again, but he didn't want to draw any attention to himself. He decided to order and wait a while before he looked back. Carefully, he turned his head and peered over his shoulder, only to see that they were all gone. What a shame. He wasn't done playing games.

Chapter 16

Kate heard people calling her name as she started to come out of her zone. She would sometimes get lost in thought, and many times it was in these zones that she did her best work. The problem was that they didn't last very long, and she could be easily distracted, which just so happened to be the case right then. Harper and a couple guys were trying to get her attention by throwing various objects at her and saying, "Earth to Kate, anyone home…? Earth to Kate…!"

She couldn't help but laugh and proceeded to joke with them. "Which one of you rode the short bus to school? Oh, never mind, you all did, didn't you?"

"Hey, we are going to grab some dinner. Do you want to grab a bite before we head over to the bridge?" Harper asked "By the time we get done, there should be a good size crowd of homeless to talk to."

"Sure, where are you going?" she asked.

"The guys want to go to the Thai place by the office. I know how much you like the place, so I figured you would be in."

"Damn straight I'm in," Kate said, even though she felt guilty eating there, knowing how much Kristen loved that place. She used to tell her that there was nothing better than a small, family-owned place with cheap but good food. Kate had to agree with her on that.

Harper and Kate headed over, with Johnson and Martin following them. As they walked in, Laila immediately came to Kate and said, "Four this time? You can sit anywhere you want."

Kate liked to pick a booth close to the front, in case she ever needed to step out to take a call or leave quickly. She always picked a seat that enabled her to see out toward the front of the place.

They continued with small talk, mostly about the guys' wives and how much they liked to nag. Kate liked being just one of the guys and hearing all their ridiculous stories. When the food came, she checked her phone again for any signs of Kristen and then began to eat. She just loved this place, and always savored every delicious bite. She stopped listening to the guys talking about hot chicks they had seen, and started to go back into the comfort of her zone.

That was, until a very strange man with cobalt eyes walked by and took a long hard stare at Martin's shield. Within an instant, their eyes were locked in a stare down. Kate followed his stare, even when she had to look over her shoulder to track him. She made it a point to never get stared down, especially being a woman in a male-dominated career. He didn't want to let it go; he just kept his gaze on her as if challenging her to a duel. After what seemed like an eternity, he finally gave in and never looked back. After breaking his stare, she couldn't even remember what he looked like, only that his eyes were so fixated on her.

Chapter 17

Lauren really hated her job. She couldn't help but think about all the homework she had and how much she really wanted to just go to sleep. Once again, she watched the seconds on the clock, and punched her timecard at exactly eight. The second she clocked out, Andy yelled from the back.

"Hey Lauren, can you wait an hour to clock out? We just got an order from a school basketball team wanting to pick up. We could really use your help!" Andy paused a second, and yelled out, "Please, Lauren…? Pretty please…?"

"Andy, you know I can't. I hate walking home late by myself. Besides, I have a test tomorrow and lots of homework."

"Oh, come on, Lauren. Just a frickin' hour, how hard would that be? After all, who gave you the weekend off? Hope I won't have to make any schedule changes." Andy laughed as he said it, and there was nothing more annoying than his obnoxious laugh.

"Nope, Andy, you know I can't. It's easy for you, since this is the only job you want. Bet your ass isn't up at six like mine will be! I am going home now. Bye bye," She scooted through the door as quickly as she could, and walked across the parking lot toward her path home.

Lauren was relieved that the bitter wind wasn't running through her like the other night. Once she reached her home, she heard Pepe's ferocious bark and laughed. Pepe could never hurt anyone - he would roll over and play dead before attacking somebody - but she was happy that he sounded so vicious.

Once she made it through the back door and secured herself inside she reached down and petted Pepe. She loved the way he was so happy to see her and she remembered the day her Mom brought him home. Her Mom had gotten him from a coworker who had a bunch of puppies and even though her Mom was totally against animals, she just couldn't resist getting one. She knew how much Lauren would love a dog.

Lauren started for the living room as she grabbed her mom's nightly note from the counter. She found herself looking forward to the notes every night and always tried to reciprocate by leaving her mom one.

It wasn't long before she had Pepe at her feet and all her books surrounding her, as she started a long night of studying.

Chapter 18

The alarm clock buzzed, and Lauren groaned at the thought of getting out of her nice warm bed and venturing into a cold bathroom. The only good news was that she got up on the first sound of the buzz, knowing that would let her steam in the hot shower that much longer.

After showering the whole place was filled with steam, and she finally removed herself from the warmth of the water and stepped out into the now-warm bathroom. She glanced at her watch and hurried to finish getting ready and just in time. Hearing the horn honk outside, she grabbed her jacket, backpack, and her usual baggy of cereal as she headed out for the day.

"Hello, Dana, how's it going?" Lauren said as she turned the blaring radio down.

"Hey, I like this song!" Dana said, turning it up again and continued to sing a horrible rendition of "You Had A Bad Day."

Lauren was thinking about the old joke of asking her who sings the song, only so she could tell her to let them sing it. However, she knew that it would probably go over Dana's head, and Lauren didn't mind not having to make conversation.

After an uneventful day of classes, she caught her ride home with Dana, and changed for work. As much as she disliked her job, she endured it so she could save some money and get through college. Her

Mom wanted her to stay home so she would finish college and Taco Tico was the perfect place so close to home. She had been saving diligently for almost a year to buy her first car, and she had almost $6,000 saved. Another six months, and she would be able to buy a car and pay for the first year of insurance.

She arrived home in plenty of time to change and walk to work; she still clocked in three minutes late. Dreading the sound of Andy's voice, she turned the corner to the backroom to get her apron, and practically ran directly into him.

"You know, if you continue to show up late, I will have no choice but to write you up," he said without making eye contact.

"Yeah, yeah, yeah, I hear you," she said with as much sarcasm as she could muster. "It's three minutes, Andy. Three minutes! It's the middle of the day, and we have one customer in the place. How about I stay three minutes later? Would that make you happy?"

"Just get to work and mop the floors. The sludge from the streets is making a mess," he said without looking at her. Luckily for her, he walked to the back office and closed the door.

Chapter 19

The morning couldn't arrive fast enough. Stan stayed in bed for what seemed like an eternity before he allowed himself to look at the clock. When he finally couldn't take it any longer, he peeked over his shoulder and noticed the clock showed twenty past five.

"Good enough for me," he said. He decided to get up and gather all the things he would need to get the day started. Even more importantly, the things he would need to end the day with a bang. Still full from the huge dinner the night before, he decided to skip breakfast and get right to work.

As he started putting things together, he contemplated how he wanted to handle the whole dog situation. Pepe was a big dog, most likely some kind of pit bull mix and undoubtedly fiercely protective. This would have to be handled swiftly because he didn't want to be overtaken by a dog making his true intentions much more difficult. After much deliberation, he decided to make it as simple as possible. He decided that he would simply use a baseball bat! He figured, how hard would it be to take down a dog if he had the upper hand? The problem was going to be getting in the house and in position to take him out.

After he packed up the chloroform, the baseball bat, a change of clothes, and a few other odds and ends, he headed for the car. The air was chilly but not unbearable. The slicing wind seemed to be at a standstill, and he could only hope that it would continue that night. He started the car and, decided that it didn't need to warm up as much as normal, so he headed straight to work.

He forced himself to drive to work without making any detours, which proved much more difficult than he thought it would be. A deep urge inside of him begged him to drive by and see his Rapunzel, but he knew that he needed to stay away until that night. Thoughts started speeding through his head as he tried to distract himself from his inner urge. He saw Mrs. Jackson on the table with blood spewing from her vein, and then he saw an image of his father's ashes some-where in a distant landfill. Ruth would have had a heart attack if she knew the ashes in the urn were not his fathers. He savored the memory of his first meeting with his new princess; she may have been oblivi-ous to him initially but she would remember him soon enough. His mind continued with an image of Sleeping Beauty and the fairy tale her eyes told him. He made himself laugh with the thought that it was more of a Grimm's fairy tale. He realized that the last image racing through his mind was of the lady at the restaurant who wouldn't let his gaze go.

He immediately went downstairs to get all his things together. He put together his trashcan, and threw the change of clothes inside, along with all the other items he would need. He secured them in the newly keyed closet and headed upstairs, knowing that Ruth would greet him within minutes.

Barely closing the basement door behind him, he heard the chimes on the door. He called out to Ruth before he even saw her. "Good morn-ing Ruth, how is your day?" he said as he headed to greet her. He couldn't help but wonder what she would find to complain about. Before she had a chance, he interjected, "Isn't it a nice day? No wind and a much more bearabletemperature."

"Oh, it may seem nice now, but they are calling for the tempera-ture to drop tonight with the big storm coming in." She headed for the kitchen to make them coffee.

Leaving it alone, Stan decided to just head to his office and get started on the paperwork for the day. After sitting at his desk, he noticed the message to call Detective Kingsley looming in front of him. He decided to make some other calls instead.

The day slowly inched along as he anxiously waited for the sun to set in the distant sky, telling him that the time was nearing.

Chapter 20

Wondering why she even tried to get some sleep, Kate got up and jumped in the shower. As the hot water splashed down on her head, she felt clarity take over and the grogginess of sleep went away. She still felt the weight of working most of the night and was happy that they managed to solve the homeless man's death. She cleared her schedule to work more thoroughly on Kristen's disappearance.

Kate kept talking to herself and asking Kristen, where are you? She must have said this to herself hundreds of times. Thinking nonstop about Kristen, she didn't even realize that she had zoned out and gone through all the details she knew about her disappearance. Pulling into the precinct, she decided to leave the guy at the funeral home another message since he hadn't returned her call. After all, he was one of the last people to see her the day before she disappeared.

After leaving her message, she headed right for the chief's office and gave him the details on the homeless case so he could call the mayor and the media could get their story. "Hey, do you have a minute?" she said, gently tapping on the door and walking in.

"Sure, I would love to get this wrapped up," he said, as he offered her a seat. "Give me the scoop!"

Kate tried to collect her thoughts, but the images in her head were of Kristen and her catching crawdads in the creek by their childhood homes.

"Just give me the brief synopsis", he said. "I need to get to a meeting."

Taking his nudge, Kate decided to give more of an overview than a full version. "Well, as you know, Harper and I went to the Kansas Avenue Bridge last night. We thought that we might be able to persuade more people to talk with an offer of hot coffee. At first, we were stressed out that we were getting there later than we wanted, but it ended up being the best thing we could have done. Upon arriving, we noticed that there were only a few people scattered around the fire, which surprised us. I thought for sure they would be trying to warm themselves for as long as they could. It was about a quarter to midnight when we started asking questions. Even with the coffee, we couldn't get any kind of warm response. So, we just kept walking up and down the bridge, until we found a woman huddled up close with her dog. Hers was the first smile we had gotten all night and, as I handed her a coffee, I knew she was the one to talk to."

"Ok. So she saw what happened?"

"Well, not exactly," Kate continued. "She first gave us her whole story which, if you ever want to buy me a beer and hear it, was actually quite interesting." Kate smiled as he raised his eyebrows, a gesture urging her to hurry up even more. "But, after a while, she finally started to get on topic a little more. She told us that, if we wanted to know what really happened down there, we would need to continue on down the bridge a ways. She said we would see a big set of cut-up boxes made into a makeshift shack."

Kate leaned forward in her chair and continued on, unable to help the rising of a climax in her voice. She knew the chief felt it, even if he acted uninterested. "We headed on down farther than we normally would ever go and, sure enough, we found box city. We approached with caution and opened the makeshift door. Upon shining my flashlight inside, we found that the homeless lady had come through with the goods. At first we thought there was a problem, because there were three piles of seven or eight people, stacked like dominos on top of each other. Many of them were sleeping, and the ones who weren't made little effort to move. When we made our presence known, we saw the start of movement, followed by a frenzy of people trying to get out of the shack.

Within no time, the walls were all down and people were moving away from us fast. I showed my badge and yelled at everyone to stop immediately, saying I would be forced to arrest them if they didn't. We ended up with four who either actually stopped or were in no condition to run from us. To make a long story short…"

"Too late, Kingsley, that was the longest story ever. I should have just read the report," he said as he started writing an email.

"Hey, if I stayed up all night to write the report, the least you can do is listen." She knew it made Chief absolutely crazy to have to sit through long, drawn-out stories. "We finally got the story of what happened. Apparently, the more the temperature drops, the more people huddle together and, sometimes, the ones on the bottom get hurt. At night, they would all draw straws to see who had to sleep on the bottom. In this case, our homeless guy was the one on the bottom, and he wasn't able to sustain the weight on top of him. He ended up suffocating, and was unable to let anyone know that he needed help. He died trying to stay warm." Kate finished the story with the rest of the explanation of what they did with the body, and looked to the chief for closure.

"Well, that is a sad story. I am glad to know that it is solved. Thanks, Kingsley. I appreciate the update."

Taking this as her cue to leave, she let herself out of his office and walked to her desk. Leafing through her messages, she was disappointed, but not surprised, that she had no leads on Kristen.

Chapter 21

Finally, the sky started to darken, and Stan knew that night would be upon him in a very short time. Just like clockwork, Ruth popped her head through his door to bid him farewell. She handed him new messages and a cup of coffee.

"Well, I am going to get going. I need to stop at the store, and do I ever have a list. With all the weather we have been having, I haven't wanted to do much but make soup and curl up by the fire…"

Stan looked at yet another message from the detective again; he started thinking about what he was going to say to her when he finally had to call. Looking up, he realized that Ruth was still talking, and he tried to engage in the conversation.

"…and then she found this hair in her salad and I said, 'Oh no, we have to call the waiter.' And then..." She continued until he was saved by the ringing phone. Stan motioned to her that he would get it, and that she should just go on.

Once everyone was gone and he finished with the accounting work, he locked all the doors and headed down to the basement. Knowing that his princess would be off at eight, he wanted to be at her house waiting at least fifteen minutes before she arrived. That would give him time to get in and take care of the dog before she arrived. He unlocked the closet door and pulled out the trashcan with the change of clothes and the plastic suit inside. He put the clothes on and laid the plastic suit on the counter next to the metal table. Knowing that being prepared was the only way to succeed, he went through the game plan in his mind. As Stan did this, he retrieved the old tools that he kept after getting the new ones for Morten. Once everything had been checked and double checked, he rolled the trashcan to the freight elevator and out the back double doors, to his awaiting car. Once everything was loaded, Stan went back inside and grabbed a quick bite to eat before heading out.

After eating, he looked at his watch and saw that the time had finally come. Practically skipping to his car, he locked the doors and headed out. The night seemed nice, and he could see the moon shining down through the clouds, glistening off the snow-covered ground.

Stan inched slowly into the alley behind her house; he pulled into the exact spot he had planned before. Everything was perfect. The clouds covered the moon just as he drove into the alley. It was as if he was being given the needed cover to stay undetected. After putting on his gloves he grabbed the towel, baseball bat, and baggy with a rag full of chloroform from his front seat, and headed for the house. He passed the back as quietly as a mouse, and kept enough distance not to alarm the yappy dog. Once he was up against the side of the house, he first checked the side windows to see if they were open. The first two were locked, but the third one was the charm. He was very lucky to have it open, he felt like the gods had smiled upon him. He opened the window ever so slowly. Climbing inside, he waited for the dog to chase him down, but nothing happened. He noticed that the bedroom had the door closed, and he could hear the rumbling of the furnace as he stood over a vent.

Slowly, Stan moved toward the door and opened it. Glancing at his watch, he noticed that it was five until eight, and she would be arriving within fifteen minutes. As he stepped into the hallway, he put his back to the side wall and started to call to the dog.

"Come here boy, come on," he said, as he made kissing noises. It didn't take long before Stan could hear him barking and running toward him. Just as the dog turned the corner, Stan raised the bat to bash him. He was caught by surprise, though, as the dog stopped and rolled onto his back, as if he wanted to be petted. After Stan regrouped his thoughts he decided that he needed to finish the job. In one swift motion, Stan swung the bat and rammed it into the dog's head. He raised the bat again and noticed that the dog was not even moving; he had blood coming from his mouth. Stan reached down and felt the warmth of the dog's blood; it gave him a feeling of happiness, but nothing like the ecstasy that was to come. He quickly gathered himself, and wrapped the dog's head in the towel he brought to clean up any mess. He also opened the hall closet and grabbed the first towel he could put his hands on. Stan quickly wiped the blood and took a garbage bag from his back pocket and put the dog and the towels inside.

Crouched in the corner behind the back door, Stan sat on the filled trash bag for support and waited, ever so patiently. It seemed like he felt time move around him as he heard the seconds tick away on the cat clock above the sink. As the tail moved back and forth, he felt mesmerized, and a new calm came over him. Stan quickly came out of his trance. He heard footsteps on the sidewalk to the back of the house. He leaned his back up against the wall so he could give clearance for the door to open. The key went into the door and, when Lauren turned it, Stan heard the lock disengage in unison with the tick tock of the cat clock's tail. He waited for the door to open and, when she entered and started to close the door, Stan jumped out from behind and grabbed her. She immediately started screaming as he slapped his hand over her mouth. Her eyes were locked on his as she scrambled for some explanation. Maneuvering around behind her, he grabbed the chloroform and switched hands.

"Just relax, darling, this will be over before you know it," he said, in a soothing voice. As he coaxed her, he applied the chloroform, and he felt her body giving way as she tried to fight it. "Just give in to it and everything will be ok."

Stan felt her body finally give up, though he held the rag in place a few seconds longer to be sure. Quickly, he grabbed the bag with the dog and heaved it over his shoulder. He moved quickly to the car being careful not to slip; he threw the bag in the back of the station wagon, making sure to give enough clearance to slide the trash can in when needed.

When he carried the trashcan in, he started to worry about the tracks it would make in the snow, and he was angry at himself for not thinking about the tracks. He was careful to remember to walk along the lines of bushes up to the house, his mind started to formulate a solution to this problem. Right before he got to the back door, he noticed a shovel leaning against the house.

Once Stan secured Lauren inside the trashcan and taped it shut, he tried to see if he could carry it to the car without rolling it. He realized that he was not strong enough to carry it and took his chances and rolled it. When the sidewalk to the back of the house ended, there was a section of snow-covered alley, about nine feet, between the car and him. He had already made numerous footprints back and forth. He slid the can into the car then hurried back to the house and grabbed the shovel, smoothing the tracks behind him. He brought the shovel with him and drove through the alley with his headlights off, heading to the mortuary. The beauty of the moon behind the clouds gave him the cloak of darkness he needed to go unnoticed.

As he pulled up to the parking lot, he took a moment to look around; nothing but pure desolation. After he backed up to the back doors, he took one last look around, and opened the back end of the car. Once he started to pull the can out, he heard a soft muffled noise coming from inside. This only meant she was awaking much faster than he anticipated; he decided to hasten his step. By the time he loaded the trashcan in the service elevator, he could hear her getting much louder.

"Help me! Who's out there? Please help me!" she pleaded in a barely audible tone.

"Shh, darling, we are almost there," he replied.

After unlocking the room, he quickly rolled the trashcan to the table. He was a little worried as she became more vocal, and wished he had taken the extra precaution to tie her hands and feet. He hoped that he could restrain her quickly, but it would depend on how awake she was. After starting up the incinerator, he started to cut through the tape that secured the trashcan.

"Now, I am going to open this lid, and I need you to do everything I say. Otherwise, I am going to kill you on the spot." He tried to sound as robust and forceful as he could. "Do you understand?"

He heard nothing but quiet for a few seconds. "Yes," she finally responded in a muffled cry.

He carefully opened the lid and peered down at her. Her eyes gazed at him with a familiar uncertainty. He could tell that she was trying to place him. "It will come to you, keep thinking about it," he said. He reached his hand down and motioned to help her out. As apprehensive as she was, she reached a hand out and clasped his. The trust she had in him was short lived, and he knew she would turn on him the instant she was free from the can. He had to secure her quickly. The adrenalin rose inside him as he helped her out. The minute her feet hit the ground, he grabbed her, and put her in a chokehold. She must have had the same thought as he did, because she decided to fight rather than run away in her attempt at survival. She started clawing at his face and, even though he tried to move, she still caught his cheek. Forcing his weight upon her, he wrestled her down to the ground.

"You son of a bitch, I am going to kill you. Leave me alone, do you understand? Leave me alone!" She gasped for air as she continued to fight.

Stan grabbed the chloroform rag out of his back pocket, then grabbed her and placed it over her mouth. This time it was much more difficult, the chloroform was greatly diluted. Finally, she started to slow down. "I still don't know you," she mumbled. "I really don't know you." Her eyes rolled to the back of her head, and he seized control over her.

He thought for sure she would remember him from Taco Tico, even if she was bored out of her mind. He felt a little deflated that she didn't remember him, but not enough to give up feeding the beast.

After he secured her to the table, he placed a piece of duct tape over her mouth. He hurried out to the car, grabbed the bag with the dog, and headed back inside. Just before closing the door, he noticed the wind had picked up, and he knew the storm was on its way. With any luck, the snow would fall and cover all traces of him being at her house.

He got back to the basement and threw the bag on the floor. Hearing the thump of the lifeless dog, he started to hum to himself...fe fi fo fum, I smell the blood of the golden one and started laughing uncontrollably.

He opened the incinerator, put the bag with the dog inside, and closed it up. He walked back over to Lauren and noticed that she was still asleep. He sat in a chair while he watched her sleep. He went over the events of the night in his head, and felt the anticipation of what was to come harden his groin. Closing his eyes, he controlled himself and waited, ever so patiently, for her to wake.

After what seemed like an eternity, but only calculated to about twenty minutes, she started to stir. He immediately hardened again, and rose so he could meet her gaze when she opened her eyes. Ever so briefly, her eyes opened, and then rolled back into her head. By the time she opened them long enough to focus on her surroundings, he was so close to her face that he could smell the breath coming out of her nose. He reached down and, ever so gently, pulled the tape off her mouth.

"Ooh, that's got to hurt, sorry about that," he said in a soft tone. "I will pull it slowly, so that it won't hurt as bad."

She seemed to come fully awake. He could see the anger in her eyes replaced with fear once she realized that she had been overcome.

"It's okay, darling, it won't be much longer," he said. "I just have a couple more things to do."

He went to the table next to her, took a hairbrush, and started to brush her hair. After he finished, he laid the brush down on her chest. Her eyes scanned his every movement, and it gave him a feeling of exhilaration. He ran her golden locks through his hands, pulled them up, and brushed them along his face. He closed his eyes, as he smelled her hair. He took the brush off her chest, and took the rubber band off the handle, and tied off a lock of her hair. He reached over for the scissors, cut the lock off, and laid the scissors back on the table. Without even seeing her eyes, he felt her fear in the heaving of her chest.

He stood up and looked down on her.

"I will do anything you want. What did I ever do to you?" she continued. "Why me…? I don't understand."

Done with words, he walked behind her, stripped off his clothes, and picked up his folded plastic suit. Never taking his eyes off her, he put the suit on and took the scalpel off the table. He carefully cut a slit in the plastic, from his belly button to halfway between his knees and waist.

He watched her strain her neck to see him.

"Rapunzel, Rapunzel, let down your hair," he said, over and over. "Rapunzel, Rapunzel, let down your hair... Rapunzel, Rapunzel, let down your hair." He was interrupted by a blood-curdling scream.

He took the scalpel and sliced it with precision across her jugular. Her scream dissipated as the blood started spewing out. He ran his fingers through the blood, and he enjoyed his hardness as it grew and grew, and the warmth encompassed every part of his being. He placed both hands through her blood, and watched death come over her, as her eyes turned to stone. He closed his eyes, took one hand and licked the blood, like a cat lapping up milk. Once the blood flow started to slow down, he took his other hand and started to move it up and down on his hardness, with a rhythm that was as much uncontrollable as it was pleasurable. He screamed in ecstasy as he reached his climax and fell to the ground. Unsure how long he laid there, he rose up and looked down upon Rapunzel. "Good night," he said. "Good night, my Rapunzel."

Chapter 22

S tan's blood pumped through his veins, as every part of his being relished the new life being born into him. The hours soon turned into days, and life became truly like a fairy tale. He would have believed the brilliant idea came to him by accident, but he knew better. He believed it was his destiny! His fame! His rite of passage!

His newfound life had him doing things that he never would have done before. He used to stay huddled in his room in the basement, praying to go unnoticed. Now as the man of the house he no longer hid in the basement, it gave him great joy when he threw everything associated with his father out. Now he was in his father's bedroom and now he was in control of his home, his life and more importantly his future. A night without having to hear his father's voice was the best night he could have ever imagined. He now realized how much living he had been missing out on. He had become quite the restaurant connoisseur, and had even dabbled in the kitchen himself. He loved to walk the streets, even in the cold. He felt the life of the city as it pulsed through his veins and as he breathed in the crisp winter air. This morning's walk was a necessity after he had the most spectacular dream the night before.

His mother was reading him the fairy tale books and the pages were so vivid and colorful. They depicted a time full of happiness. In this dream he envisioned the books and how significant they were to his newfound life. His father had gotten rid of the books shortly after his mother's death and Stan believed that it was done to hurt him. Stan believed his father was jealous of their mother and son relationship. He was saddened that he didn't have the books and believed that they were important to his life now. He decided that the books would not only guide him to his next princess, but they would also become his signature, his claim to fame.

He walked into the local used bookstore, noticing a whole collection of fairy tale books in the window. He knew he had come to the right place. As soon as he saw them, he knew he had to have them. He calculated his actions very carefully. He wanted the books, but he also knew that they could never be traced back to him. He needed to go unnoticed. He lowered his head to avoid any unnecessary eye contact with anyone. He searched for the children's section and headed in that direction. A distant voice came bellowing through the store.

"Good morning! I will be right down. Let me know if you need anything."

"Thanks, just looking," Stan replied, feeling the beginning of an opportunity forming. He surveyed the store as quickly as he could for cameras or anyone else. Once comfortable, he looked at the first bookcase and, seated on the top, was a boxed set of thin, hardback books. "The Fairy Tale Collection," he whispered to himself, as he fought the urge in his groin as it started to grow. It has them all. And they were used, which was even better. Keeping his gloves on, he took the boxed set and, without further delay, he wrapped them inside his jacket and headed for the door.

After the chimes of the door, he heard the distant voice from the back yell a quick, "Thank you."

He walked at a brisk pace, just short of a jog, trying to control his nerves and be as normal as possible — even though he felt like his stomach was going to fall to the ground. Once home, he grabbed some Clorox wipes and ran them across the kitchen table. Carefully, he opened his coat and sat the boxed set on the table. After he looked at the books for a long time, he finally picked them up. He knew what he wanted to do and he got right on task. First, he grabbed some latex gloves, a trash bag, a Sharpie pen, a box of unopened manila envelopes, and some stamps.

Sitting at the table, he took some wipes and gently went over all the books and the box. He found *Sleeping Beauty* and opened the cover. Careful not to use his normal handwriting, so it couldn't be matched someday, he started to write in the upper left-hand corner of the cardboard cover.

He wrote, *Good night, my Sleeping Beauty, you will always be the ONE who awakened me from my slumber.*

As he looked at his inscription, he felt a sense of peace come over him, knowing that it was only a matter of time before his brilliance would be noticed. Continuing on, he opened *Rapunzel* and started with his next inscription. *Good night, Rapunzel. You could never be TWO golden.*

After he blew, and eventually wiped, the dust off the box of large envelopes, he realized that his father had these for a long time. He addressed both of them very carefully, then secured the book inside, added the self-adhesive stamp, and pulled the self-stick tab off the envelope. His last touch was adding the initials "FTM" as the return address. He wiped the envelopes once more with the wipes, and loaded them into an unused trash bag.

He sat the bag on the table as he reached for the next book. He already knew which one it would be. He pulled out *The Little Mermaid* and began reading. He started dreaming of what his next princess would look like and he wondered if he would find her in time to feed the beast.

Once he finished reading the next book he carefully hid the books and headed for his car. He drove to the other side of town, and mailed the envelopes at a post office drive through. On his drive home, he realized how hungry he was. He decided to cook at home tonight. Seeing an organic grocery store, he pulled into the parking lot.

Chapter 23

If they would have gotten the call sooner than three days ago, they might have had a trail to follow. Now they were searching for this college girl, and the leads were absolutely nonexistent. Kate felt torn about having to put Kristen's disappearance on the back burner for someone else. She didn't feel like one should take priority over the other, and she just wished they could give both equal time.

"Earth to Kate, come in, Kate," Harper said, as he snapped his fingers and waved his hands. "Are you there, Kate? Wake up."

She shot him a forced smile that she knew he wouldn't let her get away with, yet she couldn't help but give it. It was all she could offer right now.

"Hey, why don't we get right to work and find this missing girl?" he said. "Burying yourself in work will keep your mind busy. That always helps me when I'm down. Sound like a deal, Kate?"

Harper always had a way of making her feel better. He had this great ability to wrap his voice around her head and calm her.

"That would be great," Kate said. "Let's start from the beginning again. What was her routine, and was it deviated? We know that her mother didn't report her missing until she received calls on the answering machine from both Taco Tico and her friend Dana. The trail may be cold, but it can't be nonexistent. Everyone leaves a clue. What is Lauren's?" she got up and began pacing. "Okay. Lauren's friend said she pulled up to the house to pick her up for school, the same as usual. She also said that she was running late and, when she honked her horn and knocked on the door, there was no answer. So she just left, and left a message on the machine. Then, Lauren didn't show up for work. That has only ever happened one time, and that was because she was sick and fell asleep before calling in. Andy, her boss, thought she had just quit because they had not been getting along, so he left her a nasty message about not showing up to work.

"That could be a cover," Harper said, tapping his pen on the notepad.

Kate nodded. "True. Then there's her mother. She works the night shift, and sometimes went days without seeing her daughter. They left notes for each other and made it a point to have one on one time once a month. Her mom noticed that the notes she left were not being picked up and that Lauren was not leaving her any. She didn't check the machine for almost two days since Lauren went missing. The mother, Lisa, had been working double shifts to save up for a surprise vacation she was planning for Lauren at the end of the school year. It was like Lauren lived an invisible life, nobody really noticed that she was gone. Harper, it is your job to keep track of me, and notice if I disappear, especially while Kristen is still missing."

"I promise," he said. "I will leave no stone unturned looking for you."

"Okay, back on track. Oh, the dog! Harper, where is the dog? The neighborhood canvass turned up nothing and neither did the nearby dumpsters. Whoever took her must have entered through the open window and waited for her. He likely killed the dog, based on the blood traces found in the hallway. We also know that there was a struggle by the back door, based on the disheveled curtain hanging on the door, and how the rug was all bundled up to the side. So he waited for her, but why her? Does he know her? We need to talk to all her friends again and make sure she wasn't seeing anyone, see if she had any enemies. This time, we need to expand, and talk to more people. It is the only lead we have. This was premeditated. He knew her, he knew her routine, and he knew when to take her. This guy needs to be found."

Kate chewed her lip, thinking of all the different things associated with premeditated murder. The likelihood of finding Lauren alive was slim. Someone wanted her, and they knew exactly how to make that happen. She felt the hair on her arms stand as she realized what the unknown assailant must be capable of.

Chapter 24

Sharon worked as a checker at the grocery store as a means to an end. Her true passion was singing, even if it was at a hole-in-the-wall bar in the worst part of town. If she wasn't over thirty, she could have tried out to be on the next *American Idol*. But those days were gone, now that she was sitting on thirty-one.

She didn't mind working as a checker. She had the opportunity to meet lots of different kinds of people. On the slower days, she tried to write new songs. Mostly in her head, but, sometimes, she had enough time to grab a pen and any kind of paper lying around to write them down. In her house, she had a box full of all the words from songs in her head, on everything from the backs of mail to toilet paper. Someday, she hoped to actually finish one of the songs that she had started.

The day had been as monotonous as any other as she continued to go through the motions of checking out customers.

"Hi, will you need any stamps or ice with that?" She looked up at the customer and put the pen and paper down below the register.

"No thanks...uh, Sharon, is it? I hope I am not interrupting you. It looks like you are in quite a train of thought." She watched his eyes leave her locked stare and slowly lower down.

"Oh, no, it is just a silly compulsion of mine. I write down song lyrics in my head whenever they pop in. I am always trying to keep track of these pieces of paper everywhere." She laughed a little.

"Hey, how did you know my…" she said, as he gave a wry smile and pointed to her nametag. Laughing, she caught those eyes again and went on to say, "Oh yeah, of course, my nametag." She felt her face filling with blood in embarrassment as she continued with the grocery scan.

Once she completed his order, he walked away, looking over his shoulder and saying, "Have a good day, Sharon." Then he was gone through the automatic doors.

After standing there feeling rather flushed, she looked up to notice a woman waiting to check out.

"Are you all right?" the woman said. "You look as red as a tomato."

"Oh, yeah, it's just warm in here. I'll be fine…" Finishing the thought in her head, she continued thinking about the charming man with the blue eyes, and hoped to see him again someday.

Chapter 25

Stan truly believed that fate was being handed to him on a silver platter. As he loaded his groceries into his car, he yearned to go back, to talk more with his princess. His mind was made up that she was the next one. She would be his beautiful, fiery, red-haired Ariel! Her pale, milky skin blushed with only minimal flirting from him. He was deeply satisfied that she was every bit perfect to help him continue his fairy tale. She would satisfy the beast waiting to be awakened from its slumber once again. A few weeks were about as long as the euphoria of his renewed life lasted. He knew it was time once again. He felt very fortunate that he was able to find Ariel so quickly.

He devoted the whole evening to thinking about his new princess. He tried to find out who this Sharon was. He decided to eat at his new favorite Thai restaurant and come up with a plan.

After arriving and ordering, he decided to call and see what he could find out. He felt sly going to the pay phone in the back by the restrooms. He looked up the number to the grocery store in the phonebook, and dialed.

"Hi, I am looking for one of the checkout girls. Her name is Sharon. Is she in?" Knowing that her shift was probably long over, he wanted to find out when she would be in, more than anything.

"No, she left at six."

The lady who answered seemed uninterested in giving Stan any more information. So he decided to take the direct approach and see what he could find out, while staying careful not to become too noticeable.

"Oh, shoot! I was hoping to catch her before she left. For some reason, I thought she worked the late shift." He tried to sound as disappointed as he could.

"No, Sharon never works nights. She is usually singing at a few different places in town," she continued. "Are you a friend of hers? I could tell her you called, or I can call her cell and have her call you. Would that work?"

Going from uninterested to seeming too interested made Stan nervous, but his curiosity was killing him, and he wanted to know where she was.

"Well, that is actually why I'm calling." Taking advantage of the opportunity, he decided to change tactics and use a different angle to get information. "I am a talent scout, and I have heard about Sharon. I'm told she is a great singer. Have you heard her?" Stan went on, trying to engage her more.

"Have I heard her? She sang at my sister's wedding earlier this year, and everyone talked about her for months. Are you like one of those people from *American Idol*?" Stan felt the urgency of her voice, waiting for his response with baited breath.

Smiling to himself, he continued. "*American Idol*, uh well, I guess you could say that I do have some affiliations with them —"

"Oh my, she will be so disappointed to miss your call. She has been wanting this her whole life, and she was so upset that she was too darn old to be a part of *Idol*." After a brief pause, not long enough for Stan to interject, she went on, "Have they changed those rules?"

He had her right where he wanted her. He knew at this point she would remember this call, but that an investigation into the call would go nowhere. "I would like to talk to her," he continued. "Do you know where she will be tonight? I can go listen to her and meet her at the same time. It will be perfect." He waited, knowing that the first one to speak lost.

"Let me see… Hold on, let me ask Tony. He always knows where she will be."

Stan heard her yell for Tony before getting back on the line. . "She is at the Blue Whale tonight. Do you know where that is? I bet you big Hollywood boys don't know your way around such small towns." Stan could hear how important she felt, being able to help Sharon. Little did she know that she had only helped Sharon find her fame as his next victim!

"I should manage fine. I have a navigator in my car that will tell me where to find it. Thanks so very much, you have been a real pleasure to talk to." Before she could respond, he hung up the phone and picked up the phonebook again. He knew the name sounded very familiar, but he wasn't sure exactly where it was.

After finding the bar's location, he went home and took a quick shower and shaved. Putting on his clothes, he began to appreciate shopping, and finding apparel that made him feel good. Not to mention how much easier it was to gain people's trust when you could charm them with you words and wow them with your appearance. After calling the Blue Whale, he found out that Sharon was actually due to sing between eight and ten. He decided to arrive about nine, in order to watch the show and leave before her set was done. That way, he wouldn't have any problem hanging out and waiting for her to leave, so he could follow her home.

Stan heard music as soon as he arrived and, as he came closer to the door, he felt the vibrations under his feet. He was very pleased to find a packed house. He pushed his way in and found that it was standing room only. He positioned himself to see the stage clearly, but so that he could be hidden among people. Someone was talking about the band, and another man going on and on about the lead singer. He understood, because he became mesmerized by Sharon's voice as soon as he heard it. It was so fluid and smooth, and it made him feel safe and warm. Watching her sing, his mind wandered into another world. A time when he had hopes and dreams of one day becoming a doctor, a time before his father could squash his dreams; back to a time when his mother took him under her wing and sang to him. A time when she whispered things in his ear when she thought he was sleeping.

Noticing that the crowd was moving around, he suddenly realized that Sharon was done singing, and no longer on the stage. Packing away his memories and hiding them deep inside him again, he wandered through the bar, trying to get a glimpse of her. Hoping he didn't miss her, he walked outside and went to his car.

After waiting only another ten minutes, he saw Ariel walk out the back door and hug the bouncer, a burly guy who clearly shouldn't be reckoned with. He followed her with his eyes all the way to her car. Stan smiled to himself, as he thought that any true harm to most people will not come in a parking lot. This was just too easy!

Her drive home was only a couple of miles, and Stan followed at a safe distance. Once he saw her pull into a driveway, he pulled over to the side of the road and parked. He watched her go inside a little house and the lights go on, and he tried to determine if she was actually alone. Could it be this easy? After about an hour of sitting, the house went dark. He drove around the block, and looked to see if there was anything that could compromise his mission.

Once he got home, he lay in bed and closed his eyes. Sharon's raspy, bluesy voice enveloped him, and he felt that warm, safe feeling drift through him. He started picturing her on the table as he debated what kind of souvenir he would need from her. He pictured cutting her tongue from her mouth as he watched the horror in her eyes. He also pictured cutting her vocal chords away and putting them in a beautiful box. However, if he did that, he wouldn't be able to see her pain, and it will most likely kill her before he could transfer her life to him. Going back and forth with the ideas, he felt a hardness growing, and he started to stroke himself in an effort to release the throbbing. But he wasn't successful and gave up.

Moments later, he could hear her sweet voice in his head, becoming a lullaby that took him into a world of sleep.

Chapter 26

Taking a much-needed lunch break, Kate drove to Kristen's condo and sat at the kitchen table with her head resting in her hands. Closing her eyes, she remembered Kristen and her skipping school and going out drinking on senior day. She remembered how they were both so drunk that they didn't know how to leave the lake. They must have driven through the winding roads ten times before finding the right turn to get out. They were laughing the whole time, until Kate wasn't feeling so good and started throwing up out the window of the car. Kristen didn't even stop the car, Kate's vomit leaving a trail behind them.

Her laughs quickly turn to tears, as she started missing Kristen all over again.

Kate yelled at the top of her lungs, "Where are you?" not caring whether anyone in any adjoining condos could hear.

After gathering her composure, Kate started to go through Kristen's mail in hopes of finding a clue. She first opened the mortgage statement to make sure that the payment Kate made was posted correctly, and that the bank used the extra to cover future payments for a year, rather than apply it to the principal.

After sorting the junk mail from the regular mail, she ended up with two piles of mail — and one manila envelope. She opened the bigger envelope, and pulled out a book, *Sleeping Beauty*. Kristen never seemed interested in children's books, and there was nothing inside the envelope except the book. She opened it and skimmed through the pages. Nothing interesting caught her eye — until she read the inside of the cover.

Good night, my Sleeping Beauty. You will always be the ONE who awakened me from my slumber.

Who the hell was this from? Kristen didn't have a boyfriend…

Kate picked up the envelope and looked at the return address. It read only "FTM."

She thought for a moment…FTM? Who are you? She looked at the envelope and the book on the table, and tried to figure out who FTM could be. Kristen would have told her if she had a boyfriend, or even a new friend. Kate felt her gut tighten as she tried to process all this information. She knew this had to be something to do with her disappearance. Otherwise, the hair wouldn't be standing up on Kate's arms, and she wouldn't feel like she was going to throw up.

She called Harper and told him to hurry over to Kristen's, no matter what he was doing. Kate wanted him to drop everything and bring the crime-scene kit. She thought she had her first clue, and she didn't want to waste any time getting it processed. She started to pace around the condo as she anxiously awaited Harper's arrival.

Chapter 27

The nice thing about working at the grocery store was that Sharon could make her hours whatever she wanted them to be. Finally climbing out of bed at ten, she went downstairs and started the coffee brewing. Turning on *The View* and putting it on soft mute, she made her morning call to her mom. She had been Sharon's biggest supporter through all her years of trying to become a professional singer.

After a rather uneventful conversation, she headed for a quick shower and then it was off to work. Arriving promptly at eleven, she started daydreaming about becoming someone famous. Many people dreamt of winning the lottery, but she would have been happy just to be able to support herself by singing.

The workday inched by, but her final work hour neared, and she started rehearsing the songs she would be singing that night. Before long, she found herself humming some of the familiar melodies she had grown to love. Clocking out, she started back through the store.

"Hi Sharon, I have been meaning to talk to you since I got here," Mary said, running up to her, "but just haven't had a chance."

Sharon stopped walking. "What's up?"

"Have you talked to the scout?"

"Uh, no, what do you mean?" Sharon replied.

"The gentleman who called last night said he was a scout for *American Idol,* and that he was looking for you. I told him how great you are and that you sang at my sister's wedding and brought tears to everyone. Anyway, I told him where you would be, and I thought he would show up last night. He seemed very interested in meeting you."

"Really, do you know his name? Was he with *American Idol* for real?" Sharon could hardly contain herself.

"No, he said he would go see you himself. Maybe he meant tonight. Now that I think about it, I must have been confused."

"Thanks, Mary, I appreciate it." She tried to recall her set the night before. Oh, she hoped she didn't blow it. If only she could have known, she could have given the performance of her lifetime.

While she was driving to the club, she tried to convince herself that she didn't blow it and that he really was coming tonight. Or, maybe he'll want to make sure and see her one more time; just in case, she started preparing for the show of her life.

For the second time that day, time inched by as she awaited show time. Once she stepped up to the microphone, the whole world vanished around her, and she sang her heart out.

Chapter 28

Daydreaming at work was one of the best parts of Stan's day. It was also the most productive in helping him establish timelines and get things in order. His room was ready for his new princess, and everything had fallen into place beautifully. He enjoyed receiving new life from his princesses, but he also enjoyed the planning of how to bring them in. The seed he planted with the old lady at the grocery store was a sure way to get Ariel to talk to him. Dressing in his best casual-but-dapper clothes, he formulated and mastered his plan.

The good thing about a funeral home was that everyone who worked there was always eager to go home. After a day of death and sadness, people wanted to be with their families. Ruth was the easiest; all Stan had to do was tell her she could leave, and she was already headed for the door. From that moment, it only took one long, drawn-out story for her to be on her way out.

Stan watched the clock practically stand still for hours, but it was finally time to be born once again. After driving to the Blue Whale, he headed to the back parking lot and parked a couple of cars down, in the darkest part of the lot he could find. This time he had to be faster because there would be no time to spare. He rolled down his windows, and listened to the music resonate from the club. He closed his eyes and pictured Ariel, beautiful Ariel. Once the music stopped, he waited for her to come outside. It took longer than the previous night, and he started to worry that something had changed. After he heard the creaking of the back door open, he noticed the bouncer walking her out the back door rather than standing post at the front door. As she started walking to her car, he could hear her conversation with more and more clarity. Something about his girlfriend and how he should call her.

Stan crouched down in his seat as he intently waited for the bouncer to go inside, but he could see that he was a stickler for watching her to safety. Finally, she waved at him as she opened her car door and yelled, "Goodnight, Bull!"

The door was barely closed when he jumped out of his car and headed for hers. As she fumbled for her keys, Stan lightly tapped on her passenger window.

"Hi, my name is Kent. Do you have a minute?' He tried to sound calm as he turned on the charm and showed her his pearly whites.

She looked unsure.

"I am with *American Idol*," he said, prepared to charm her socks off. "I talked to someone at your store, and they told me to find you here. I came last night and missed you, so I wanted to make sure I caught up with you tonight."

"Oh, yes, of course. Mary told me you called. I thought I had missed you, or that you didn't like my show." She sounded like she was going to burst with excitement, and Stan knew he had her.

"Would you like to go have a coffee and talk? I have some demo tapes from a couple of songwriters I would love you to hear. I think that your voice would be perfect for them. Come on, I'll drive. We can listen to them in the car, and you can tell me where to go for coffee." Stan watched for hesitation in her eyes. There wasn't any.

"Oh, sure, we can even go to my house, if you want. Let me get my things." She reached behind and grabbed her purse, opened her car door, and followed him to his car.

Once she was inside, Stan started the car and drove before she even had her seat belt on.

"So, you have demos in the car?" she asked. "I wish I would have brought mine. You know, I am a songwriter as well."

Amazed at how anxious she was to jump in bed with the big bad wolf, he smiled as he drove down a couple side streets, waiting for an opportunity to subdue her.

"Oh, I am sorry," she said. "You should have turned back there."

"Oops, I get so turned around in unfamiliar places."

"No problem. Where are you from?"

"A little bit of everywhere. I guess you can say I have lived in many places." He saw the dark church parking lot he had scoped out before. "Let me just pull in here and I will start one of the demos."

He parked the car and undid his seatbelt, then reached behind with his right hand, as if to grab the demos. Instead, he pulled the chloroform out of the bag and slowly transferred it to his left hand, just outside her peripheral vision. He quickly braced his right arm around the back of her seat, and slammed the chloroform onto her face.

Her eyes went wild with bewilderment. She started clawing as she fought the fight of her life. Slowly, her struggle slowed, and she slumped down in the seat in total submission.

Feeling total dominance, he took an old blanket from the back seat and put it on the console between them. He gently laid her head down on it, as if she were taking a nap. He then reached back, grabbed a bottle of vodka, poured just a little in her mouth, and lightly dripped it on her clothes. He figured if anyone stopped them on the way, he could always say she had too much to drink and passed out.

Heading for his special room, he took care not to draw unneeded attention to himself. He turned on the radio and started to daydream. The drive to the mortuary went very smoothly. He noticed that there was nothing out of the ordinary as he pulled into the garage. Once inside, he opened the trash container and placed her inside. Happy not to have to tape it closed, he entered the mortuary.

As he walked through the hallway, he enjoyed the silence of the dead. No one here at night could stop him. He headed for the elevator, and down to his special room.

Chapter 29

Sharon heard movement around her as she tried to open her eyes. She smelled a musty odor and tried to remember if she was in her basement. It smelled familiar, even though it seemed surreal. As she became more coherent, she started to remember what happened. She remembered the man with those eyes, and that smile. She remembered his car and the parking lot. She started to scream, not sure whether it was out loud or in her head. She realized that she was not anywhere she had ever been, and that her arms were strapped down to a table. Her screams were out loud because she heard them echo off the walls. She also heard soft laughter coming from someone nearby.

After focusing, she turned her head and saw him, that man, that *American Idol* man.

"Ok, ok, shh there is no reason to scream," he said. "Anyway, no one can hear you from down here. So, all you are going to do is ruin that voice, that beautiful voice of yours."

The terror screams slowly turned to a quiet calm, as she tried to see what he wanted. "But, I thought you were a talent scout," she said.

"Well, my princess, if it is fame you want, then I will give it to you. You see, we could both help each other out. I give you fame, and you give me life so I can live on in infamy." He said it with a most sincere tone that chilled her to the bone. Sharon knew she was not going anywhere.

Chapter 30

Stan thought to himself how much he loved the point when they resigned themselves to the fact that they were not going anywhere. The power they gave to him fueled the beast inside, and he could barely contain himself. The defeat in their eyes was his proof that he had won, and he knew that the best part was coming soon.

He had already prepared all his necessary tools and arranged them in the precise manner needed. The incinerator was rumbling in the background. He leaned down and asked one simple question: "If you want to live, you have to do one simple thing for me. I want you to sing me the most beautiful song you can, as if it was for your life. Can you do that for me? After all, you don't want to make me angry, do you?" He looked in her pleading eyes, trying to convey reassurance that everything would be okay.

After contemplating for a long minute, she started singing. It was really rough at first, but after a while, she started singing from her heart. He knew he would never forget her as she sang "The Wind beneath My Wings" and, as the song neared the end, he opened his eyes and pulled the sharpened knife from the big pocket of his coveralls.

He couldn't blame the girl for suddenly stopping the song after he laid the knife on her chest. He wasted no time grabbing her jaw and pulling down. Her resistance was futile as he pried her mouth open and placed a small rubber ball, about the size of his palm, between her upper and lower back teeth. Then, without hesitation, he took the knife, grabbed her tongue with his left hand, and sliced through it, taking it in his hand. She was gurgling an ear-deafening scream as she started choking on the blood.

Saddened that he couldn't relish the prize in his fingers, he dropped it down and made the cut through her jugular. He could feel the warmth of her blood as he ran his fingers through it. Leaning down, he gently touched the spewing blood as her life surged through every part of his being. Once the blood started to slow, he wrapped his hand around his groin and started to stroke. The warmth of her blood and his hardness became one as he released once again and became whole.

Once it was all over, he looked down at the mess he made, and smiled as he picked up her tongue. The warmth of it made him hard all over again and, for the first time, he reached ecstasy twice in the span of minutes.

"Good night, Ariel, my beautiful nightingale."

Chapter 31

As Kate was sitting in her favorite Thai food place, she couldn't help but notice the flowers lining planters along the shops on the street reminding her of spring and the warm weather. She had three case files opened and closed one only to go on to the next. She looked for clues in the files, at the victims' homes, and at their workplaces. She walked the routes they liked to walk and drove all the different routes they could get from one place to another.

"Hello Kate, are you there Kate? If so, please pick up," Harper said, looking down over her.

"There has just got to be something we are missing, Harper. Here, look at Kristen's file. It could use a new set of eyes." She continued reading Lauren's file without even looking up at him.

"Will it be the usual, Kate?" the waitress asked.

"Of course, that sounds great," Kate said as she continued reading.

"How about you, sir?"

"I'll have the number four, please," Harper said.

The waitress walked off, and they continued to look through the files as they passed them back and forth to each other.

"Ok, Kate, let's start at the beginning. Going back to Kristen, who was the last person to talk with her? We have checked all the mail, right?"

"Yes. The only thing unusual was the book. The only ones to talk to her were her friends and family at the funeral service. She also talked to the funeral home director. Who, now that I think about it, still hasn't returned any of my calls." Kate closed Kristen's file folder and looked at her notes on the front cover. "I've left him a few messages. For a persistent guy, he sure hasn't shown any persistence in getting back to me. I need to talk to him to see if he can shed some light on her state of mind, aside from the obvious grief." She added a note to make him her next priority.

"Do you want me to go by there and talk to him while you talk with the families of the victims?"

"No, I'll go by there. Why don't you stop by the club where Sharon sang and see what you can find? We can meet up later and compare notes. How about we meet back at that taco place where Lauren worked, Taco Tico. I would like to also stop by the grocery store where Sharon worked but, since it is farther out, we can do that one last."

They finished their lunch and set out on their missions. There had to be something that they had missed. There had to be a slip up somewhere that told them who the kidnapper was, how he picked his victims, or what he had done with them.

Kate hurried to the mortuary so she could cover as much ground as possible before meeting with the chief for a debriefing the next day. She was thinking she would need to call a press conference to warn women about this predator out there.

Chapter 32

Sometimes Stan's destiny was all too clear for him; these beacons of brilliance came to him in waves. Today was no different than any other day — except for one new opportunity, something he would never have thought of before. Driving into the parking lot for work, he saw the same scenery as always. He saw the mortuary in all its magnificence, with the extra-large parking lot to accommodate all those sad and vulnerable families with the same big yellow farmhouse at the edge of the parking lot. Nothing new this time, except a "For Rent" sign was up in the front of the farmhouse. A sign that told him what he needed to do. It was at this point he realized he was going to sell his home, which had done nothing but accumulate bad memories from the time he was born. A home where he watched his mother die of cancer, a mother who was his lifeline, one who let him dream and be who he was. His dreams died the same day as his mother, but for his father that day was nothing more than business as usual. Stan spent almost his whole life having his father tell him how to think, how to live, and how not to ever dream. If not for Sleeping Beauty, he would never have known what life could be and what it felt like to truly live.

After slowing through the parking lot, he wrote the number down, headed straight into work and made the phone call. Acquiring the home as a renter proved easy; owning a mortuary was not too bad on an application. The next step would be to get his house listed and sold, which shouldn't be too hard. It was located in a very nice historic district and, from what he had heard, it would sell quickly, even in this distressed market.

He pulled out the phonebook, knowing exactly who to call. How could he forget a name like Nichole Nickels? Especially since her name was all over every billboard, parking bench, and grocery cart in his area. She seemed to specialize in the historic district, and her slogan was, "Your home may be as old as George Washington, but I promise to get you more than a million quarters." Damn right, Stan thought to himself. His home should be worth at least two or three million quarters. He made the call.

After setting up a meeting at seven, he realized that this was going to be a great day. He continued working all morning and through lunch, softly humming "Wind Beneath My Wings." The only thing that pulled him out of his own world was the sound of the bell on the door, and he realized that Ruth must already be back.

"Did you have a good lunch with your son?" He called out.

The voice that answered wasn't Ruth's. "Hi, my name is Detective Kate Kingsley. I am looking for Stan?"

His mind started to whirl around as he jumped up from behind his desk and headed for his door. He was surprised by how calm he felt.

"Then, I suppose you came to the right place. I'm Stan." He headed out into the hallway. "Nice to meet you," he said, reaching out to shake her hand. "Please come in and sit down."

Looking her up and down, he was disappointed that he couldn't think of any princess who looked like her. She had the long, dark hair of a princess, but she was way too confident and rugged to actually be one. He was taken back when he caught her gaze. Her eyes were dark brown and serious, and her body language showed that she was anxious to get on with the task at hand. He continued to his office, and motioned for her to have a seat.

"I left you a few messages," the detective said, clearly irritated. "Why haven't you returned any of my calls?"

"Well, I am running this place on my own since my father's death. It's not that I thought to myself, 'Hey Stan, don't call Officer Kingsley back.'

I have been really busy and, to be honest, I forgot. I didn't know that this was such an urgent issue." As he turned his back to her to close the door to his office, he couldn't help smiling and enjoying this just a little.

"Actually, it is Detective Kingsley, and this is regarding Kristen Jackson."

"Oh, my apologies, Detective, I had no idea someone so young and beautiful could be a detective so soon. How long have you been on the force?" He could see she was clearly annoyed at his intrusion. He kept trying to picture what princess she could be, but he just couldn't place her. Kate was definitely in a league of her own. The beast had not called on her.

"I am sorry to take up your time, but I just need to ask you a few questions. You knew Kristen Jackson's mother, right? I mean, you prepared her after her death?"

"Yes, I helped in the preparation for her viewing. Then they sent her off the next morning to the church." He knew what she really wanted was information about Kristen, but he wanted to make her work for it.

"I was more interested in her daughter, Kristen Jackson. You did talk with her extensively, didn't you?" She watched his every move, and her hard gaze continued.

"Only to the extent of making sure she was happy with her mother and how she looked. Miss Jackson was very adamant about making sure she looked the best she possibly could. I couldn't really blame her. I would want the same for my mother.

"I am sure Kristen appreciated your efforts. How did she seem to you when you talked to her? Was there anything unusual? I mean, I know that she had to be grief-stricken, as anyone would be. But I am looking for anything unusual that you may have noticed, since you deal with grief on a daily basis."

"Well, she was so worried about everything going perfectly," he said in the most sincere voice he could come up with. "I didn't notice anything out of the ordinary. I just wanted to make it the best for her, as I do for all my grief-stricken families."

"Also, I saw you called her repeatedly on her cell phone the afternoon before the viewing," Kate said. "Is that usual for you to do? I mean, why not just call once and leave a message?"

"Well, as I said before, I wanted to make sure she felt comfortable with all the arrangements we made for her mother. She was so upset, and I wanted to ease her mind from some of the stress of planning her mother's funeral. You know, Detective, we stay in business primarily from referrals..."

"So, it was a marketing technique? You called her so many times because you wanted to make sure she referred all the people she knows who die to you?"

"You make it sound like I'm a used car salesman. That is not fair at all. I go the extra mile, because that is how I have been taught. This place has been in my family for generations, and we have great pride in our reputation." He paused for a moment before trying to get back to the point of the conversation. "That's all I know about Kristen Jackson, except she hasn't even paid her final bill yet. Has something happened to her?"

"She's missing," the detective said. "I'm just trying to find out what happened to her."

"That would explain the bill. I thought it had something to do with her being unhappy with our service. Just another example of how far behind I have been since my father's death. If I recall, Detective, my father passed the night before Mrs. Jackson's viewing. I was the only one who could take his place and, to be honest, I am learning as I go. The paperwork is a mess here."

"Stan, I am sorry to hear about your father. I had no idea. I didn't mean to sound like you did anything wrong. It's just that Kristen was also a friend of mine, and I know she would never just pick up and leave..."

Kate looked down. When she looked back up, Stan noticed her eyes seemed much tamer, and she softened as she looked at him.

"Do you have any clues?" Stan asked, feeling almost giddy inside from learning that they were friends. He felt exhilarated, but kept his emotions in check and put on the most concerned face. "This is just horrible. I had no idea that was why you were calling. I am so sorry, Detective. Is there anything I can do? I would be more than happy to provide you with a copy of the guest list from the viewing. Do you think that might help?"

"Stan, that would be very helpful," she said. "I can't believe I hadn't thought of that."

"Not a problem at all. I'm sure this has been very trying for you."

"It has," she said. "When do you think you could get that for me?"

"No more than a day or two. If you give me your number, I will make sure to call as soon as I find it."

Kate reached across his desk to shake his hand, and Stan more than happily obliged. They said their goodbyes, and she left.

Oh, how lucky he felt that she had not called to his inner beast. After all, as Hannibal Lecter would say, the world was more interesting with her in it. He whispered to himself, "Catch me, Kate. Catch me... if you can."

Chapter 33

Kate was not sure how she felt about Stan. The man answered most of her questions with more questions. Something about him seemed familiar, and Kate tried to recall if she had met him before. He was no doubt a handsome man, but he had all the charm of a snake. Those piercing blue eyes put holes right through her when he talked. The good news was that he was going to give her the guest list. She couldn't believe that she hadn't thought of the guest list before.

She started driving toward Taco Tico, and gave Harper a call on her way. "Hey, old man, where are you?"

"Well, old lady, I was just driving the area around the taco place. Nothing new came from revisiting the old workplace. I was waiting on you to call, to see what you want to do."

"Well, I am heading that way now. Why don't we just meet at the coffee place on the other corner? I could really use a coffee, and then we can drive out together to the grocery store where Sharon worked."

"Sounds good, I will order your usual and see you in a few."

Harper hung up, and Kate continued to think about her conversation with Stan. What an odd bird. How awful to lose a father, and then have to figure out the family business so quickly. She supposed she understood why he didn't call back, but she did leave a few messages.

Once she met with Harper, she inhaled the fresh aroma of coffee and took a few long sips before engaging in conversation.

"So, any news on the places you went?" Kate asked.

"Nothing really great, I talked to the bouncer at the club, Bull Grantham. He said he walked Sharon out that night, like he does all other nights. He said he always watches until she gets in her car. The only thing he remembers was that he thought there might have been someone in a car further back in the parking lot, getting ready to leave. He said it wasn't anything unusual, and he always figured that, once she was in the car, then it was safe to go inside. He seemed very protective of her."

"How protective, did he seem capable of anything?"

"No, no, I don't think he is our man. He has a pretty steady girlfriend, and the rest of the staff said he's a good guy all around."

"Those are the ones to worry about."

"Just the same, I was going to check his alibi and talk to his girlfriend. I don't think he is our guy, but no stone unturned, right?"

"Yep, that's the way to do it. No stone unturned. How was the taco place, anything there?"

"Nothing new there. I don't think those kids even know what day it is. They already have two new employees."

"Well, we'll just keep going with this. We have to meet the chief at four, right?"

"Yeah, we should have just enough time to get to the grocery store and back to the precinct."

"Oh, I talked to Stan at the mortuary, and he offered us the guest list for Kristen's mom's viewing. I thought that might be helpful. Other than that, I didn't get anything very useful, but I guess it is something."

As they pulled up to the store, Kate was happy to find a parking spot up front. When she had a cart full of groceries, she always wound up parking a mile away. It was ironic, but she supposed she should never turn any good fortune away.

As they walked into the store, she looked for the nearest employee so she could ask some questions. She noticed a young kid standing at an empty register, waiting for someone to check out so he could bag their groceries.

"Hello, I'm Detective Kingsley. I would like to ask you a couple questions," Kate said.

"Sure, I guess," the kid said, looking nervous.

"You guys have a checker by the name of..."

"Sharon? Have you found her?" he asked with an eager expression.

"No, I am sorry. But we are looking for her, and we wanted to talk to people here to see if they could give any clues. Did you notice anything unusual about her recently?"

"You mean other than she is gone?"

"How about at work, was there anything unusual? Or, was anyone hanging around who was out of place?"

"No, I can't think of anyone," he said, after thinking a moment. "You could ask Mary in the office, they are pretty close. I think she's there now."

"Thanks, is it this way?" Kate pointed over to customer service and, after he gave a nod, she headed in that direction. She motioned to Harper to keep talking to everyone and she headed for the office.

After only one knock, an older woman answered. She saw Kate's badge, and it only took a second for the tears to start coming.

"Ma'am, is something wrong?" Kate asked.

"Oh no, Sharon is dead, isn't she? I just knew it would be the worst."

"Dead, why would you think that? Do you know something?"

"Why else would you be here? Police don't come to people's work asking questions if they aren't dead," she said while grabbing a tissue and wiping her eyes.

Kate walked into her office and closed the door behind her. "She is missing, but we are trying to find her. Can you tell me anything about Sharon that might help us?"

"She's such a nice girl. Did you know she is a singer? A beautiful voice, she even sang at my sister's wedding. Not a dry eye in the room when she finished. And I mean a good cry, not a sad one."

"How about at work, was there anything unusual? Or, anyone hanging around who didn't seem like they belonged?"

"No, nothing that I can think of, and I would know. She tells me everything."

Kate asked her a few more questions, gave her a business card, and headed for the door. As Kate opened the door, she said, "What a shame, too. After all these years trying to become a singer, she was finally getting her chance."

Kate hesitated, "What do you mean?"

"Well, that *American Idol* scout called and wanted to know how to find her. I knew she was going to make it big once he heard her sing. I guess that won't happen now —"

"*American Idol*, do they send out scouts? This seems quite unusual that they could track her down at work. He certainly couldn't have heard her sing at work. Did he leave a name?" Kate said, and the lady got a look of horror on her face. "When did this man call?"

"It must have been the night before she disappeared. I remember because he was so disappointed that he missed her."

"Did you give him any information about her?"

"Well, yes, I told him how she sang at my sister's wedding and how there was not a dry —"

"Anything else, did you tell him anything else? This could be important," she said impatiently.

"I told him she sings at the Blue Whale, and when she would be in next. How else was he going to find her and hear her sing?"

Kate picked up her cell phone and dialed Harper.

"I need you to get a dump on all the phones here at the store for three days prior to the disappearance. I think we just got our first lead. It may explain how he gained her trust." Kate's blood pumped as a glimmer of hope emerged. "Also, Harper, I think he went to the club to hear her sing. We have to see if anyone saw him."

After giving Mary all the information on how to reach her, Kate got a promise from her that she would ask everyone who worked at the store but wasn't in to give her a call. Kate wanted to talk to everyone. No stone unturned.

Chapter 34

L isting his home was a walk in the park. Stan was actually quite surprised to find that it was worth much more than he initially thought. It would make for a nice nest egg, if he ever needed a quick getaway. Although Kate did seem smart, he knew she was no match for him. However, he also knew that it was always better to be prepared.

The next few days would be hectic, as he tried to put together the things he wanted to keep and the things he would give away. He also had some business to tend to that he had been neglecting; he needed to clean the ashes and bone fragments out of the incinerator. There were pieces of bone that could link his princesses to him, and he needed to make sure that didn't happen. He decided to do it after work that night. In the meantime, he made a note to himself to stop and pick up a sledgehammer. He figured that if he used the hammer to break up the bones, and then move them into various dumpsters throughout the city, they would be at the landfill within a few days. He thought this was much safer than burying them somewhere. Too many things got dug up.

Moving through the home was more like an obstacle course these days, and he realized that it was sometimes more work looking for things than just improvising. So, when he found his favorite old baseball cap in a half-open box, he couldn't resist putting it on. He remembered wearing the cap in high school and how it made him feel like he was invisible when he pulled it down over his eyes. He always tried to remember to take it off before the teachers told him to, so as not to draw attention to himself. His father hated the cap and always said that only cowards who couldn't look people in the eye wore caps. Eventually, he couldn't find it anymore. He always knew that his father had taken it. After Stan cleaned out his father's crap, he found it in the back of the closet. So, finding the cap that morning was meant to be; he put it on and headed for the door.

After arriving at work, he tended to business as usual. Still, he couldn't help but think about Kate. He wondered who she was and what she was about. His curiosity got the best of him and he decided that, after all these years of work, he deserved a day off.

Walking through the hallway, he looked for Ruth. He knew it wouldn't take long to find her because, at any given time of the day, she would stop for a refill of coffee. She was incessantly making coffee. Stan found her in the kitchen.

"Hey Ruth, I think I'm going to take today off. The Williams viewing should all be set for this afternoon. I'm confident you can handle things in my absence."

"Oh sure, Stan, I hope you are feeling okay. I hope you haven't come down with the swine flu. Oh, I hear that is horrible. My friend from church group said that her sister's friend's daughter might have it. They think she got it from another boy at school who was just visiting Mexico. I think they even quarantined..."

His mind started to wander; he was thinking about Kate again. She had so much confidence, but he could see she had so much pain by the loss of her friend. He was solely responsible for her pain, and it exhilarated him. He couldn't help but smile.

"Staaaan, this is nothing to smile about. Do you know people are dying from this? I bet you didn't know that, did you?"

Coming back to the present, he realized that Ruth had taken his happiness as somehow mocking her.

"Oh Ruth, I am so sorry. I wasn't smiling about this. I was thinking about something else and lost track of our conversation. You are right, maybe I don't feel well. I should get going before I make anyone sick." He knew saying this would scare Ruth half to death.

"Yes, you should go right now. No sense for all of us being sick now, is there? As a matter of fact, you should take a couple days off. You sure do deserve it."

"Thanks, Ruth."

Heading straight to his car, he knew exactly how he was going to find information about Kate. He started to drive the short distance to the library. Spring was a nice time of year to really enjoy the weather. It was not smoldering hot and humid like the summer, and not bitter and freezing like the winter.

Arriving at the library, he approached the closest employee he could find. The young kid wore a sloppy nametag that said his name was Matt.

"Hi, I was looking for the best way to find out information on a friend of mine who I have lost contact with. How would I go about doing that? Do I need to use those microfilm things to look up past newspapers?"

"Dude, where have you been? Use the Internet. You can find out anything about anyone. It is actually kind of creepy how much stuff is on the Internet."

"Can I do that here?" Stan asked, feeling embarrassed about being so behind the times.

"Just go down that hall and turn left and you will see a bunch of computer stations along the wall. Do you have a library card? If not, you will need to go up to the checkout station and get one. Then go and sign in with the computer area librarian." he said.

Stan took a chance that he wouldn't be asked for a library card, he didn't want his name out there or to show any identification. It didn't take long to find the computers, and it took even less time to feel the rumblings of the beast deep within calling out to him. As he looked at his new princess sitting at the computer help desk, he knew he had found his Belle. Luckily, signing in was easy and he didn't need a library card after all.

It had been weeks since the beast had been fed. Stan had been getting worried that he wouldn't find his next princess. He had taken days of walking aimlessly around in the hopes of finding her. It wasn't until he wasn't actually looking that he realized he had found her. How perfect, he thought.

"Excuse me, could you help me get started on a computer? I am kind of new to this," he said.

She looked up from the book she was reading and gave him the softest, most sincere look. He felt himself melting right in front of her. She was beautiful with a quiet essence about her. He knew he had to have her.

"Sure, follow me and I will get you set up," she said as she handed him a clipboard. "Just sign in here."

He followed her over to a computer desk with a small privacy wall. Once she got him set up with a quick tutorial, he got started. Closing his eyes, he could still smell her lingering scent as he sat there. Looking up periodically, he noticed that she had gone back to reading her book, while she twirled her hair with her free hand. It reminded him of how his mother used to play with his hair as she read to him.

Chapter 35

Harper and Kate drove back to the precinct in a state of silence as they thought about all the information they had just learned. Feeling anxious about their meeting with the chief, Kate used the lights on the car to help them maneuver through traffic. Her phone rang, and she picked it up immediately, "Kingsley here."

"Kingsley, is Harper with you?" Chief Broxterman asked.

"Yep, we are on our way to meet you, what's up?" She was sure that something bad had happened if this couldn't wait. "Please tell me there isn't another victim."

"No, but the Blue Whale received a book, just like the one you found before. It's *The Little Mermaid*, and the envelope is specifically addressed to the 'big, bad bouncer.'"

"Looks like this is his calling card," she said, knowing a calling card meant there would be more victims unless they caught him. "What does the inside cover say?"

"It says, 'After a special dedication, THREE is now off key.'"

"Do you still have the book? Or has it been sent to forensics? I really want to see it."

"We literally just got it in," the chief said. "However, it's most likely contaminated. They had it sitting on the bar while they waited for us to show up."

"Well, I guess they'll find as much with this one as they had with any of the others, which is nothing."

"There is more, Kate. The Blue Whale is swarming with reporters because the bouncer contacted the media. This was why I called. I need you and Harper to head over and talk to them, make sure this doesn't become a panic. We could meet after, but, right now, I need you there."

"On our way right now, Chief, ETA is about ten minutes."

Chapter 36

Absolutely amazing! This computer stuff was as important as the missing link everyone was always talking about. Stan could literally find out anything about anyone from anywhere. The only thing that held him back was his clumsy fingers. He noticed young children around him typing the letters much faster than he could. It only took a couple of searches before he realized that he was hooked and he knew his next purchase would be a computer. Another thing his father was too cheap to buy and another thing he would enjoy buying with his father's money.

He had been at the computer for hours, even though it only seemed like minutes. He had looked for every opportunity to go talk to Belle. Sometimes what you are looking for is right in front of you. Walking up to her, he pointed to the guide on vintage books she was reading, using it to start a conversation.

"So, you like vintage books, huh?" he asked.

"Oh, yes! The older the better," she said, as her eyes sparkled. "This book explains how to find the true rare books from the many forgeries out there. I have already gotten a few good finds in the last few years. I have also seen some really good forgeries out there, but I've been fortunate enough to stay away from them."

"That sounds very interesting, good luck with it. I hope you find some great books," he said as he headed back to his station. He immediately started searching the Internet for information about rare books. It didn't take long to find one that he could entice her with. Almost giddy, he headed back to her.

"You know, I have a bunch of vintage books that have been passed down through the generations. My father recently died, but I know he has some really old stuff. I don't have as much interest as my family did, but I do know that one of the books is worth something. My father used to tell me the story, but he would never read me the actual book, because he said he wanted to preserve it. You may not even be interested…"

"Oh, what book is it?" she said with utmost curiosity.

"Do you know the book, 'The Count of Monte Cristo'?"

"Yes, it has always been one of my favorite stories."

"All I know is that it is a hardcover print from like 1896." Once he told her the year, she got even more interested.

"Oh, that is quite old. And you say it's a hardcover? Sounds like you really have something."

"Yeah, I am just not much of a bookworm. The truth is, I am selling my family home and moving. I just can't move all those books with me. They may be my family's tradition, but I am trying to start over and create my own traditions. You wouldn't be interested in any of them, would you?"

"Oh, I would be very interested. But I don't make much money here." She shrugged. "So my budget for my passion is really limited."

"Well, I am not interested in making a killing on these books, but I really would like to get rid of them. How about we work something out? I would rather have someone like you have them than some dealer who would take advantage of someone later. We could do an exchange. I sell you the books, the ones you like, at a discount. In return, you can give me some computer lessons here at the library, so I can become more proficient. What do you think?"

"Oh, I don't know if I would feel right about that…"

"It's totally up to you. I don't want to pressure you. Either way, I hope you can still help me with the computer lessons." He allowed a moment of silence, waiting for her very important response.

"Well, of course I will still help you with the computer. That would be my pleasure. I would love to see the books. Do you want to bring them in, and I will look them over? I promise I will let you know if you have anything of great value. I could even refer you to someone who will give you a fair price."

He knew the next moment was of the utmost importance. Getting her to come to him would be tricky.

"I am sorry, but I never even caught your name," he said as he put his hand out.

"Rose" she said as she reached out and shook his hand.

Rose, how perfect was that? She was destined to be a part of him. She was undoubtedly the next one.

"Rose, that must be a very special locket," he said as he pointed to her necklace.

He felt himself getting hard, as she put her hand to her necklace and rubbed it between her thumb and index finger. She massaged it with so much love, and he couldn't help but feel the beast within start to rumble, and he knew he had to have it. For a moment, he thought he might have to excuse himself so that he could gain control, but reality came back to him, and he heard her talking.

"I was named after my grandmother, who was named after her grandmother, and this locket was passed down through the family to me. We are all named Rose. Except for my mother, because my grandmother was actually quite the rebel and she wanted to break away from the traditions of the family. Much like what you want to do." She smiled at him as she said it, but kept the locket tight in her grip.

"So, does it open up, the locket?" he asked.

As she pulled her other hand up, she took the vintage rose locket and opened it. He could see a very old picture inside. "This was my great grandmother, Rose; she was the first one to wear the locket. My grandmother never wore it, but my mother has always been intrigued by family tradition, and she named me Rose in an effort to keep it alive. I never really understood tradition but, after my grandmother died, I received the locket from her in her will. That was just a couple years ago, and I have worn it ever since. I am sorry! I just keep rambling on and on, and you are being so polite just listening to me…"

"Are you kidding me? You are making me want to rethink this whole family tradition thing." He smiled.

She smiled back at him and started to talk again. But she was interrupted by an old lady who didn't seem very personable. Now this was how Stan remembered a librarian.

"I am so sorry to be late, Rose," the old librarian said. "I've had one heck of a day. I should have called, but I kept thinking I will be there any minute. Thanks for waiting."

"Oh, my, I have completely lost track of time!" Rose said.

"I'm going to run and put this stuff in the break room, and I will be right back to take over." The old lady was off and running, as quick as an old lady could run.

"I should let you get going," he said. "Maybe I can get your number so I can call to make arrangements. Or should I just call the library?"

"Hmm, probably best not to call here," she said. "We're not supposed to receive personal calls. I can give you my home number. I don't have a cell phone."

"Me neither, I don't want people to be able to get a hold of me all the time." He chuckled, causing her to laugh. He didn't feel the least bit bad about lying to her about a cell phone. Of course he had one; he was always on call with the mortuary.

"I know, why be available to everyone?" she said, as she wrote her name and number on a piece of scrap paper.

"Actually, do you have any plans this evening?" he asked. "I mean, I know it is presumptuous, but we could order something to eat and go through the books at my house. That is, if you want to. I totally understand if you can't." He maintained the smile he knew she liked; he could see she loved the flirting.

"Well, I don't really have plans tonight. I really would love to see your books. Do you live far from here? I don't have a car with me at work, but I could just go home real quick and meet you at your house."

As fate would have it, this was a perfect opportunity. His mind gathered all the information and quickly converted it as the beast within began to rumble. Stan wasn't even sure of what he was saying, but knew that something that felt so right couldn't be wrong.

"Seriously, I live only a few blocks from here. I actually walked as well. I like being outside." He was telling the truth about where he lived, but being deceitful about how he got there. "We could actually enjoy the walk to my house, and we can stop at a restaurant and pick up a couple burgers on the way. Do you like greasy burgers?"

"I could really go for a greasy burger," she said, and he could see the excitement building within her. He guessed she was thinking this was becoming more of a date than a business transaction.

"Great, how about I just meet you out front and we can go from there?" he said as he walked off toward the exit.

He passed the old lady as she headed back to relieve Belle. Happy that she never even noticed him, he kept his head down as he exited through the sliding doors.

"How was surfing?" the boy from earlier called out as Stan left. "Did you find what you were looking for?"

"I found exactly what I was looking for, thanks," he replied. Stan knew he was taking a great risk here. He would be remembered, maybe not by the old lady, but definitely by the bratty kid. For a brief moment, he considered making him part of his infamy, but quickly decided that he was not worthy. He would take his chances. After all, no one here actually knew who he was.

Stepping to the side of the building, he waited for Rose, his beautiful Belle!

Chapter 37

It wasn't very often that guys flirted with Rose. She did feel lonely many nights wishing she had someone to share her passions with. However, the truth was that for Rose there wasn't much else in life other than reading and she didn't put herself out there too much to meet people. She almost felt ashamed to be having dinner with a man who was clearly flirting with her. She knew she was not interested in a man who didn't understand family or traditions. However, she couldn't stop thinking about his books. What if he did have great books, she felt it was an obligation to her to at least check them out. In the end she knew that she would have to let him down easy and tell him she wasn't interested in him romantically. Rose knew she was somewhat using him for his vintage books but she just couldn't help herself. She thought he was cute enough with those eyes but just not her type, she couldn't see them cuddled on a couch reading books for fun. She finished gathering her things and made one last walk through the computer section, as she finished up her shift.

Noticing that the guy never signed off, she signed off for him. That would also give her a chance to see his name since he didn't sign in with the clipboard. Pulling up the signoff screen, she noticed that his login name was Edmond. The computer signed off before she could notice his last name.

"Goodnight, Judy, all the computers are secure," she called out. "There are people on computers two and five. Other than that, it seems really quiet."

"Thanks again for being so understanding, Rose," Judy said. "I am so sorry for being late. I hope I haven't held you up from anything."

"No worries, Judy, I will catch you later," she said as she headed out to Edmond.

She continued through the automatic doors. Looking around, she didn't see Edmond and felt a bit of relief not to have to lead him on when he was clearly interested in her. However, she then noticed him leaning against the side of the building. She walked toward him, and the guilt of leading him on almost took over until she thought once more about the books.

"Hi, Edmond, long time no see, huh?" she said, smiling.

He gave her a curious look, but then he smiled. "It's Ed," he said. "Edmond is way too formal, don't you think?"

"Sorry, hope you don't mind," she said with a sheepish grin. "I saw it when I logged you off the computer."

"No problem, shall we get going?" He extended his arm for her to wrap hers in.

He was definitely flirting. She couldn't help feel a little ashamed. Her mind started wandering, trying to picture what his home looked like. Would it be one of the old homes in the historic district right around the corner? Oh, she hoped so. Old charm was one of her favorite things.

As they walk up to the little drive through burger shop, they proceed to the side window to order. He looked at her with a gesture to go first.

With dinner in hand, they headed to his home. Not even noticing that they were walking down the alley, she admired the historic homes and dreamt of someday living in a place like this.

"Well, here we are. Watch your step. Some of these pavers are a little loose from age." He held her arm gently, but kept her sturdy at the same time.

"I just love it, Ed. It looks much like the way it was originally built. I would give anything to live somewhere like this."

"Well, you can have it, Belle. Oh, I mean, Rose."

Rose was taken back slightly from being called Belle, but figured it was an honest mistake. "What do you mean? You're not really selling this, are you?"

"Yeah, it is way too much for me and, now that my father is gone, I just want to start new. I have it on the market to sell right now."

As they walked in the door, she let her eyes wander and take it all in. He proceeded to a small table in the kitchen, and set the food down. He pulled a chair out for her, and she sat down.

She soon realized that the burger hit the spot. She didn't realize how hungry she was. They both ate in silence, catching each other's eyes and shyly looking away. Yes, he was flirting. He was thinking this is a date more than anything else. She was anxious to see the books because she started to regret leading him on.

"You will have to forgive the mess. I have boxes everywhere, since I have been packing up to move." Wiping his mouth with his napkin, he crumpled the wrappers and tossed them in the trashcan. "If you will excuse me for just a minute, I am going to the restroom."

"I think I could manage just looking at all the wonderful things in your home," she said.

"Feel free to look around," he said. "I will be right back."

She took him up on the offer, and walked through the archway into a formal dining room. Looking around, she saw old-world furniture, including an antique desk. It had old-world charm, but was covered with new-world books. The collection of children's books seemed odd, and she chuckled to herself and wondered if these were the books he was talking about. Now she started to wonder if Mr. Charming was married with kids, divorced with kids, or just a happy uncle. Before she could wonder too long, he came back.

"If you want to follow me, I will show you the secret room full of all the great stories of all generations." He extended his hand to hers.

Focused on nothing more than seeing the books, she had no concern where he was taking her. She took his hand and walked slightly behind him.

"Sorry, you must be careful, these steps are very old. Oops! Let me turn the light on."

Letting go of her hand, he moved around the corner, and she could hear him rustling with something. She patiently waited at the top of the landing. As he came back, she noticed that he had one hand behind his back and a large smile on his face. Within a split second, she felt fear rising from her stomach and spreading like cancer through her body. Her knees started to buckle, but she couldn't take her eyes off his blue eyes, which now seemed distant and cold. His smile was ravenous as he grabbed her by the hair and pulled her to him.

By the time she realized what was happening, she was within his space. She started to scream and tried to pull away, as her arms flailed in all directions. She felt a damp cloth over her mouth, and she realized her time was short. Immediately, she fought, and she caught him with an elbow smack in his nose. She heard a crack as he screamed in agony.

"Ouch, you little bitch! Just stop fighting it. It will be over sooner than you know it."

She took this opportunity and wrestled free from his grip. The only place she could go was down the stairs, the dark stairs. She ran down them, and fumbled through the basement for somewhere to hide.

After a few moments of what seems like an eternity, she could hear him methodically coming down the creaking stairs. She could hear him humming and calling out. "Oh, Belle, come here my princess. You are my destiny." He kept saying it, over and over. "Belle, Belle, Belle, Belle…"

Belle, what was he talking about? She remembered that he called her that earlier.

"I can smell you my princess. Prince Charming is coming for you. Are you ready?"

She made her breathing as shallow as possible, the closer he came. How did he know where she was? Could he really smell her? How else could he know? Before she knew it, he was upon her. He grabbed her by the hair again, and pushed her to the ground, knocking down everything around them. She felt the damp cloth again, and she could hear him calling out.

"Belle, Belle, Belle. Let it go, my princess. Belle..."

She could feel her body going limp, everything around her blacking out. His chanting got softer and softer; she could feel his hot breath upon her face. Sleep took over, the chanting stopped and the last thing she thought was 'there are no books...'

Chapter 38

Arriving at the Blue Whale, Kate could see that there was a feeding frenzy of press surrounding the place. She saw the bouncer outside, talking into microphones from all the different stations around him. One reporter Kate worked with before, Sara, saw her and dropped Bull like a lead balloon. She just about tripped and fell, trying to catch Kate before any other reporters could.

"Kate, can you tell us anything? Is this case related to the other missing women? Do you have any suspects?"

The questions kept coming as she continued walking toward the entrance of the bar. She motioned for Bull to come with her as she opened the door and waited. She wanted to talk with him before answering any other questions.

"Listen, I will answer questions in a few minutes," Kate told the gathered reporters. "I want to talk with some people inside first, but when I am done, I will come out and answer questions, starting with you." She pointed to Sara. After all, they did have a history, and she had always been fair when Kate asked her to keep things off the record. Those kinds of alliances were hard to find.

"Please, let's have a seat, Mr. Grantham," she said once she closed the door. "I just have a few questions."

"Sure, I answered questions from the other officers. Anything I can do to help."

Kate asked him the usual questions, starting the process from beginning to end, then from the end to the beginning, trying to find any gaps that they could fill in. He was very eager to help, which was a plus.

"I'm sure you have gone over this a few times," she said. "But when you say you saw a car out in the parking lot, did you see anyone inside?"

"Well, not exactly."

"Then what was it that made you remember it?"

"Well, it was running, but it looked like it was just sitting there idly. No brake lights or backup lights. So, I could see the exhaust, but it didn't look like they were actually ready to leave."

"Why do you remember this?" she said, "Did it worry you at the time?"

"No, I don't think I even noticed it at the time. I think that I remembered it later, when I looked back on it."

"Do you remember what kind of car it was?"

"Well, it was hard to see, but I am pretty sure that it was a dark car. I think it was a big sedan of some sort. I can't remember much more than that. I wish I could, but the information is just not in my head. I have tried and tried, but all I come up with is what I have told you."

"I understand," she said, trying to reassure him. "It is really hard to want to help but not be able to come up with anything."

Once she was done talking with everyone at the bar, Kate headed for the door and walked past Harper, who was still talking to the bartender. She could hear him asking the usual questions, trying to get some clarity on anything that might be useful.

The questions started coming as soon as Kate walked outside. She decided to make a statement, rather than answer the same questions a hundred different ways. She walked up to Sara's microphone, and everyone else came over with theirs. Addressing the whole crowd, she started her impromptu statement.

"As you all know, we are in the midst of a very high-priority investigation, and we encourage anyone who can contribute any information to please step forward and call the police department. We are working diligently at trying to find whoever is behind these abductions. We have three confirmed disappearances, and we also have a calling card from the killer. It seems he wants to take credit for his work. We are advising all women to take extra precautions, and be extra aware of their surroundings and people around them. We believe the perpetrator has taken two women from their homes, but it also appears he is cunning and manipulates women to come with him. However, we also believe that he has made many mistakes, and one of these will bring him to justice. We will be making more statements very soon, but that is all we have for now."

As she walked to her car, she knew Harper was following without even seeing him. They were always so in sync with each other. She could hear the questions continuing, even as she shut the car door and headed to the precinct. She was anxious to get to work on this, and she anticipated a long night.

Her mind wandered on the drive, as the silence brought back memories of the past, memories of Kristen and her. She couldn't help but feel a lump in her throat as she fought back the tears.

Harper put his hand on hers, "We will find him, Kate, I promise, we will find him."

Kate felt comfort having Harper around. She started thinking about the first time they met. Kate was newer to the force and Harper had already been around the block a few times, even though he wasn't much older than her. They originally weren't partners; that happened by Kate's request after he saved her life. She felt indebted to him and hoped that someday she could return the favor.

She was a rookie when they first met and he was newly married with his first daughter on the way. Kate and her partner, Officer Neil Harris, were heading to a routine domestic abuse call. Her partner filled her in on all the details on the way to the call, and it sounded to Kate rather routine as well. When they arrived at the house and knocked on the door there was an eerie silence. When no answer came after repeated knocks, Kate tried the handle on the door, her partner letting her take the lead for the first time.

Kate opened the door and immediately felt something was wrong. She started to back out and tripped and fell over Officer Harris, who was on the ground behind her. By the time she realized what was happening, she was pulled up by her hair and thrown in a choke hold. She saw a glimpse of her partner on the ground and couldn't tell if he was alive or dead, and for the first time in her life, she felt fear.

She was dragged through the front door, her boots scraping across her partner's unmoving body. Once inside, the door closed and she was thrown to the ground. When she looked up she saw the barrel of a gun pointing at her face. It didn't take long for her to realize that it was her gun pointing at her.

After being hog tied and bound, Kate could hear the soft murmurs of someone else in the room. Trying to adjust her eyes, Kate could see someone sitting in the corner with their arms wrapped around their legs, as they were drawn up to their chest. Kate knew it was the battered wife.

"You should do what he says." she said. "If you don't, it will only get worse."

"Do you know where he is?" Kate asked. "Please, come untie me and I can help you."

"Oh, no I can't do that. He will kill me." She said.

Kate started to talk, but the lady pleaded for her to be quiet because he was coming back.

When he arrived, he was pacing the floor and looking at Kate every few seconds. Kate decided to try to reason with him, and that was when she saw the other officer crouched down in the room, behind the man. Kate knew she had to keep the attention on her, or the officer was going to get shot.

"You know, things are not as bad as you think. The way I see it, there is still a way out of this," Kate said.

"My ass, there's a way out, do you think I'm stupid?" He raised the gun back at her.

That was all it took and the man fell to the ground at the same time she heard the gunshot. It took her a second to figure out what happened, and she could feel his blood as it sprayed all over her face.

Within seconds, the officer was at her side, telling her that everything was going to be ok and that it was all over. As he was untying her, she saw his nametag; it said Officer Harper. From then on he was always Harper to her, and she was Kate to him. At the time, she didn't know he was trying to calm her down by asking her first name, and saying it over and over. He never stopped calling her Kate.

Kate found out later that Harper had been there by accident. He had stumbled upon her like a scene from a movie. He was following up on a cold case file down the street on his day off, and noticed the police car. After he finished, he drove past the police car and thought he saw someone lying on the porch. He turned, parked and, headed up the sidewalk to double check.

Once he saw that there was an officer down he called in and proceeded to the house. He found a window open in the back. Realizing that backup may take a while, and an officer could be in trouble, he climbed through the window. He heard people talking and cautiously entered the darkened room, crouched low with his gun drawn. He then saw an officer hog tied, and he knew she had a visual of him because she immediately started talking to distract the man while Harper crept in.

It wasn't long after the incident that Kate requested Harper to finish training her. The chief agreed and made it happen. They had been partners ever since. Kate was at the hospital within hours of all of his children's births. She knew Harper's wife, but more importantly Harper's wife knew and trusted Kate with her husband's life. Kate considered Harper's family her own, and often spent holidays with them when Kristen was unavailable.

Kate couldn't help but notice that the longer they were on the force, the more Harper became a family man than a Police Officer. He was nothing less than proud when Kate was promoted to detective and left him as an officer. Eventually he, too, was made detective, but he was chasing Kate's heels from then on, and he was happy to do it. Harper loved his family, and Kate believed that his children softened him to be more careful, which was fine with her. She didn't mind doing the more risky things because she didn't have the responsibilities that he had.

After years of being partners, Kate felt she knew Harper better than anyone else, other than his wife. She learned that he was actually a very smart man. He never received anything less than an A in schooling. His only regret in life was disappointing his parents when he said he wanted to go into the Police Department. It had always been a passion of his, and he knew what he wanted at a very young age. His parents were furious, and they believed he was throwing all his education away. They couldn't understand why he would pick this over medical or law school. Harper never could explain why he needed to join the Police Department; he just knew that it was what he wanted. He had received a great deal of grief from his family over the incident, and it took many years for his family to come out of it.

The only person in his life who always supported him unconditionally was his high school sweetheart, who became his wife and the mother of their children. They had a marriage that worked off of respect and trust; Kate envied this. She was thankful to have met Harper that horrible day and to have him as her partner. Right now, he eased the pain of missing Kristen.

Chapter 39

Feeling the blood dry in and around his nose made Stan furious, he was tempted to just kill her right then. He realized that there was no time to waste. Now that she was subdued and downstairs, she was going to be much more difficult to get back up the stairs and to the mortuary.

After tying and gagging Belle, he decided it was safe to head back to the library for the car. He walked back, careful that he walked down as many alleys as possible, so he would stay unnoticed. Once the parking lot was in view, he started to feel relieved as he headed for his car.

"Hey, surfer dude, I thought you left?"

Without looking up, Stan knew that Matt was standing behind him. Feeling a sickness build in his stomach, he continued on to his car. "Yeah, running later than I thought," he said, without looking back. He meandered through the parking lot at a slow pace until he heard the kid's car door open and close. Then, out of the corner of his eye, he saw him leave. Once he felt safe, he got in his car and hurried home. After he backed the car in through the alley and to the back of the house, he headed to the back door and let himself in. He heard a muffled scream and prepared another dose of chloroform as he headed to the basement.

"Shh, we can do this the easy way, or the hard way." he told his princess in an even tone. "Either you settle down, or I will break your nose just as you did mine."

She stopped trying to scream, and the struggle started to slow.

"Belle, my precious Belle, we are going to be famous. We have all night together. It will be just you and me, my princess." Then he put her back to sleep.

Getting her up the stairs and to his car was much more of a struggle than with any of his other princesses. Once he had her secured, he realized that darkness had finally descended. Cloaked in it, he drove the short way to the place where fairy tales came true.

This time, the chloroform worked for much longer. He had plenty of time to secure her to the table and get everything prepared. He started the incinerator and actually had a moment to change clothes and sit for a bit. He felt exhausted and almost fell asleep in his chair before he heard her stir.

"Hello, my Belle, have you had a good sleep?" He rose to catch her eyes in his.

"What do you want?" she pleaded. "Please Ed. Please let me go."

"Well, for starters, my name isn't Ed. You, Belle, of all people, should have caught that. I used the name Edmund Dante. Get it, Belle? "Edmund from the *Count of Monte Cristo* —"

"You are no Edmund, whoever you are," she said indignantly. "You are Montego if anyone."

"I see myself more as the Count. You see, he was the one who tricked everyone into believing that he was actually someone different. However, I am sure you can understand that I can't quite sign in on the computer as the Count of Monte Cristo. Clever, don't you think?"

He saw the rage in her eyes and relished every minute of it. He reached down and unlatched the locket around her neck. "This will be a very nice addition to my collection," he said.

"You're that man they're looking for, the one who sent that book to the bar," she said. "I heard it on the radio in the break room."

"Good to know that you listen to the news. Now you know your fate. So, basically Belle — you don't mind if I call you, Belle, do you? No, I don't suppose you would mind under the circumstances, you being tied up and me here with all the power. Anyway, Belle, it will actually be quite simple. You will just disappear into thin air. Poof! You will be gone!"

As he said it, he enjoyed every moment watching the fear in her eyes. "So, Belle, do you want to know what will really happen to you? Or, do you want it to be a surprise?" He walked over, past her line of vision and checked on the temperature of the oven. "Oh, I wish you could see over here, but I suppose I could just tell you. This here is a great big oven used to cremate people. Do you know where you are now? Or, would you like a hint?"

"You know, you will never get away with this. You will get caught. The police are not as stupid as you think they are. You will get caught." The rage in her was growing stronger. They all went from one extreme to another, he thought. Either they were scared to death or mad as hell, always one or the other.

"Too bad for you, Belle, you won't be able to witness my big capture. However, just so you know, I will not be caught. You see, it is my destiny to be infamous, and you are only a step leading me there. So, what will it be now? Are you going to beg for your life and cry, or are you going to just give up and accept your fate? Which will it be?" He walked back and peered down at her. His eyes caught hers, and he could see that she was going to do neither. He heard her trying to escape the bondage, as she struggled in an attempt to get free.

"Oh Belle, I wasn't expecting this from you. You are a feisty one, and you are going to try to fight. All the more fun for me; fight for your life, Belle, fight!" He couldn't help but laugh as he watched his little Belle fight for her life. He opened his hand and looked at the locket that was now a part of him, He laid it on the table next to her. "Thank you, Belle, for the wonderful gift. I will remember you always with it."

He could feel the beast within rumbling to a point of no return. It was time to be born again. He quickly grabbed his knife and cut through her vein. Watching her while he did it gave him immense pleasure. However, her reaction was not what he expected. He was waiting for the scream. Instead, he received nothing more than a low, guttural whisper.

"Go to hell," she said with barely enough strength to finish. "I hope you burn in hell."

"Wait for me, Belle. I will see you there," he said, as he watched her eyes turn stone cold. He reached down and began to relieve himself. The more he thought about his Belle, the more pleasure he received. He could feel the warmth of her blood fill him with life. The beast had been fed, and Belle would live on now through him, in infamy.

"Good night, my Belle."

Chapter 40

It had been a couple days since their press conference and, as expected, they found no prints or evidence left behind on the "Little Mermaid" book. They kept following up leads as the phone calls kept pouring in. Most of them ended up leading them to dead ends.

Once again, Harper and Kate decided to split up and hit the pavement. Harper was going to canvass the neighborhood of the Blue Whale and Sharon's home. Kate was heading back to the mortuary to see if Stan had her list done.

She opened the mortuary door, and walked in as the chimes rang. She started to pass an office, noticing a woman sitting at a desk, with the phone to her ear. "Yes, I will hold," Kate heard her say.

Lingering outside the door, Kate waited to be noticed. After a few moments, Ruth looked up and seemed startled to see her standing there.

"Oh, hello, I am so sorry. I didn't hear you come in. Can I help you with something?" She motioned for Kate to come in, but continued her phone conversation. Putting up a finger in a gesture to have her wait, Ruth tried to finish up.

"Yes, I am still here. I just don't understand. You have been out a couple times and checked the meter, and you have even replaced it. There is something really wrong here. Our gas bills have doubled. Look at the history of our usage. Well, there is nothing different now than there has been for years. I need to speak to a manager, but I have someone in my office now. Can you please have someone contact me?" There was a long pause. "Yes, that is correct. You can reach me at that number during normal business hours. Please understand that I will not let this matter go. I will call back tomorrow, if I haven't heard back." She then put the phone down on the cradle, gave a big sigh, and turned to Kate.

"I am so sorry about that. I have just been on and off hold with this damn gas company for over an hour now. How can I help you?"

"I'm Detective Kingsley, and I'm here to see Stan. He's putting together a list for me, and I just wanted to see if it was ready."

"He must be down in the basement. Let me ring him."

Kate heard her on the phone talking to him, agreeing with whatever he was talking about.

"Stan is in the middle of something he can't get away from," she said to Kate. "He asked if he can touch base with you later today. That boy is always doing something, always busy."

"Well, I really don't mind waiting. Can you please call him back and let him know I'll be waiting?" Kate said with an emphatic tone. "This is official police business."

"Oh, let me call him back and let him know," Ruth said as she picked up the phone and dialed the extension. "Hi Stan, did you know this lady is with the police? It sounds really urgent. She said she will just wait for you. Should I have her wait in your office?" She hung up the phone, said that he would be right up, and asked Kate to wait in the lobby. It was only a few minutes before Stan appeared in the lobby. He had a big smile on his face, despite a swollen nose that looked as though it was broken.

"Oh, jeez Stan, it looks like you got the worse end of a fight," Kate said, as she examined the dark bruising that clearly had set in over a couple of days. "What the hell happened?"

"Well, this mortuary business is very dangerous," he said with a charming smile, but without really answering her question. "I suppose you want that list now? Follow me, it's in my office. You were actually on my mind today. I'm glad you stopped by."

They walked through the lobby and continued to his office. Stan motioned for Kate to sit as he went around the desk and sat down. He started thumbing through some papers on his desk, until he located the one he was looking for. Before he handed it to her, though, he started in with the questions.

"So, how is the investigation going? Do you have any news on your friend Kristen's disappearance?"

Kate leaned forward quickly enough to grab the list from his hand. She hated being toyed with.

"We are still following up on all the leads," she said, as she started reading through all the names on the list.

"Do you even have any good leads? I mean, with this bad economy, I bet manpower is down and there aren't too many people to help with the investigation."

"Oh, we seem to manage just fine. He will make a mistake and slip up. They always do. In the end, they really just want to get caught. This guy seems like a real amateur. He has already made a few mistakes. It's just a matter of time."

"What kind of mistakes?" Stan said.

"I can't talk about that since it's an ongoing investigation. I really should get going. There are never enough hours in the day." she stood up and started to leave.

"Sorry, I forgot about that whole silence during the investigation. I am just anxious for this man to get caught, and I find this stuff interesting."

For a second, Kate wasn't sure how she wanted to respond. "You find what interesting? Missing girls who are most likely dead?" she said it with a clear irritation in her voice.

"No, Kate, that is just ridiculous. I find it interesting how the police are able to track down clues in investigations. Sheesh, I am just trying to help. Anyway, I am busy, and I need to get back to work. Good luck, Kate. I am sure you know your way out." With that, he walked out of the office, and on down the hall.

She was left standing in his office and, after finishing reading the guest list, she let herself out. She couldn't help but think that he was one strange bird.

After leaving the mortuary, she called Harper, who answered before the end of the first ring. "What's up, Harper? Do you have any news on canvassing the neighborhoods? Please tell me you have something."

"Well, they have something, but you are not going to like it. We received another book."

After hearing this, Kate's mind turned to mush for just a moment as she contemplated what he had just said. "But, we don't have a missing-person report yet," she said, sounding as confused as she felt.

"Not yet, anyway." Harper said. "This time the press hasn't gotten wind of it. It was left in the night drop of the library, and it is addressed to the 'pigs' at the police department. The lady who received it never opened it; she called us immediately. I am on my way there now. Do you want to meet me there? Oakdale Public Library, you know where that is, right?"

"You are talking about the library in Potwin, Right?"

"Yeah, that's the one. See you in a few."

Luckily, she was not too far from there and arrived even before Harper did. Kate showed her badge to the first lady at the library counter and was immediately directed through the swinging doors and into an office. After closing the door, the lady walked behind her desk. She pulled an envelope out from her drawer and handed it to Kate.

"I'm the only one who knows about this, other than my manager, who is home sick today. I called her first, and she told me not to tell anyone and to call the police. I'm the only one who has touched it. Do you think it is him?" She looked at Kate with pleading eyes.

"I really don't know, but I hope not. I am going to just ask you a couple questions, and then I will most likely send someone over or come back later myself to follow up. First of all, do you have any cameras on the premises?"

"I am not aware of any," she said. "We just don't have the budget for them."

"Have you seen anything suspicious around here lately?"

"I haven't seen anything out of the ordinary. Do you want me to ask around?"

"No, it would be better to let us ask the questions. I think it's best for you to just keep this to yourself, for the time being. My last question for right now is, do you know of any reason why he would have dropped that off in the return slot here?"

"No, I don't know why he would want to leave it here," she said apologetically. "It doesn't make any sense. I wish I could help more."

"I'm going to go ahead and take this now so I can get it back to the precinct and have it analyzed. You did really well here, really well. Thanks for calling us first. It gives us more time to investigate without the media hounding us. Oh, one more thing. Do a roll call of all employees and let me know if there is anyone missing."

Kate shook her hand and headed for the door, holding the bagged envelope. As she started for the door, a young kid stopped her.

"Whoa, that is one big gun you got there," he said. "You must be a police officer."

She turned to face him, and read his nametag. "Hi Matt, stay in school, don't do drugs, and work hard." Before he could respond, she was already out the door and heading for her car, which was parked in the fire lane. Wasting no time, she called Harper and told him to meet her at the precinct so they could get this book analyzed.

Chapter 41

The ride to the precinct was a somber one. Kate knew she would be receiving a call any minute about a missing person. It made her stomach turn as she thought about which fairy tale princess would be the next victim. Her mind started going over all the facts that they had, and she tried to find something that could give them a good lead. She decided to call the precinct, and check on the phone dump from the grocery store.

"Hi, this is Darla."

"Hey Darla, this is Kate. Do you have those phone records for the grocery store yet?"

"Yeah, I had them placed on your desk this morning," Darla replied. They had the kind of relationship that was all business, unless it was a social call.

"This morning?" Kate said. "Why wasn't I notified earlier?"

"The receptionist was supposed to call you when they delivered it. She didn't call? Kate, I apologize. I know how much you were waiting for this."

"Do you still have a copy?" Kate asked.

"Sure, what do you want me to look for?"

After going through the dates and times in question, she came up with the answer she was looking for.

"Thanks, talk with you later." Kate hung up and immediately dialed Harper.

"Guess what I found out from the phone records at the grocery store?"

"I can only imagine," Harper replied. "Go ahead, give it to me."

"It is the payphone at the Thai restaurant. It's the one in back by the bathrooms."

"You are kidding. Are you going there now?"

"Yeah, I am on my way. Tell the chief that I'm going to follow up with this lead real quick on my way to the precinct."

After hanging up with Harper, she drove to the restaurant. She didn't feel the same excitement she usually felt walking through the doors and smelling the wonderful spices from the kitchen. As usual, Laila was there to greet her.

"Hi Kate, how are you, just one today?"

"Unfortunately, Laila, I am here on police business."

"Oh my, please come sit and tell me all about it."

They sat at the front booth, and Kate explained what had transpired in as much detail as she could. "So, I am going to have to dust the phone for prints, even though I realize I most likely won't get any that are useful," she said. "I will also need to get everyone at the restaurant fingerprinted, so we can rule them out."

"Anything you need, Kate. I know some of the dishwashers and a couple of the cooks actually do use the phone. They are only allowed to when they are on break, or in case of an emergency."

Kate headed back to the phone, opened a case with all the fingerprint equipment, and got right to work. After finishing all the dusting of the phone, she started on the cover of the phonebook hanging below. When she started flipping through the book, a page that was folded in half fell out. When she reached down to pick it up, the bathroom door flew open, and one of the waitresses she recognized came out. Kate jumped back for a moment.

"Oops, sorry," she said. "Oh, that darn page keeps falling out, and I keep putting it back in. I have been just sticking it back in the phonebook, but it always ends back up on the floor." She shook her head and walked away.

Kate picked up the phonebook page and, after scanning it, she realized that she was holding the same page of the phonebook that their suspect held. She carefully held it with her fingertips, and asked the waitress to come back. "Your name is Anna, right?"

"Yes. Do you need something? Which table are you sitting at?"

"Oh, I'm not eating. I'm here on official police business." Anna's eyes opened wide. "You say this page keeps falling out. Do you know when you first noticed it?" Kate asked.

"Sure I do. There was a customer who sat in one of the back booths who used the phone one evening. I know it was him because when he got up to leave, he had it in his hand while he paid the bill. However, he somehow dropped it when he walked away. I remember thinking how rude it was to tear those pages out. So, I took the page, and stuck it back in the phonebook."

Kate asked her about the dates when this may have happened, but Anna was unsure of anything exact. Kate motioned for her to sit at the booth nearest the payphone. She leaned way forward on the table, still holding the page by the corner.

"Anna, this is a very, very important question. It could make a big difference in our investigation. Do you remember what this man looked like? Was he familiar? Had he been here before?"

She sat there for a long minute, really thinking about what to say. "He didn't seem familiar, but there was something about him…"

"Ok, let's break this down. Do you remember the color of his hair?"

"No, I am not seeing it. He was tall, though. I remember because he was on the phone, and he had to bend down to talk on it."

"Good, that's good. So, how much was he leaning down?" Kate walked back to the phone and picked it up off the cradle. After lifting it up to its tallest height, she looked at her, "Was he leaned way over or just a little?"

"Um, he wasn't way bent over, but he was enough that it looked uncomfortable. I know that he was on long enough that I thought his food was going to get cold after I brought it out."

146

She started calculating an estimated height, and she came to the conclusion that he would have to be more than six feet tall. "How big was he?" she asked. "Was he thin or heavy? Was he muscular like someone who works out, or mushy?"

"He was average, that's all I can remember. Definitely not fat, but I am just not sure about the rest."

Kate motioned for Laila to come over and asked her to look up all credit card transactions that took place that evening in the hopes he used a card.

"Oh, also Laila, how often is the phone emptied? Could you get me the name of the company that services it?"

She was off as fast as lightning, as she went to gather the information Kate requested.

"Detective, his eyes," Anna suddenly interjected, "He had the bluest eyes, and I think that's why I can't remember any more about him. His eyes were so captivating that I didn't notice much more."

She made a note to herself, blue eyes and more than six feet tall. That was definitely a start, much more than they had until now. Laila came back with all the credit card receipts from that night, and handed them to Kate in a bag. She also gave her the name and phone number of the servicing company for the payphone.

"I called the repair hotline on the payphone, and their records showed that it was actually emptied yesterday afternoon," she said. "I am so sorry Kate. I wish we could help more."

She looked back at Anna and asked, "Do you think that you would recognize him if you saw him again?"

"I am not sure. But if he looks at me with those blue eyes like he did that day, then I will remember him."

"Good, here is my card," Kate said, as she handed it to her. "Be sure to call me if you see him, even if you are not sure." Kate grabbed her case and headed for the door. She stopped on her way out and gave Laila a big hug.

"Have you eaten, Kate?" she asked.

"Thanks, Laila, but I really need to get back to the precinct."

"No, wait right here, just a minute." Within a few minutes, she was back with a bag of food clearly meant for more than just Kate. "It is your favorite and a couple other things. You guys must get hungry."

Kate started to dig in her purse for her wallet, but Laila touched her hand and shook her head.

"No, this one is on the house. You catch this horrible man and, any time you guys are hungry, you just call Laila and I will bring you something to eat."

"You are so sweet, thanks so much," Kate said, as she gave her another hug and started out the door.

Chapter 42

Kate arrived back at the precinct without even remembering her drive there. They had recovered a lot of new information, but her thoughts kept going to the latest book, worried when she was going to hear about the next missing victim.

She went right in and headed for the chief's office, passing Harper on her way. He jumped up out of his chair and followed her in. Without words, she laid the bag with the unopened envelope down on the chief's desk.

Chief Broxterman looked up and then opened his drawer. He pulled out a long piece of plastic, some gloves, and a tiny knife. He carefully took out his camera, and snapped pictures of the front and back of the envelope. The only things written on it were the "Pigs at the Police Department" where the address should go and the initials "FTM" where the return address should be. Right before cutting the envelope open, he looked up and took a big breath. "Ready?"

"Not really, but let's get it done," Kate said.

He carefully opened the envelope and pulled the book out.

They all mumbled, *Beauty and the Beast*, as the chief held up the book and opened the front cover. Harper and Kate strained their bodies over the length of the chief's desk to read the inscriptions on the inside cover.

"Belle rings no more. FOUR gives the Beast even more."

"That son of a bitch," she said. "He's sending books out now before we even know they are gone. He is escalating."

She started filling Harper and the chief in on what she had found out from the restaurant, and the potential description she'd come up with. As she talked, the chief closed up the book, and put it back in the envelope. Within minutes, he had it all secured in a bag. He then made a quick call, and a young assistant came in to take the package to forensics.

Once they were back at their desks, Harper turned on his laptop. As it powered up, Kate started dishing out some food. While they ate they tried to formulate a plan for finding this missing girl. Once she was done with her food, Kate went over to the white board and started adding all the new information. The new book, the new description, and anything else they could find of importance.

"Good work, Kate, really good information," Harper said.

They sat for what seemed like an eternity as they talked about different scenarios. They were so immersed in their mission that Kate was startled when her phone started to vibrate.

"Detective Kingsley," she said.

"Hi, Detective, this is Mary from the library. I met you earlier today when you came in and picked up the book."

"Yes, Mary, I remember. Have you thought of some new information?"

"Well, it is most likely nothing and I didn't know about it until all the officers left a little while ago."

"Okay."

"I looked up all the employees today and looked to see if anyone had called in sick. Well, the only one who called in sick was my manager."

Kate waited impatiently for what she really called to tell her, but didn't want to rush her.

"However, we also had one employee who didn't show up today. Her shift was covered before I knew about it. Everyone had been busy with police interviews, so I just now found out. They just didn't think it was important."

"I need a name, Mary."

"Her name is Rose Ferarro. She works in the computer section, monitoring the computers. She is a really sweet woman. We all love her to death, and it is very unlike her not to call in if she's sick."

Kate listened to Mary as she watched Harper on the computer, going through online images of scenes from the *Beauty and the Beast* story. When he came to an image of a rose in a glass cover, she felt a chill go through her.

Kate put her hand over the phone and whispered to Harper, "I think we found her."

After she got Rose's address from Mary, Harper and she grabbed their things and headed out. Without a word, they both knew where they were heading, and they both knew that the outcome would not be good.

Chapter 43

Stan couldn't help but wonder how long it would take them to find out about his last princess. He couldn't believe she hadn't been reported missing; poor thing really should be missed by now, he thought. The news stations definitely didn't have any idea about it and, as tempting as it was to send them a hint, he decided not to.

Instead, he decided to take his lunch hour, and use it to buy a computer. The information on computers was unbelievable, and he couldn't wait to get one and surf the Web whenever he wanted. After finishing up with his morning routine, he was just getting ready to leave when he got a call from Morten.

"Hey Stan, could you come down to the basement? I want to talk with you about something," Morten said.

"Sure, on my way." he felt a sickness in his stomach, as he wondered if he had left something behind or forgot to put something away. What if Morten found blood somewhere that he had missed? Stan hurried down the stairs.

"What is it?" Stan asked.

"Hey, I was just wondering if the oven has been on."

"That oven?" Stan pointed to the incinerator. "Why do you ask?"

"Well, it's strange because the door was open a few inches and, when I went over there to close it, I noticed there were ashes in it. Have you been turning it on? Or using it?"

Stan felt angry with Morten for spying on him. It was none of his business what Stan did with his property, and Stan tried to hold back the fury within him. "Well, Morten, I don't start up the oven any more than necessary. I know you wanted to get rid of it, but it was part of my tradition. My father used to start it up just to keep it working. Sometimes I will throw newspapers or trash in there to kept it working. Why are you so concerned with this?"

"You know, Stan, it is really dangerous to use that thing. It's so old, and it hasn't had any kind of inspection in years. You really should have it inspected if you want to use it."

"Thanks for the input. I will keep it in mind," he said. Stan needed to leave the room before his anger took over his actions. He left the basement, headed right out to the lobby, and yelled back to Ruth that he was going to lunch and would be back later in the day.

After driving around aimlessly for a few minutes, he started to cool off and was no longer having visions of killing Morten by throwing him in the oven. He laughed to himself at the thought of Morten inside the oven, looking out the tiny window as Stan started it up. He bet the questions would stop, and the pleading and apologies would start. But, of course, by then it would be way too late.

He arrived at the electronics store and went to the computer section where he got the rundown on the many different kinds of computers. Once he made his big purchase, he started to feel less angry and hungrier. He decided to get some lunch, and headed for the Thai restaurant.

"Hi sir, will this just be for one?" the familiar old lady said.

"Just me, can I get a booth?"

"Sure, please follow me."

After looking over the menu for a few minutes, he decided what he wanted to order right about the time the waitress came to his table.

"Hi, what will it be?"

"Can I have the number three, and also a side of the house soup?" As he looked up, he noticed she was not one of the usual waitresses. "You must be new," he said.

"Well, not new, I just usually only work weekends," she said. "But they called me in to cover the other girl's shift. I guess she was all freaked out over all the police business."

"Police business? What do you mean?" he could feel the world closing in on him. First Morten, then this, was his time coming?

"Oh, you know that crazy guy out there. You know the one who sends those books?"

"Of course, who hasn't heard of him?"

"Well, he apparently made a phone call from the payphone by the back restrooms. They have taken it out now. But, anyway, the other waitress actually remembers him."

He couldn't help but feel all the blood drain from his body, and he started to feel light headed.

"So, if she saw him, then she can give a description to the police, and they can actually catch him."

"Well, it's not that easy. She does remember him, but only a few things about him. Like he is tall, and he has blue eyes. Oh, you have very blue eyes as well."

"Yeah, I get them from my mother's side." He had to shift gears. "Do you know what time it is?" After she looked at her watch and gave him the time, she started to turn to drop off his order.

"You know what, could you just make this to go? I really lost track of time, and I need to get back to work," he said.

"Sure, where do you work?" she asked, and he started to get annoyed by her questions.

"A really boring job, but at least it pays." He looked away, as if to tell her he was done talking.

He decided to keep his head down while waiting for his food, in case the other waitress showed up. He felt sick to think he could have left a clue behind. At the time, he was more worried about leaving prints on his quarters or even the phone. He was never worried about getting recognized by a waitress.

His food arrived and he paid with cash and a nice tip. He couldn't get out of there fast enough, and felt sad that this would be the last time he ate there. However, he also knew that it was his own fault.

He headed back to the office and immersed himself in work. Still feeling angry with Morten, Stan decided to keep his distance from him until he knew he was over it. He also decided to dial Ruth's extension.

"Ruth, can you check on something for me?"

"Oh sure, Stan, did you have a good lunch?"

"Yes, it was nice," he lied, not wanting to tell her that he actually didn't have the stomach to eat after the information he found. He ended up throwing the food out. "Ruth, do we have Internet service here?"

"I don't think so. Do you need it?"

He got so tired of everyone treating him like a kid. Did he need it? He owned this damn place and, if he wanted it, he should have it.

"It doesn't matter, Ruth. I want it. Can you make the arrangements?"

"I will take care of it, Stan, right away."

Just as he was about to hang up the phone, she interjected, "Stan, you really should let me know when you are running that incinerator down there. We should have permits and have it inspected. No one knows we are using it, and you could burn the place down using that rickety old thing. You know, my sister's husband's friend had this house and it was the simplest thing but it caught…"

Stan's mind started filling with a fog of fury. He could hardly concentrate long enough to respond to her. He wanted to fire her right on the spot, but he knew better.

"…anyway, Stan, I wish I would have known you had been using the incinerator because I've been fighting with the gas company about the bill. It was crazy high, and I thought for sure they had a leak or problem."

"Ruth, there is no problem. You just worry too much," he said it with as much composure as he could muster. "If doing the bills is too much for you, then I can take them over. I don't want to micromanage you like my father did, but if you are going to worry about every little thing, then I will have to. Do you understand?"

"Stan, I didn't mean to offend you…" she started before he interrupted her.

"Just get the Internet and forget the little stuff," he said as he hung up the phone.

Stan spent the rest of the day in his office behind closed doors. No one tried to bother him, and all the phone calls were routed away from him. He took his time to gain composure and think about the day's events. A few hours before, he felt like it was D-Day but, after a few hours of contemplation, he came back down to reality and realized that the police only had a few clues, and the likelihood of tracing them back to him were really slim. If anything, it would make the game more exciting. He decided that he was safe again, and he started to go back to Belle. He started thinking of her, and how different she was from the others. Sure, Rapunzel fought back, but Belle was so much feistier than he had thought she would be. He always missed the game after they were gone, but knowing they were a part of him forever brought a surge of life into him. He decided to ride this euphoria out as long as he could because he knew it wouldn't be long before the beast needed to be fed again. He realized that the beast's satisfaction was lasting a shorter and shorter amount of time after each princess.

He packed up his things to leave and, when he opened his door, all the lights were out and everything was ready to close up. He saw two sticky notes taped to the hallway in front of his door. One message said to call his realtor; apparently someone wanted to see his home. He had to make viewings by appointment only, just to make sure he had everything in perfect order. The second message was to let him know that the cable company was coming out the next day to install the Internet.

Taking the sticky notes back to his desk, he called his realtor and made arrangements to meet her and a client at his home in a few hours. He was anxious to be done with this sale.

Chapter 44

Harper and Kate arrived at Rose's address and started the careful canvass of the area around her house. They were well aware that this was going to be a long night, and they were prepared to leave no stone unturned.

Kate first went to the front door and knocked to make sure Rose was not really home sick. Getting no response, she went to the front windows and tried to open them. Luckily, one window was unlocked. She opened it, climbed inside, and opened the front door. Harper and she moved through the house, checking for Rose. After a few minutes, they determine that she was not home — not that Kate expected her to be. They also noticed that the home didn't look like there had been any kind of foul play. Kate decided that they should start on the outside and work their way in.

"You take the front, Harper," she said. "I'll take the back." He nodded and headed to the starting point of his grid.

Kate walked to the back, looking for anything that would indicate foul play. After many hours of tedious searching, they came up with absolutely nothing. The closest thing to a lead was a nosy neighbor who kept watching them out the window. However, after talking to her, they realized she had no information to add. She couldn't even remember the last time she saw Rose.

After finishing up what they needed to do, they handed the home over to some other officers to complete the process by collecting fingerprints.

"I think we need to head back to the library and start interviewing everyone again," she suggested. "What do you think?"

"You mean in the morning, right?" Harper said.

"Unfortunately, we don't have any choice. At this hour, no one is there anymore. Let's make that our top priority in the morning."

Kate drove back to the precinct to drop Harper off at his car and decided to head home to try some more brainstorming. First, she made a stop at Kristen's to check the mail and make sure everything was still in place.

She locked herself in Kristen's apartment and started going through all her mail. She checked her cell phone and home phone, only to find nothing. No one even left messages for her anymore. She went to her bedroom and looked through her closet. After finding a few photo albums, she sat on the bed and started flipping through them. Her reaction went from laughter to tears within seconds. She wanted to stop, but she also wanted to keep looking. It had been a horrible emotional roller coaster losing someone she cared about.

Waking up in the wee hours of the morning, well before the sun was up, Kate realized she had fallen asleep on Kristen's bed. Getting up was difficult because she was so exhausted. However, there were so many things she needed to do, and she wanted to get a good start. She grabbed her things and headed home. A quick shower and a change of clothes would do her wonders.

After showering, she once again grabbed her things and headed out to work. She pulled out of her driveway and saw the sun rising over the horizon. When she got to the precinct, she found Harper standing at the white board, making notes.

"Harper, you look like shit. Did you even go home last night?"

"Yeah, for a while, but I couldn't sleep. So I decided that it would be better to be here instead of lying there awake all night. You're here early as well. You couldn't sleep?"

"I stopped by Kristen's to check on things on my way home, and I fell asleep there. I kind of thought the same thing as you. If I'm awake, I might as well be here. Have you thought of anything new?"

"Not really," he said. "I was just trying to clean up the timeline. Did they ever hear back from any of Rose's family?"

"Not yet. I left messages late yesterday, but haven't heard back."

"What time does the library open?"

"Nine," she said, as she thumb through case files, in the hopes of something jumping out at her.

"How about we go eat at that little diner in Potwin while we wait for them to open? What do you think?"

"Actually, that sounds good. I could always go for some more coffee in the morning." They headed out with their files and got in her car. She said, "How is Megan holding up with you gone all the time?"

"I think she's more scared about this guy out there, and she wants us to catch him. She has actually been very understanding."

"She sure is a good catch, Harper. You should keep her."

"Eh, she's all right," he said, as he smiled back to her.

Sitting in the diner was actually rather relaxing. They took a bigger table and laid out all the files while they ate. The only good thing about a missing-person case was that there were no gruesome pictures to worry about with others sitting around. Actually, the files were really rather skinny. There was not much information when the people just come up missing with no trace.

They ate a huge breakfast with the unspoken understanding that they might not get to eat again that day. She drank enough coffee to energize her through the morning and soon, it was time to go to the library. They both talked over the game plan of how they were going to handle the interviews. By the time they pulled up, they knew exactly what they wanted to do.

The first person they ran into was Matt. He was clearly waiting for them.

"Hi," he said. "I'm supposed to show you where the conference room is for you to use. Mary is already in there, getting things organized for you. Do you know when you will want to talk to me?"

"Not sure, but we will let you know," Kate said, as she headed for the conference room.

Harper lagged behind her, making a complete canvass of the library and the layout. He also went outside to the drop box and looked around for anything they could have missed. He wasn't gone very long before he came back to the conference room, empty-handed.

They started by interviewing everyone who worked at the library. They talked to the evening cleaning crew, the day crew, and the volunteers. The most they could gather was that Rose hadn't been heard from or seen since her last shift. No one could remember any unusual activity or anyone hanging around the library. They felt at a loss, deflated because they were not able to come up with anything.

Kate asked Mary to show her Rose's desk, and she started going through all the items on and around it. She was also aware that this was a community desk and that anything she found could belong to anyone.

"So, Mary, what was Rose's job exactly" she asked.

"She ran this help desk and the computers in this area. They are free for people to use, but many times people need help and the area needs monitoring. She was a very patient person to do a job like this."

Kate looked up and down the aisle, and noticed that there were four computers along a wall.

"Is this all the computers?"

"Yes, we are very much in need of funds. Many times there are time limits and waiting lines for the computers, depending on the time of day and how many people are here."

"What are the busiest times?"

"Weekends are the worst, mornings are the best times," she said. "But, to be honest, I am not sure other than that. Rose runs a tidy ship. I've never had any issues or complaints."

"I know this might not make you very happy, but we are going to need to take those computers to have them analyzed. I am sorry to do this to you, but we really have to look at all possible leads."

Mary immediately motioned for Matt to come over from across the lobby. She quietly told him to go make a sign saying that the computers would be unavailable until further notice.

"I understand, Detective," she said. "We want to help in any way we can. My manager told me to give you all the cooperation you need."

"I really appreciate all your efforts. You have no idea how well you have done in helping us."

"Do you think it is Rose, Detective? Is she the next one?" she said, her eyes filling with tears.

"I really hope not, Mary, and we are still checking for places she might be. We are just not sure yet."

"It's very unlike her to be just gone without a trace. She has the same routine every day and, as far as I know, she doesn't deviate from it. I think he has gotten her. I have been praying for her nonstop, and I don't even go to church."

"When you say routine, what do you mean?" she asked.

"Well, she always walks to and from work, she always brings her lunch, and she is always reading everything she can get her hands on. She's an avid reader and book collector."

"That's good information that gives me something to work from. Thanks again, Mary."

They finished up a couple more rounds and cleared up some things. The day was finishing up as the sun started to set. She knew they had lost another day, and all she could do was hope for a better day tomorrow. At least the computers were on their way to the lab and would be ready for them to dive into tomorrow.

"I think we should come here first thing in the morning and walk the route to her house," Kate said to Harper as they walked out of the library. "I just want to see if anything jumps out at me. No stone unturned."

"Yeah, no stone unturned, Kate," Harper said, and she could hear the disappointment in his voice.

Chapter 45

Stan felt tired in the morning, since he stayed up cleaning out the incinerator, washing and scrubbing the inside; just in case nosy Morten or Ruth started snooping around. Luckily, Morten didn't look too far inside the incinerator, or he would have found the remains of bone fragments, and then Stan would have had to kill him.

He pulled up to work and got everything opened. He was happy to see that the cable man was actually waiting for him when he arrived.

"Hi, I'm Stan," he said "Let me get this opened up so you can get started."

"Thanks," the cable man said. "Just show me where you want the service hooked up."

"Well, did Ruth tell you I want service here and at my residence across the parking lot?"

"Yeah, that shouldn't be any problem. I was setting it up as well. You do know about the extra fee for that, right?"

"Just let me know what I owe you, and I will take care of it. Follow me and I will show you where to set it all up. You know I bought a wireless router?"

After finishing up with the cable man, he decided to dive in and get some work done. He had lost interest in eating out for the time being and was trying his hardest to keep the beast in check. So far, the beast hadn't summoned him, but he also knew it was only a matter of time.

"Hi Stan, how was your morning?" Ruth asked. She seemed tentative, as if testing the waters with him.

"Good. And you?" he said, giving her a small smile to make her feel like everything was peachy.

"A little tired, I hope I am not coming down with something. Did you get my messages last night? I see the cable man, so you must have known he was coming. Did you call your realtor back?"

"Thanks, Belle. I did. I actually should be getting an offer today, so keep your fingers crossed."

She gave him a curious look.

"What's wrong?" he said.

"Well, you called me Belle. Stan, do you have a girlfriend you haven't told us about?" She smiled and waited for his response.

"No, not yet, but I am still looking for Miss Right," He walked to the basement to get the room ready for the next delivery. It actually gave him solace when they got deliveries, because he was left alone to do his work and relive all his memories.

Getting people ready for viewings didn't bother him, but it was also no fun for him when they came to him dead. He liked the opportunity to connect with them and actually transfer their life to him. It was a moment they shared unlike any other, he thought.

By the end of the day, everything had fallen into order. He received an actual apology from Morten and a sheepish apology from Ruth in her own way. He had Internet at both his new home and his office. The best news yet was that his house had finally sold. The buyers wanted a quick closing and were going to pay cash. They were Canadians who apparently had lots of money to spare. The next couple of weeks would be crazy; he had to work hard to move into his new place and get rid of most the stuff in the old.

On his way home, he was still wary about stopping and eating at restaurants. But when he saw a little bakery hidden in the corner of a strip mall, he swore that he could smell freshly baked bread. After walking in the door, he heard a ding. He started looking through all the great pastries and breads, and already knew that he was going to have a hard time choosing.

"Hi, can I help you?"

He looked up and lost his train of thought when he saw a beautiful woman standing there. She was in an apron with flour all over it and had a few sprinkles in her hair. He gestured that she had something on her nose, and she blushed as she reached up and wiped it off.

"Guess this is one of the hazards of being the baker and the help," she said, dusting flour from her hands.

"Oh, that is too bad," he said. "So you are the owner?"

"Well, it is me and my sister, but she works another job. This one isn't quite enough to make ends meet for her."

"But it is for you?"

"Well, I guess I don't need as much as she does." She laughed and continued. "Did you decide what you want yet?"

"There's way too much to choose from here. What do you recommend?" He felt the beast within calling to him. He felt like he was going to explode with happiness.

"Well, these are my favorites," she said, as she pointed to some pastries in the window.

"Then that is good enough for me. I will take two of those, a loaf of bread, and some of those donuts over there. How about a half a dozen and you pick them?"

"Sure." She got right to work, wrapping everything up for him, and he caught himself mesmerized by his next princess. He had found her much sooner than he really wanted. But, when the beast called, he listened.

After paying, he headed for the door and said goodbye. Under his breath, when the door was almost closed behind him, he whispered one word to himself: "Cinderella."

Chapter 46

When Kate woke up from her slumber, papers and files were piled around her, and the light was still on in her room. She didn't even recall falling asleep, but she knew she had slept hard. She looked at the clock; it was after seven. She had meant to get an earlier start than that, but she also knew that her body needed the extra sleep to work at its best. She jumped in the shower, got ready in record time, and made a call to their lab tech.

"Hey Joe, have you received the computers from the public library? They should have been delivered by now. Once you get them up and running, I would like to come by and check out what is on them."

"Sure, Kate, I will let you know when they get here," Joe said with the urgency she needed to hear. "I promise to put a rush on it."

After hanging up with Joe, she gave Harper a call to meet at the library. Once again, she was not surprised that he had already beaten her there and was starting another canvass.

She drove through a Starbucks, picked up her usual and grabbed Harper one out of habit. She drank half her coffee before she even met up with him. She found him walking the grid around the library. Handing him his coffee, she asked him if he was ready to walk Rose's route home. They started walking, with coffee in hand and their eyes peeled for anything that could help. Kate kept checking her phone, to make sure she hadn't missed a call from Joe.

"So, are we even sure that he met her in the library? Could he have just stalked her outside and followed her home?"

"Well, I suppose that is a possibility," Kate conceded. "But if that was the case, then how did he earn her trust? There was no evidence of any struggle at her home. He could have followed her home and taken her somewhere along the way, but that doesn't make sense. Someone would have seen something. I suppose he could have followed her in a car, but how did he get her in the car? No, Harper, she trusted him. She went with him willingly."

"Well, it looks like he's escalating. The first two, he takes from their homes. Now, it looks like he's twice found ways of establishing trust with these women. Where do they go, and what does he do with them? Do you think he's keeping them somewhere alive?"

"Well, if that is the case, then why send the books? The language seems to indicate that they are no longer with us."

"Then where does he put them? We have dragged all the lakes, searched the local wooded areas. What could we be missing?" Harper said it as if he was talking to himself as much as to her.

They arrived at Rose's house, losing hope of finding a clue, and the desperation of finding this fairy tale madman weighed heavily on them. Her car was still parked in the garage, and there was no evidence of any struggle anywhere.

"He had to have earned her trust, Harper. She met him somewhere, or went with him willingly like Sharon did. It's not like with Kristen or Lauren. He knows how to manipulate them. I think he was at the library. He had to have met her at the library."

Her cell phone rang, and she reached for it. "Kate Kingsley."

"Hey, it's Joe. The computers are in the process of being dusted and processed on the outside. I gained access to the hard drives, and I was just starting to gather all the data. Do you want to come now? Or should I go ahead and start compiling the information?"

"On our way, Joe, go ahead and get started, and you can bring me up to speed when we get there." She could feel hope inching its way back into her. They headed to the library for their cars and then on to the precinct.

Chapter 47

Marilyn felt most happy in the early morning hours when she got up before dawn to get started on baking. She was done with all her baking by six, which was when she got her first customers. They were usually the same people who lived in the neighborhood or they stopped in on their way to work. She also had a delivery boy who showed up in the morning so he could deliver pastries and donuts to some local businesses. A few times a week, she put together sandwiches and pastries for luncheons. That delivery was what really kept her in business doing what she loved. Work was calming for her and, when things got chaotic, she found that baking made things better.

Marilyn wished she had enough money to buy her sister out because she created too much stress and drama. They had opened the bakery together — not because Marilyn wanted to be business partners, but because she wanted to bake. Her sister really had no interest in baking. She was more of a silent partner who did not work at all, but collected weekly paychecks. Marilyn heard the ding of the door from the back baking room, and quickly walked out to greet a customer.

"Back so quickly? This can only mean one of two things. Either you disliked your order, or you want more. I am hoping for number two. Which is it?" She smiled.

"Definitely, number two," Stan said. "It was so good that I ate all of the bread last night and some of the pastries this morning. I decided that, since you are on my way to work, I would bring some donuts to the office."

She felt mesmerized as she picked up a box and opened it. "Same as last night, do you want me to pick them for you?"

"Yes, please, that seemed to work perfectly."

She started picking and choosing the donuts, and she could feel that he was watching her. As the phone rang, she sat the box down and looked at the caller ID. "Ugh," she said as she put a finger up to the customer, asking him to wait a second. She rolled her eyes and answered the phone.

She could see him mouth the words "no problem" back to her, and he gave her a great big smile. Even as she turned her back to him to answer the phone, she could feel him watching her, and her heart started to race with excitement.

"Hello," she said, "No, not yet, I will go to the bank later this morning."

After listening to a long explanation of nothing, Marilyn realized that her sister was not going to stop until she got the answer she wanted, she interrupted her, "Cindy, I am with a customer. I will have to call you back later." Marilyn continued to try to get off the phone with her sister, but was stuck answering questions: "Yes, Cindy, you can pick your check up later today. It's just not going to be as much as you want. I haven't had as much business, especially with this economy."

She finished the call and turned back to the customer. His gaze was still on her, but his eyes took on an apologetic look as he said, "Bad call?"

Feeling bad that she had to divert her attention from him, she quickly got back to work.

"Sorry about that," she said, as she continued putting the donuts in the box.

"No, don't worry about it. Who was that?" he said.

"My sister, she is the half owner. Our father left us both a small amount of money when he passed, and we invested it in this bakery. Unfortunately, I needed her money to open the business, and she believes in the philosophy of not working to earn a living."

"Oh, I am so sorry. Why don't you just buy her out? I bet it makes your mother very unhappy to see you working so hard," he said earnestly.

"I wish! I just can't. The bakery barely makes enough money to support itself. After I pay her share, I am left with the crumbs. You are right that my mother would not like it, but she passed from breast cancer a couple years back..."

"Ah, family," he said. "That explains it all. It's difficult doing business with family. Anyway, at least the crumbs she leaves you with are tasty crumbs. I can tell you, right now, that I would rather have your crumbs than her money any day."

"Well, thanks, that is good to know." She could feel a little bit of happiness come back to her with just a simple kind gesture.

"So, you do all the work and she reaps most of the benefits? How many hours do you work, and how many does she work?"

"Work, she has no idea of the concept. She comes in for the ten-to-two shift. I come in at the break of dawn and get everything baked for the day. Then, when she finally does come in, I head to the bank, and sometimes to the store to pick up supplies. Once two comes, I go back to work until seven. At least we are closed Sundays." She said as she helped other customers with their morning orders.

"Maybe you can find an investor to buy her out. Have you thought about that?"

"I think about stuff like that all the time. I just don't know how to go about it. I figure someday I will be able to get out from under her." Realizing that she had started to bring her problems onto the customer, she quickly changed direction. "So, here are your donuts. Now pick out something, anything, for yourself. It's on the house, for the counseling session we just had." She started laughing.

"How about you pick out your favorite for me?"

"Well, I suppose I can do that." As she looked down at the case, she could feel him watching her — again. She wasn't use to having so much attention and it embarrassed her.

As she rang him up and gave him the total, she almost felt sad to see him leave.

"Don't worry, we can continue our session next time," he said. "After all, you have made me an addict for your baking now, haven't you?" He laid a hundred-dollar bill down on the counter and, before she could give him change, she heard the ding of the door and knew he had left. She found herself feeling happy again, and she started to whistle a tune as she went back to the baking room.

Chapter 48

What a morning, thought Stan. He had found his next princess, and she just might be his best catch. He loved her subtle nature and the way she blushed with attention. Her shyness was a very cute quality.

He sat at the computer, looking up ways to take care of a broken nose. The Internet gave him very helpful hints. He soon found himself surfing the Internet every chance he got. It was amazing how much information was out there, and how easy it was to access. He had started spending as much time online as he could, in the hopes of laying low for a while.

He had the house almost packed up, and had already made a few trips to the new house with many of the essentials. The movers were coming the next day to complete the move. With any luck, he would be sleeping in the new home very soon.

He'd been trying to think of a way to hide the proceeds from the home sale in a safe place, and ultimately decided to hide it in a couple different places. The first place was in the basement of the new rental. The brick walls in the basement were old and crumbly so he would chip away the mortar on one wall and clear away a section behind it to stash some of the money. Worst-case scenario, he could always break a window in the basement to get in and retrieve the money. The next place was a safe-deposit box at a bank not affiliated with him at all. The last place he was thinking about was a local church. He figured many churches were open only during the day. How easy would it be to make his way down into the basement area and find a hiding spot?

Sometimes the small details could be so tedious, but, in the end, he also knew they were the ones that were most important. Hiding the money was crucial, because it gave him a large sum accessible in smaller amounts in a few different places. Any one of those amounts was more than enough for a getaway, and a new start with a new identity.

His drive to work went by quickly as he thought about the details of hiding the money. He was almost disappointed to arrive and realize that he had wasted all that time thinking of those details rather than day-dreaming about his new princess. He would make up for it by looking up all her details on the Internet. He parked the car, grabbed his laptop, and headed inside

Once he was inside, he heard the silence of the dead. He loved that quiet when he first got to work before anyone else arrived. He could sometimes feel the energy of all his princesses as he relived all their moments together. The mortuary started to come alive as he went through his normal routine of getting all the lights on, setting the temperature, and putting on some music. After all was done he sat down, and booted up his computer.

Stan's first search was always the same: Detective Kate Kingsley. There was usually a new article about her investigation. The articles very rarely gave any bit of new information about the case, which told him that they really didn't have much to go on. So they had a phone call made from a restaurant. So what? That was hardly enough to convict anyone of murder.

He also liked looking into Kate's past. He saw all her swimming and basketball accomplishments. She was a star on both teams and there were numerous articles. She won State two years in a row for swimming and her basketball team won State in her junior year, but came up short their senior year, even though they hadn't lost any players. Kate was quite an athlete and she had the body to prove it. She looked fit and he wondered if she still had to work out to maintain that body or if it came naturally to her.

He also searched his next princess, Cinderella. He didn't even know her name yet, so he typed in the name of the bakery, Bakers Delight. It took him much longer to find her than he expected. He was frustrated and kept getting redirected to different Web pages. He was almost ready to give up when he finally landed on what he was looking for.

"Well, hello, Marilyn Morris, my Cinderella," he said. Once he found her name, it didn't take long to find her address, phone number, and much more information than he could ever possibly need.

He heard the ding of the door, and realized that he was not alone anymore. He quickly closed his laptop and called out to Ruth.

"Good Morning, Ruth. How are you?"

"Hi Stan, how is the packing coming?" Ruth said.

Her voice trailed in the distance as she headed toward the kitchen for her morning coffee. He didn't even bother responding, knowing that she wouldn't hear him anyway.

Once he found all his information about Cinderella, he started formulating a plan; a plan to make her part of him, a plan to release the beast.

Chapter 49

When Kate arrived at the lab, she was happy to see that Joe had all the computers ready to go. He had even started downloading the contents.

"Hey, Joe, how's it going?" she said, as Harper followed her in.

"It is going. How are we going to go through these?" Joe said. "I started with the Internet history, since the library really doesn't let anyone save anything to the computer. I guess my question is, how far back do you want to go?"

"This 'FTM' seems to be picking his victims rather quickly," Kate said. "Let's just start by going back about a week, and we can keep going back from there later, if we need to. I honestly think that, if he used a computer here at all, it will be within the last few days."

They each took a computer and started going through the downloaded history. Most of it was rather easy to eliminate. There were a lot of searches for kid stuff, information on the book and movie *Twilight*, Club Penguin - all kinds of predictable searches.

After about an hour of going through the histories slowly and methodically, Kate came across some searches related to rare books. She noticed that one search was for *The Count of Monte Cristo*. Kate paused for a second and tried to remember what Mary at the library told her. She said that Rose was interested in books, that she was an avid book collector. She started to go back to where the searches for the rare books started, and slowly went through them. After looking through a few things, she called Joe over.

"Hey, Joe, can they see who signed on to the computers at certain times?"

"Sure, let me pull it up," Joe said. After a few minutes, he matched the records to their source. "These searches are under the sign-in name Edmund Dante."

"You are kidding me! Edmund Dante? He's a character from *The Count of Monte Cristo*," Harper said as he headed over to Kate and looked over her shoulder. "Do you know the story, Kate?"

"I know enough of it to know that this must be him. We have a huge lead here, guys. Let's not take any chances of missing anything. Let's do this right and go slow with it." She felt that dangerous feeling of hope fighting its way through her. "The prints for this computer are being processed, right, Joe?"

"You bet," Joe said, as they all remained glued to the information in front of them.

"Look at this — he actually did a search on rare books! I bet he used this information to entice her. This is how he did it. He acted like he had rare books," Kate said "See, look, this book has an edition in the 1800s worth some real money."

"I believe that this is not something he thought could be tracked," Harper said.

"I think you're right," Kate said. "This is not a clue we are supposed to have. He did this for a completely different reason. This is him in raw form."

They anxiously continued through all the browsing history and, the further they went, the more they were convinced that it was him. He searched many different things in the time he was on the computer.

They found searches on all the victims and their family members. The hairs on Kate's arms stood up as they found his searches for Kristen. He searched for her and also for Kate. No one said a word, but she felt Harper's hand on her shoulder in a gesture of acknowledgment.

They printed everything they could, and Kate also made special notes of certain things she found along the way. She wrote down the names of the victims' family members and anything else that seemed relevant. She also found a few other interesting searches, including a search on Swiss bank accounts.

"Do you think he is putting money away in an offshore account?" she said.

"I'll have someone check on that and see if we can find anything out," Harper said, adding, "Be right back, have to make a call."

"Look at that, Joe." Kate pointed to the screen and saw the searches he had done about Kate's past and her family. She felt violated immediately, and she wanted to throw the computer across the room. He knew her address, her phone number, what car she drove, and so much information. Kate felt sick to her stomach.

"Harper, you need to see this," Joe said, when Harper walked back in the room.

Harper read the history and then said, "Why did he pick you, Kate, why not me?"

"He probably just saw me on TV and wanted to find out more information." She tried to sound like it wasn't a big deal, but she felt sick. "Did you see this as well?" she said.

"What's that?"

"He searched all the mortuaries and funeral homes in the area."

Kate just thought of another lead and immediately got on the phone. "Hi, can you please check to see if any of our victims have had recent deaths in the family?" she asked the officer on duty. "I want to know if they had visited a funeral home recently." Kate finished the call, after making sure they understood it was an absolute emergency.

"I wonder if this is how he finds his victims," she said.

"It's possible, but I don't recall any of them having a recent mortuary visit," Harper said, "other than your friend Kristen."

"But, it can be something that we overlooked. It is possible."

"You bet it could be. It is a damn good possibility," Harper said.

They meticulously went through all the browsing history, well aware of the urgency to get out and investigate. After a few grueling hours of reading through the entries, they decided they had enough information for now. They both knew that this would be revisited again and again in the future, until they caught him.

"Okay, Harper, I think we need to hit the streets again," she suggested. "How about you start visiting the victims' families? Make calls, go in person, and do as much as you can as quickly as you can. I'm going to meet Lauren's Mom for coffee. I have been promising Lisa for a couple days and I really need to follow through. After, I'm going to the funeral homes and mortuaries. Whoever gets done first can go back to the library and start asking for descriptions of anyone interested in the computers recently." Harper gave her thumbs up. They both headed out and said, simultaneously, "No stone unturned."

Chapter 50

S tan started preparing the embalming room for Ms. Marsh as he waited for her body to be delivered. As a habit, he looked into the oven to make sure there was nothing left behind, even though he knew he had thoroughly cleaned it out. He now realized that he couldn't be too careful with snoopy people in the office.

After about an hour of preparing, he heard the phone ring with the interoffice tone.

"Hi Ruth, what do you need?" he said.

"That detective is here again, and she wants to talk to you. She's on her way down now."

"Down here? Ruth, you know it is forbidden." He slammed the phone down and headed for the door. He could hear the detective's footsteps coming down the stairs. Her audacity infuriated him.

Stan tried to open the door to greet her in the hallway, but she just let herself into his room, his special room. His mind raged as he thought, this room is not for her!

"Hi Stan, hope you don't mind, but I have a few more questions," Kate said, as she scanned the room. "So, this is where they go before the viewing? It seems so gloomy and cold here in the basement."

Stan moved in front of her, to stop her from coming in any further. "Let's go upstairs, I don't allow anyone who is not an employee to come down here. Insurance reasons, you understand." He motioned for her to follow him upstairs, but she didn't budge. She walked in even further.

"So, what happens in here, Stan?" She walked over to the corner where the incinerator was.

"What do you mean?" he said, as he tried to calm the beast inside. "That is private business, and you can't just barge in here and do what you want."

Smiling, she looked at him and said, "Calm down, Stan. There's no reason to get so upset. I am just curious, that's all." She walked around him once again, just far enough to see the oven in the corner.

That, Detective is none of your business, he thought to himself. He was tired of being nice. He knew his rights, but he also knew he had to be careful not to raise any suspicion.

"All right, Stan, we can go upstairs. I'm just curious," she said. She turned back to the door, and he felt a huge sense of relief come over him as they started to go upstairs. Ruth, who looked as if she had been waiting patiently for them to come back up, intercepted. She had a nervous disposition about her. He was sure she knew how upset he would be for her letting the detective barge in unannounced.

"So really, Stan, what is that in the corner down there?" Kate asked him. Feeling like his hands were tied, he knew he had to respond, especially with Ruth right there.

"It's an old incinerator that probably doesn't even work anymore. This place used it many years ago, but we don't use it now. It's too dangerous." He gave Ruth a look that could kill. She turned and headed to the kitchen, keeping her mouth shut.

He followed the detective back to his office, and he started to feel relief as they walked in and sat down. Knowing what would irritate her, he turned and said, "So, Officer, what can I help you with?"

"Well, Steve, I just have some questions. They're just routine questions in this investigation."

He stopped himself from smiling. When she called him Steve, he knew he had gotten to her. He watched her look around, waiting for her to speak again. He thought that was all she did was look around and look around and look around. Good grief!

"Do you ever go to the library in Potwin?" she said as she looked up directly at him.

"No. Why do you ask?" he said, as he held her gaze.

"I'm just curious, because your mortuary came up in a search done on a computer at the library." She continued to gaze into his eyes, and he felt her cold demanding stare.

"Why would I go to the library to use the computer?" he said as he tapped his hand on his laptop. "I have one here. Besides, why would I be looking myself up?"

"Do you know why someone would want to do a search of all the mortuaries in the area, other than the obvious reason of needing one?"

He sat for a moment, attempting to give her the impression that he was thinking about what she said. After a few moments he responded. "I really don't know, Detective. I am sorry I can't help."

She started to get up. "Well, please give me a call if you have anything that might help."

"Will do," he said.

She headed for the door without looking back. He decided to have just a little more fun.

"Hey, Detective, whatever happened to that friend of yours? Kristen Jackson, wasn't that her name?" He could see her body language become rigid and uncomfortable.

"Remember, this is the whole point of this investigation. We haven't been able to find her yet, but we'll never stop looking. Even if we have to go back to all the places we have been a million times." She caught her breath and started to get control of her emotions again.

He was amazed to see how much control she really did have. He couldn't help but wonder if she would have this much control, if she knew who he really was. He wondered if she could handle the beast.

"Not looking good, is it? I mean, don't they say that after so much time the victims are usually dead?" He spoke in the most sincere way he could muster, but all he got in return was a hard look.

"No stone unturned," she said before walking out.

Chapter 51

Country Haven left Kate with an uneasy feeling. There was just something about this snake charmer Stan that really rubbed her the wrong way. She tried not to let her dislike of people get in the way of her job, but for some reason, Stan got to her. She found herself playing his little mind games and getting off track from her main purpose. His answering questions with questions got annoying, and she never felt any closure when she left him. She was unhappy with her inability to have clarity on this case and it concerned her that she may be missing clues because she was so close to the case. Stan was the epitome of the type of men she disdained the most. He was egotistical and arrogant, she disliked being around those kind of people.

Moments later, she was in her car and headed to the next stop. She noticed the light blinking on her phone, and she dialed in to check her messages. The first one was from Harper. "Hi, Kate just wanted to let you know that I am batting zero again on this case. I haven't found anything out that we haven't already learned. I still have a few calls to make, and I will keep you posted. I hope you are doing better."

She felt disappointed, and that bit of hope from earlier today was fading fast.

The second message was from Lauren's mom, Lisa, looking for her weekly update. "Hi, Detective, I really hate to bother you. I am just having one of those days, and thought it might be good to talk to you. Thanks for meeting with me, could we meet again soon?" She had met Lisa for coffee before, to see if she might remember anything else that could help them, but more just to help her cope with her daughter's disappearance. Kate understood what Lisa was going through, and she knew how difficult it could be. After listening to this last message she was not in the mood to call Harper back. Neither of them was finding the answers they needed.

She decided to take a detour from the next place on her list. She figured as long as she got to all the mortuaries today, she would still be making good time. She picked up her phone and dialed Lauren's mom. While she waited for her to answer, she thought about Stan's basement. There was something so creepy about it, just like something out of a horror movie. Just like him.

"Hello," Lisa said, her voice sounding either sleepy or heavily medicated.

"Hi, Lisa, this is Detective Kingsley. Are you going to be home for a while? I thought I would stop by."

"Oh, Detective, how about we meet at the usual place? My house is a pig sty and I'm embarrassed. I am glad you called, no one understands like you do. I need to change out of my PJ's and I can meet you." Lisa said.

"I would kill to be in my PJ's still. I am just pulling up out front right now. How about I ignore the mess?" Kate said.

Within seconds Kate was ringing Lisa's doorbell and looking around the outside of her home. It was clear that it hadn't been kept up in a long time, and the home had a deserted feel to it. There was tape residue on the door where something had been posted and later torn away.

Kate hadn't actually been back to the home since the incident happened. They had both lost loved ones and the comfort of talking to each other helped them both deal with the losses. The other thing they had in common was their love for coffee; they often met at a local coffee shop and talked. After time, they started actually talking about things other than the obvious connection and built a nice friendship.

Lisa opened the door, and Kate could feel the sadness and despair in the house. Lisa's eyes were puffy as she stood there in her pajamas with a blanket wrapped around her. Kate reached out and gave her a long heartfelt hug while Lisa broke down in tears. Eventually, she said, "You said PJ's was fine, please come in and excuse the mess, I just haven't been much into housekeeping these days."

Kate sat down next to Lisa on her couch and noticed how cluttered and disheveled her home had become. It reminded her of one of those shows about hoarders. However, she also knew that this was nothing more than pure depression, a sign of someone who had given up on life. Her home was now in foreclosure because she couldn't get out of the house to work. Her kitchen table was so full of mail that had started to pile onto the floor.

Lisa must have seen her looking at the table. She said, "Oh, those are just pesky bills. I should just throw them away. The mailman fills the mailbox at the curb then when it gets full he kindly delivers the mail in a plastic bin to my front door. I know he's just trying to be nice, but I really couldn't care less about the mail, my daughter is missing and that is all I care about. So, I just throw them on the table."

"When was the last time you checked any of your mail?" Kate started thinking about Lauren — and how they didn't get a calling card after her disappearance. She realized that they didn't have a book for her, only for the other three. Kate felt her heart start beating faster as she stood up and headed for the table.

"I will throw them out," Lisa said, as she watched Kate walk to the table. "I am so embarrassed you even had to see me like this."

"Do you mind if I look through these?" Kate started going through the pile.

"Nothing but bills in there, but look all you want."

Kate sifted through the pile, knowing that what she was looking for would be near the bottom. As she continued looking, she asked Lisa, "Have you been watching the news about the other girls?"

"The missing ones, like my Lauren?" she said, and Kate saw the tears welling in her eyes again.

"To be honest, I turn the news off the minute they start talking about the girls. Kate, you are the only one I want to tell me about what is happening. I don't trust the news; they only tell you enough to scare you." Lisa got up off the couch and joined Kate.

It didn't take Kate long before she saw the familiar initials "FTM" on a large envelope. "Stop, Lisa, don't touch anything else!" she held up one hand, and dialed the precinct with the other.

After making arrangements for someone to come collect the evidence, she waited with Lisa, who was in a near-comatose state.

"How important is that envelope?" Lisa said after a long period of silence. "Could it have helped find Lauren sooner?" she said with despair in her voice.

"Look at me, Lisa. You didn't do anything wrong. You need to understand that. You have no control over what other people do. Yes, this is important evidence, but this guy is good. He has not left any trace of anything on any of the other envelopes."

"So, you think that it is a book?" she said.

"Most likely, yes, I think a fairy tale book."

Kate felt relieved to hear the door and see the officers arrive. It didn't take the team long to collect the evidence and be on their way. She felt guilty about leaving Lisa in such a state, but she also knew the day was growing short. Most businesses would be closing their doors soon, and she couldn't take a chance of losing any more time.

After hugging Lisa and saying goodbye, she was in the car again and headed to the next stop. She pulled up to the next mortuary on her list, headed inside, and started to ask the same routine questions.

Chapter 52

The day had been busy, especially since Marilyn's sister never showed up to work, again. Her sister didn't call or even give her a heads up that she wouldn't be showing. Marilyn felt irritated every time she thought about how she did all the work and her sister shared all the benefits. She wished she could just buy her out.

"Marilyn, I am here."

"Nice of you to come to work!" Marilyn said in a flat tone.

"Oh, sorry about that, I figured you wouldn't mind. I can't stay long. I just came by to pick up my check. We're going to a nice dinner tonight, and I need to cash it before we go."

"Check? I haven't been able to make it to the bank since you didn't show up and relieve me. There isn't any money to cover a check yet!" Marilyn said, irritated at her sister's audacity. She continued to knead the dough for that evening's bread.

"Just write me a check and make the deposit in the morning!"

"There's not enough to cover a check that you are going to cash right away! We will bounce checks that we already have out. No way. You will have to wait until tomorrow." She felt proud of her ability to speak her mind for a change.

"I want it now. If you don't write it, I will," she said, walking toward the back cubby of the office.

Marilyn quickly wiped her hands on her apron and walked over to intercept her. "I said no. The funds will not be there until I make this deposit."

"Then just give me cash." Her sister unzipped the bag with the money and rummaged through it.

Ready to explode, Marilyn grabbed the bag out of her hand, zipped it closed, and walked back to her baking table. She shoved the bag into the drawstring of her apron and got back to work.

"Are you kidding me? I need that money. I want it now, Marilyn, I am not kidding. Frank will be furious when he finds out how you're acting. The money in that bag is half mine, and I want my half…"

Marilyn tuned her out, and was relieved when she heard the ding of the door. She immediately walked past her and headed out front. She looked at the clock and noticed she was about an hour away from when the evening crowd came in for fresh bread. After helping the first customer, she had a few minutes to run and put the loaves of bread in the oven to bake. Her sister had left, but she knew she'd be back.

After about a half hour with a slow trickle of customers, she savored the aroma of the bread baking. She felt so much pride when the customers went on and on about how good the bread smelled. She never failed to sell fresh bread when the customers could smell it baking.

Chapter 53

Stan found himself pacing in his special room. His meeting with Kate made his mind wander to places darker than ever before. He had to gain control quickly because Morten was expected in soon and he had to have it together when he arrived. He would need the room to get this afternoon's viewing ready. His anger surfaced again as he started to think about sharing his room with someone else. This was his space, his mark on history, and he didn't want it tainted. The phone rang for what seemed like the hundredth time, and he knew he would need to talk with Ruth and answer her damn questions.

"Hi Ruth, are you trying to reach me?" he said in a calm and almost cheery voice. She always responded to his cheeriness.

"I hate to bother you, Stan, but I am worried. Both Morten and I have been concerned about you. You seem different, and we just want to know if there is anything we can do to help."

"Well, for a start, you guys could cut me some slack and stop nagging me. I am not my father, and you have to realize that there are going to be some changes. I hate to say it, but you guys are driving me crazy." He immediately regretted letting the emotions of the moment get the best of him. He quickly tried to backpedal. "Ruth, you know you have always been the next best thing to a mother to me, and you know how much I respect you. I guess it hurts my feelings that you don't have enough faith in me to trust my decisions," he said it in his most sincere and wounded voice.

He felt the tension in her voice fade away as she said, "Oh, Stan, you know you have always been like a son to me. I guess I am just not used to all the secrets and locked doors. Don't get me wrong. I know how important your privacy is; I am just not use to all the changes."

Feeling the anger emerging again, he closed his eyes and pictured his princesses. The anger started to melt away. "You remember my father, right?" he continued, "Well, he never let me have anything of my own. I never got to go to college. I never had play dates. I always worked for him on his terms, and I lost my childhood over it. I just want to make this place my own. All I need is a little support. Can you give me this, Ruth, just a little support?"

"Of course, Stan, I will give you some space. I never really thought about it. Don't worry about Morten. I will take care of him."

"Thanks, Ruth," he said, anxious to get off the phone and start daydreaming about his next princess. "Is there anything else?"

"Nope, that should do it. Let me know if there is anything you need."

"Great, Ruth, thanks —"

"But," she said, with some hesitation, "I had just one more question, Stan."

"What?"

"Why did you lie to that nice lady cop about the incinerator?"

He felt like someone punched him in his gut, and it took everything he had to keep his composure. "First of all, both you and Morten have been all over me about this damn incinerator, and how the gas bill was higher, and all about inspections and blah blah blah. I don't know all the laws, but I do know that if there is a law to have it inspected and I have been using it, I could get this place in a lot of trouble and big fines. Or, worse yet, Ruth, I don't want to take a chance of anyone coming in here and trying to take away a piece of my family history. So, I lied to that cop because I am trying to protect all of us. This place is a second home to all of us, and I don't want to jeopardize our reputation or cash flow. Especially since I know you haven't had a raise in a very long time, and I know that it is not because you don't deserve one. I know you depend on this job, and I also know that my father was so tight and didn't take care of you financially. How about we sit down soon and talk about your much-needed raise?"

He felt like he needed a nap after that speech, but he knew how much Ruth would eat it up. She was actually rather easy to manipulate.

"Well, if you think so. I would love to get together. Thanks, Stan, really, thanks. I mean it."

"No problem, Ruth. Let me finish with some things, and we can get together in the next day or two and decide." Knowing he had reeled her back in, he hung up the phone and started pacing again. However, this time he was pacing in excitement. Cinderella's time was coming, and he had to mentally prepare, and plan the next release of the beast. Ruth would be off his back for a while, but he was going to have to pay special attention to make sure she stayed off track. This meant he would have to engage and be interested in all her boring extended conversations. The thought of that made him want to take the scalpel to his own jugular.

Chapter 54

Kate couldn't help but think that talking to a piece of wood would be more interesting than engaging with the staff at funeral homes. All the polyester made her itch just thinking about it. She felt exhausted as the evening came upon her after an unproductive day, and she knew she should stop for takeout on her way back to the precinct. She opted for a venti coffee instead. She figured staying awake was much more important than eating her way into a slumber.

Pulling into the precinct, she checked her messages again, always in the hopes of hearing something, anything, from Kristen. Disappointed again, she headed into the station.

"Great work, Kate, great work," Harper said as he greeted her.

Gathering that he had heard about the book, she said, "Thanks, I can't believe I didn't think of it before. I had to have known that Lauren was connected. I just hope that we haven't lost any time because of missing this. I am just not on my A game with this. I feel like I'm missing important clues. "Do you think I am too close to this?"

"Don't think like that Kate, you may be close to it, but I also know you can't ever let it go," Harper said.

"Jeez, Harper, you should have seen her mother's place. It was the saddest thing I have seen, other than Kristen's empty apartment. Oh, and I am sorry I didn't call you and let you know. I was just so anxious to get to the funeral homes and get some questions answered." She started going through the piles of paperwork on her desk.

"And?" Harper said.

"And what?"

"And? Did you get any questions answered?" He looked at her anxiously.

Kate shook her head, dropping her shoulders in shame. "Not only was it unproductive at the funeral homes, I had to talk to that snake charmer Stan again," she said as she continued looking through mail. "For some reason, that guy really makes my skin crawl."

"Yeah, well, my day was uneventful. I didn't find another clue, like you did," he said. "Don't be so hard on yourself."

After filling each other in on all the events of the day, they checked on the status of the latest book find, only to learn that there was nothing available forensically. Only the inscription:

Good night, Rapunzel. You could never be TWO golden.

"Well, it's pretty clear we have them all in order now," she said. "We just have to find his weakness." In a whisper, she said, "Just what am I missing? No stone unturned."

"Right, no stone unturned," Harper said, as they both just sat there and looked at the book.

"Go home to your wife, Harper. Maybe it will do us both some good to get some rest." She patted his shoulder and headed for the door. "Fresh eyes tomorrow couldn't hurt."

Chapter 55

"So much preparation and so little time," he said to himself as he let out a chuckle. He was giddy when he was in his fantasy mode, as well as anxious to arrive at the little bakery and check in on his next trophy. The inner beast rumbled deep in his groin; he was going to have to satisfy the craving soon, or he would not be able to have as much control as he needed to continue living this fairy tale. He weaved in and out of traffic as he headed toward the bakery. He passed the Thai restaurant and felt a small pang of sadness that he wouldn't be able to eat there again. He really liked the food, and he couldn't help but think about that copper he saw there that day. He remembers her eyes locking onto his, that's when he remembered! Could it really be? Of course — it was Kate. He couldn't believe he had missed that.

The realization only reinforced his need to continue. He then realized that she was part of his destiny and that they were destined to intertwine in this fantasy. He only hoped that she didn't become a problem because the world was a much more interesting place with her in it. He found himself talking aloud in the car, asking questions to himself:

"So, my Kate, what is it going to be? Do you come so close to catching me that your fate does you in? Or are you always just so close to catching me that we can continue to live in this destiny together?" He pondered these possibilities as he drove into the parking lot of the bakery. He knew that Cinderella had a destiny as well, and he relished the moment when she got to meet his beast. The hunger was so strong now that he knew it had to be done soon. He started formulating a plan as he walked up to the door and heard the chime.

"Coming, just a second," he heard from the back room.

He peeked through the swinging doors, but all he saw were shadows from behind. He waited and waited for her to come out.

"Sorry about that!" she said as she looked up and caught his eyes. "Oh, hi, back so soon? I think I like you making a habit out of this."

"I think you are trying to fatten me up. These pastries are so damn good. Do you have a special ingredient you use to keep everyone coming back?" Stan smiled at her.

"I wish I had some magic potion to make everyone come back as often as you do." She leaned on the counter and smiled back at him. He couldn't help but notice her interest in him, and he couldn't help thinking of satisfying the beast. He had to get control, or he was going to take her right here and now. Then she said something that caught him off guard.

"Why don't you come back here, and I will show you how I make the breads and pastries?"

She motioned for him to follow, and he couldn't help himself. As she started towards the back he ran to the door and flipped the sign to closed, just in case he lost control.

"Are you coming?"

"Right behind you, darling," he called back to her. He was worried that there was not enough willpower in him not to feed the beast. He started saying a chant in his head, trying to warn the beast that tonight was not the night. Don't kill the princess, don't break the spell, don't kill the princess, and don't break the spell. He kept saying it over and over as he walked through the swinging doors.

She immediately started giving him a tour of everything in the kitchen and how it worked. Delirious with the swelling of his groin he tried to pay attention as he watched her flutter around the kitchen talking with excitement.

"Oh, forgive me for talking so much. I hope I am not boring you. I guess I assume everyone is as interested in this stuff as I am," she said, as she walked around the kitchen.

"It smells really good in here. What's in the oven now?" Stan envisioned her kitchen oven being his incinerator.

"Oh, those are peach pies. They're usually a hit for the lunch crowd."

Not being able to control the pain in his groin he knew he had to release himself or he wouldn't be able to not kill her right then and there. He walked closer behind her as she was looking at the pies in the oven.

He tossed her ponytail away from her neck and kissed it. She pulled away and moved closer to the oven.

"I am so sorry, I shouldn't have done that. It's just with all the aroma of the pies in the oven and the beauty of you I just can't help myself. "Stan said, moving closer to her and kissing her neck again. He turned her towards him and away from the oven. It gave him comfort to see the oven behind him and he felt like he was going to explode in his pants.

He couldn't control it much longer so he started moving his hands up from her waist and up to her breast as he continued kissing the side of her neck. He felt her breathing increase as he caressed her and kissed her lips. Once he felt the wetness of her mouth, he immediately increased his speed of kissing and caressing and she hesitantly obliged him.

Undoing her apron behind her and pulling it over her head he started unbuttoning her shirt when she responded in a winded voice.

"Oh, this is a little fast, don't you think? I have customers who may come in and I am not sure this is a good idea."

Not thinking that he could make himself stop he said, "Don't you believe in fate, Marilyn? I mean I think there is an honest connection here and I have never been as spontaneous as I feel like being right now. Doesn't it just feel right to let go? I think we shouldn't hold back." Stan continued unbuttoning her shirt.

"I just don't know Steve. I am not this kind of girl. What will you ever think of me after?" she said, as she let him continue to unclothe her.

"I will think that I have finally met the right one for me, my true love, just like the fairytales." He undid her bra and moved her towards the table in the kitchen.

"I don't usually do this, but I think you have me in a spell," she said, returning his kisses. "Have you cast a spell on me?"

"A spell, don't break the..." He welcomed her kisses as he once again felt the wetness of her tongue slide into his mouth, and the beast inside him started swelling to the point he thought his pants were going to rip open. He slipped off his shirt, enjoying the naked feel of her breasts against him. He lifted her cotton skirt and she kissed him harder and with more urgency. The beast was almost out of control now.

Stan felt like he was going to explode as he took her hand and placed it on the outside of his pants. She undid his button and zipper. The throbbing was almost unbearable as he grabbed her by the waist in a big bear hug, and sat her on the table full of bread dough and flour. With his boxers down around his ankles, he laid her down on the table, grabbed her underwear and yanked them down as quickly as he could. Now she was completely naked and vulnerable. He stood at the edge of the table, grabbed her by the hips, and slid her through the flour, as he went inside her, hard and deep. He could hear her moan as she lay back and moved her hips back and forth in a rhythm. He didn't have to do much but just stay deep inside her, as she did all the work. He watched her scream as she hit one orgasm after another and, right before each one, she arched her back and held her breasts. He continued until he knew she was done and then slowly withdrew from her. He was still hard and unsatisfied. It was so painful to put his pants back on without releasing the beast, but he also knew after going inside her that he wouldn't be able to climax. Not this way. However, he also knew that this was a means to an end, and the intimacy it created would make the final transformation that much better. She would come with him anywhere, now that she had been satisfied and experienced such ecstasy with him. She would be dying to get back with him and, next time, she would live in infamy with him, on his terms.

After finishing, Stan could see how embarrassed she was. They exchanged glances as she quickly looked away.

"Thank you for that. Wow! What a great way to start the day," Stan said.

"I don't know what came over me. I am just not that kind of girl. I hope you don't think differently of me."

"Are you kidding me, I am not that kind of guy either. I think we just got caught up in the moment. I find it refreshing to be spontaneous for a change, don't you?"

"I suppose, it's good to be out of your comfort zone every now and then."

After they were both fully clothed again he gently reassuringly kissed her cheek and headed back out the swinging doors and towards the front door.

He turned the sign back to open and winked at her as he left.

"Until tomorrow," he said to himself in a whisper. "Until tomorrow, my Cinderella."

"I hope to see you soon," she said.

He bet she couldn't wait. He bet she couldn't.

Chapter 56

The cool, brisk wind blew against Kate's face. She realized that there was someone next to her holding her hand. She turned her head slightly and smiled as she looked at Kristen. She smiled back at her and said, "Go higher Kate, much higher."

Not wanting to disappoint her best friend, she started to soar higher and higher until they were up with the clouds. As they leveled back out, they looked down on the city and noticed that all the lights looked so beautiful.

"Just like the Peter Pan Ride, Kate, remember?" Kristen said, extending her arms while still holding Kate's hand.

"How could I ever forget? We were eight and we went on that ride over and over and over, until I thought they were going to glue us to the seats as permanent fixtures," she said, realizing how happy she felt and how she never wanted this moment to end. She looked over at Kristen and felt so complete with her next to her. She felt her hand start to loosen, and she looked over to her. "Don't let go Kristen," she said. "Don't ever let go."

She let go of Kate's hand and started drifting away from her. The harder Kate tried to catch her, the farther away she went. Though she couldn't see her anymore, she could hear her in the distance. "We can't stay like this forever, Kate, and you have worked hard to find him. Find him, Kate. Find out who did this to me. He is out there, finding his next one. I love you forever."

Then she was gone, and Kate heard the rain pounding on her window. She opened her eyes and realized that there was a big storm hitting. Looking at the clock, she was surprised it was already seven, as it was still dark and gloomy. She thought the storm clouds must be fierce to block out the sun this late.

Kate started the shower and tried to remember the dream, how she felt having Kate next to her again. She wanted her back. She wanted her best friend back.

Feeling drained and tired, Kate didn't even bother making her own coffee and went to the drive through, the rain coming down in sheets on her windshield. When she rolled down her window to get her coffee, she took a deep breath and smelled the rain. She used to love rainy days, but now they made her feel lonely and sad. She paid for her coffee and headed toward the street when her phone started vibrating. She pulled over to the side and answered.

"Hi, Kate, I'm going to be late coming in today, if at all. Megan started having contractions, and we spent most of the night in the hospital. She's stable now, but I need to be here today to keep an eye on her. I can call her mother…"

"No, Harper, you need to be a husband and a father now. You take the day off, and I will keep at it. Let me know if you come up with anything. Otherwise, I don't want to see you today. Comprende?"

"Well, at least for the morning. If she is doing better, I will have her mom come take over." From the tone of his voice, she could tell it was killing him to not be there for her.

"Harper, you have to take care of your family. Don't worry about me. I have a lot of paperwork to go through, and I am going to go back and randomly go through some of the crime scenes. The library has been nagging me. I think I will start there."

"Well, keep me posted. You know how much I hate being out of the loop."

"I wouldn't dream of not keeping you posted. Otherwise, we both know you will nag me to death and not take care of your wife. Harper, hold the ones you love close. You never know when they may be gone."

She hung up before he could say anything else. She knew Harper would try to stall her on the phone, because talking to her made him feel less guilty about not coming in for the day.

She continued through the city, being careful while driving in the crazy rain. Her mind started to wander through all the different crime scenes and all the different girls. What did they have in common? How did he pick them? So far, all her leads were taking her in circles. She tried to think about what things kept coming back up in her circle. The books kept coming up, the girls kept missing, and something else…

She pulled into the parking lot of the library and reached for the umbrella hidden somewhere in the back. Having it in her grasp, she stepped out of the car and opened it in one smooth move. She dashed inside, shaking the rain off the umbrella. Before she could look up, she heard someone talking to her. "Don't do drugs, right?" he said. She saw the young kid at the information desk. "Remember me? I remember you, the big gun." He smiled and pointed at the gun on her hip.

"I do remember you now. You are Matt, right?"

"Wow, a big gun and a good memory."

"A good cop never forgets anything, Matt. Don't ever forget that." As she walked up to him, she decided that he was as good a place as any to start. "So, Matt, you know why I am here, right?"

"Yeah, about the whole Rose thing, it has this place torn up. People are crying everywhere, or calling in sick when they can't cope."

"Matt, why aren't you crying?" She watched him very carefully, looking for a tell, but all she got was a young kid too absorbed in his own drama to comprehend the magnitude of this.

"Me? I barely knew Rose. Plus, she's like my mom's age. It's not like we hung out or anything. Just because I'm not crying doesn't mean I don't care. Crap, she could have been my mom or one of my aunts or something. That would've been real bad."

"What I would like to do is go through the last day she was here at work. You were working that day, right?" He nodded in confirmation. "I thought so. Now I would like to start with the beginning of your shift."

199

She motioned for him to sit with her in a couple of nearby chairs, and continued. "You have a really good view of the door from where you are. Did you happen to see anything unusual during your shift? Like anyone who looked out of place or hung around too long, anything like that?" She noticed he wasn't looking at her. She pointed her finger up to her face and said, "Focus here, Matt. I need you to fully engage. This is very important. What you know could really help the investigation."

He shrugged. "I didn't see anything any more unusual than usual," he said.

"What would you consider unusual?"

"Well, I didn't see any mean-looking people who looked bad. No one had any guns or weapons that I could see."

Kate averted her eyes in an attempt not to smile. He was so sincere about what he was saying, and she didn't have the heart to make him feel stupid. Instead, she tried to guide him in a different direction.

"Very good, Matt, you are doing great. Now, I want you to think of everyone else who might have seemed normal. How many people can you remember noticing as they came through the door?"

She saw that the question really threw him; a look of panic swept across his face. "You mean you want me to remember everyone who came through the door?" He looked to her for confirmation.

"Just everyone you can remember, Matt. There is a big difference. Also, you are not in any trouble, I just want to pick your brain. You seem like a pretty observant guy," she said, as she tapped her gun and smiled.

"Well, I guess I do notice things, but not from here. Everything is so damn boring here. I just do it while I'm in school."

"How about the people you talk to? Do you remember talking with very many people that day?" She didn't want to lead him too far with this, but she wanted to know if he saw anyone around the computers or if anyone talked to him about them.

"Let me see… There were some old ladies asking about botanical garden passes. Then a teacher who needed to ask about getting her class library cards. Then there was the Hooters girl." He smiled as if with a memory of her. "She wanted to see if she could borrow a computer. I remember thinking that was funny, because they don't loan them out like books. Oh, and then there was that dude who was asking about microfiche. I mean, who really uses those things anymore? Seriously!"

"Tell me more about this guy with the microfiche. Whatever happened with him? Where did you send him off to?" Her heart started racing, thinking this could be something. She stayed calm, so as not to rattle him and have him freeze up.

"Oh yeah, this guy was seriously from a time capsule. He looked at me like I was crazy when I told him, 'Google it, dude.' I even had to point toward the computers. He looked like he had never seen one before. I remember telling him that he could sign up to use them over with Rose at the computer desk." He stopped and gazed at her. "Oh my God, do you think that's him?"

"I don't know, but it's very important to stay calm, very calm. Just answer my questions as we work through this. What color was his hair?"

"Hmmm, maybe light brown or sandy blonde. I can't remember for sure."

He sat there for a moment and concentrated. She knew that this bit of information was crucial, so she remained still and let him take his time.

He then blurted, "He was wearing a hat."

"Very good, Matt," she said in a very soft voice. "Do you remember what the cap looked like?"

"Hmm, I am not sure, I guess it was a baseball cap," he said. "I don't even remember what color it was, though. But I do know what color his eyes were. Even I couldn't forget how blue they were."

"Great, that is good information, very good. Now how tall was he? Compared to you, how tall was he?" He closed his eyes and focused.

"He was maybe a hair taller than me, and I am almost six-two," he said.

"Size, how big or small was he?"

"Not as thin as me, but not fat either. I would say average." He seemed to be on a mission to answer questions now. He was alert and anxious to answer each question. "Did he talk with an accent, or was there anything distinct with his voice?" she asked.

"No accent that I can remember. I do remember thinking that, as dumb as he was, he sure seemed arrogant."

Kate knew this was her guy. She could feel it with every bone in her body. She wanted to call the sketch artist right away, but she didn't want to lose Matt's momentum either.

"Smell anything odd or out of place?" she said.

"Nope, that I don't remember, I don't normally smell people."

"How about a car, did you see him drive in or leave, by any chance?"

"No, I never saw a car. But, now that you mention it, I did see him in the parking lot after my shift was up. I remember thinking that he left the library hours ago, but was still in the parking lot. I just thought he must have forgotten something."

"Interesting, what time did you get off work?" She looked at her notes for the hours that Rose worked that day.

"I got off at eight. When I saw him in the parking lot, he was kinda rude with me, like I was annoying him."

She remembered that Rose got off work at five. That might have given him enough time. "Do you happen to know what kind of car he got into?"

"No. I was in such a hurry to leave, I never looked back to see him."

"Do you know if Rose drove a car to work that day?"

"Rose always walks, rain or shine. I don't think she lives far from here."

Kate's thoughts started racing, faster than she could process them. He must have left with her when she left work. They walked somewhere, but where? She knew they didn't go to her house. And if they left by car somewhere, then why would he be back in the parking lot later? Her mind was racing until she eventually looked up and met Matt's eyes. She caught herself talking out loud through the whole process. "He must live nearby. They walked to his house, not hers." She realized he is hunting close to home now. He is so sure that he won't get caught that he is hunting down the street.

"You think he lives around here?" Matt said, with an appalled look on his face.

"Matt, you have been so helpful. I am going to send an officer over to have you help them draw a composite of this guy. I can't tell you how helpful you have been. You've given me a really great lead to work with." She shook his hand and started for the door. She turned back to him and said, "Matt, stay in school. Also, slow down on the pot. It kills your brain cells, you know." She was out the door before she could make out what he was saying, but she was pretty sure that he was denying the whole pot thing.

She picked up her phone and dialed Harper's number. He answered on the first ring.

"Yeah, I am here, what do you need?"

She proceeded to tell Harper all about the conversation she'd had with Matt.

Chapter 57

When Marilyn woke up, the rain was pouring down, which normally would be the start of a depressing day. This morning was different. It was the beginning of a new day, a change for the good, she thought, as she continued to knead the dough.

Every time the chime sounded, her heart skipped a beat, waiting for him to come. She almost felt disappointed when she came out and saw that he had not shown up. Nonetheless, she continued making the bread and pastries, and found herself singing songs with words she made up as the morning passed. She felt like a giddy schoolgirl.

She heard the keys going in the back door, and she knew it was her sister again, here to bleed her of more money she didn't have.

"Look, the bakery barely pays its bills and you still make more than me. Something has got to change. Either you start working more, or I am going to start paying you less. You decide, but enough is enough." Marilyn didn't even need to see her reaction. She felt her sister's anger as she took a moment to formulate her words.

"First of all, you are not my boss, and you cannot tell me what I am entitled to. I need money because, unlike you, I have a family and a husband who need to be taken care of. Unlike you, who has no one."

Normally this kind of conversation would sting, but not today. Today she would not let her sister get the best of her. Today was the day for change. She never looked back as she continued singing her made-up song and dancing to a rhythm that only resonated in her own head.

Before long, her sister continued on out the door and slammed it closed behind her. Marilyn knew it was only temporary, but every little bit helped. She continued baking for the customers who came in slowly throughout the day. Hopefully, he would come soon.

Chapter 58

S tan had so much to prepare for the big night ahead of him. The only thing that made him a little sad was the thought of missing out on the homemade bread. She could bake, but it was a small sacrifice he was willing to make.

He intentionally avoided going to the bakery in the morning. He expected that she was anxiously waiting, however, he would have much more control over her tonight if she sat and waited for him all day. That way, when he showed up in the evening, she would be ready to come with him, without hesitation.

He made his usual rounds and got through the tedious work of managing the business. After Stan hit the lull in the day, when everyone was at lunch and he was left alone, he headed down to his secret room. He unlocked the door and closed it behind him, sat down, and started working out all the details.

His mind wandered as he tried to stay on track and come up with a plan. He couldn't help but reminisce about all the times he had fed the beast in this room. He went through many different scenarios for how he would get Cinderella there. He wanted to take her willingly from her business rather than carry her out in a trashcan. He decided that a surprise was what she needed, something to look forward to and something to look nice for. He immediately changed his mind about waiting until tonight to see her, and decided to call ahead and make a date. After all, a date with "Steve" wouldn't get traced back to him.

The problem was he needed to call from an untraceable phone. He decided to close up and escape while he could. Ruth would be back from lunch soon, and he didn't want to have to explain his actions to her. After riding the service elevator up to the garage, he pulled out of the driveway.

Since he knew that this call would likely be traced back to the originating phone, he decided that it had to be from the perfect place. It couldn't be just some local payphone. After driving aimlessly, he finally figured it out. He would call her from Kristen's apartment. He had been doing his homework, and he knew that Detective Kate had been keeping the place up in the hopes of her friend's return. This would be the ultimate slap in the face.

The rewards far outweighed the risks in this situation. He decided that he needed to gain access quickly, make the phone call, and exit just as quickly. He couldn't take a chance of getting caught up in enjoying the scenery.

He pulled into the driveway with every intention of waiting a while for someone to leave the building's back exit so he could sneak in. He pulled a janitor jumper out of the back and slipped it on over his clothes. After putting a baseball cap on and pulling it down over his eyes, he headed over to the door and waited.

It only took about ten minutes before someone came out the door with a cell phone to their ear. They didn't even take notice of him as he slipped in behind them. Remembering the last time he was there, he quickly moved through the halls to the elevator. After arriving at her door, he looked around to see if anyone had noticed him.

He pulled the crowbar out of his sleeve where he was resting it in the palm of his hand. He figured it could work as a weapon or as tool, though he was hoping that it would be just a tool. Within seconds, he broke open the door and let himself into Kristen's apartment.

He took a moment to breathe in the emptiness. It exhilarated him to reminisce about old times, and he could feel the beast within starting to stir. He moved quickly through the apartment and did a quick check. He made sure the jumper was zipped all the way up and covered his head with his cap. He looked at his gloves in detail to make sure they were not torn or ripped.

Feeling confident and ready, he picked up the phone and dialed the bakery.

"Hi, Bakers Delight, can I help you?"

"Can you give me some more of that special desert you made for me yesterday?" he said, knowing that she would love the attention.

"Well, I wondered if I scared you away. I was hoping to see you this morning," she said, as if wounded from his not showing up. "Yesterday was so out of character for me."

He hated it when people were so needy. He had to control his response because he knew how important this next step was. "I really wanted to come this morning, but work got busy." He added in a pouting voice: "How can I ever make it up to you?"

"Well, I am just happy to have you call."

"How about we go out on a real date tonight?"

"Really, I would love that. What time?"

Good grief, woman, you sure are easy, Stan thought. "How about I pick you up when you close, and I will plan the surprise of your life. Would you like that?"

"The only thing I don't like is that I have to wait all day in suspense. I will go home and get a change of clothes so I am ready. If you like, I can try to close early. It's just that I have to get all the pastries done tonight for tomorrow morning's business run."

"No, no, my princess, that will not be necessary. Nine will be fine." The darker the better, he thought. He knew that this one would be one to enjoy. He would take his sweet, sweet time with her.

He exited the apartment as quickly as he entered, and it wasn't long before he was pulling back into the mortuary garage and closing it behind him. He made notes of things to get: blindfold, chloroform…

Chapter 59

Not feeling like going back to the precinct, Kate decided to stop off at Kristen's to check her mail and messages. She had been back to many of the crime scenes today, going over things in her head. She even stopped by Lisa's, but didn't go to the door. Instead, she just wandered around in the alley, again trying to get a feel for what happened.

She also drove through the neighborhood around the library. She was always amazed at how different all the historic homes were from one another. Much different than the new, cookie-cutter homes they were building everywhere now. These old homes had so much character, and she loved looking at the way people had so much pride in maintaining them. She also noticed that most all the real-estate signs in the yard were for a Nichole Nickels. She must do pretty well to have this many listings in such a bad economy.

After getting tired of driving the neighborhoods, she headed over to Kristen's. She stopped for a coffee along the way and continued to make mental notes from her conversation with Matt earlier in the day. After pulling into Kristen's place, she strolled through the complex and headed to the stairs, climbing them by twos until she came to her floor. She searched through her keys, but quickly realized that she didn't need them. The door had been pried open.

She stepped back and radioed for backup. She pulled her gun from her holster and pushed the door open. She hesitated before crossing the threshold. After a clean sweep, she determined that whoever had been there was gone now. She sat down at the table and waited for backup to arrive.

Nothing, as far as she could tell, seemed out of place or missing. She didn't understand. If this were some random burglary, then there would be things missing. People didn't just break doors open for no reason. She could feel in her gut that this was not random. She picked up the phone and dialed Harper.

After she got only a couple words out, he said he was on his way and practically hung up on her. She didn't even try to argue with him, because she wanted him there. She needed him there to help her sort through it. She was too close to the situation, and might be missing something.

The officers arrived and started with the dusting and usual basics. Evening was already setting in, and she wondered where the day went. She felt like she was spinning in circles, even though the kid had been a great source of information.

Harper finally came through the door and sat down next to her. "Let's go through this. If nothing was missing, then why come here?" he said. "We have to figure this out before we leave this apartment."

Tears welled in her eyes. "It is a condo, not an apartment."

Harper then told the officers not to miss anything. He wanted them to look under and over everything. He concluded with, "No stone unturned."

Kate repeated that phrase in her head, over and over, until it was almost like a Buddhist chant.

Chapter 60

Where has the time gone? Marilyn asked herself as she looked at the clock. Steve would be there in no time, and she still had to change her clothes and spruce up. She'd felt like a machinist, kneading the dough and baking the pastries in record time. Working was so much more enjoyable when she had other things to look forward to in life. No TV dinner tonight, she thought. She was going on her first real date in years.

To make the day even more enjoyable, her sister never showed up or even called. She kept waiting for her sister's husband to show up and give her an earful, but not even that could take away the elation about her big date coming up.

The bell chimed and she looked at the clock again. She realized that Steve would be there in less than an hour. She headed through the double doors, and greeted the customer waiting in the lobby.

"Can I... Oh, hi, how are you?" she said as she greeted Tanya, one of her regulars. "Let me guess? A loaf of bread, a container of milk, and a stick of butter, right?" She started to laugh as she said it.

"Aren't you the happy one today?" Tanya said. "You know, I saw a rerun of that *Sesame Street* episode the other day when my little one was watching it. Girl, don't get me started, or we will be quoting lines all night. Besides, by the looks of you, there are some big plans in the making."

Tanya was one of her first customers, and she had been one of the most loyal. She began loading her usual order up as she started telling Marilyn all about her deadbeat boyfriend. Usually, Marilyn would take the opportunity to complain about her sister, and before long they would have a nice little pity party going. But tonight, nothing would spoil Marilyn's mood.

"… enough about me now, tell me about whatcha got going tonight. It's something big, right? So, give it up now. What's his name? What does he do for a living? What does he drive? And, yes, it is important what they drive. You don't want an old beater car that the fellas think they can do all the fixin with. Okay, okay, and now back to the beginning, what's his name?" She finished without even taking a breath.

"You are right about the hot date, but girl, I don't have near enough time to get into it. Oh, but he is so dreamy, so damn cute. He has these blue eyes that just melt your heart. His name is Steve. To tell you the truth, other than that, I really don't know much about him. He'll be here soon, and I need to get my face on, so you need to get going."

"Good enough for me just be careful. There is that crazy man out there. People are saying that he's keeping all those girls locked up somewhere as prisoners."

"Well, trust me, Steve could keep me locked up as his prisoner any day," she said as they both started laughing again.

After Tanya left, Marilyn flipped the sign on the door and locked it. She ran back to the bathroom and started with the makeup transformation. Within seconds of finishing, she could hear the light rap at the door, and she knew he was there. She couldn't help blushing in excitement as she flipped the lights off behind her and made her way to the front.

"Well, hello gorgeous," he said.

"You know how to greet a girl," she said.

She noticed he had a scarf in his hand.

"Remember how I said that this is going to be a surprise?" he said.

"Oh yes. Do I get to know now?"

He smiled and winked at her, and she felt her heart flutter.

"In time, dear, in time, let's start with keeping it a surprise until it is time." She felt him maneuver behind her starting at her hips and pulling the scarf up her body. She felt him getting hard up against her back and she softly moaned acknowledging that she felt him. Pulling the scarf up and over her breast he hesitated around her neck as he moved it up to cover her eyes. Approving his gestures she put her head back and pushed her back into his groin. She could feel he was excited as the scarf made its way over her eyes and was secured tightly. Within minutes, they were in the car driving.

She couldn't wait to see what was to come. She hadn't had a surprise in a long time, and she felt like a child on Christmas Eve.

Chapter 61

Silence took over as they sat at the kitchen table. Kate had her head in her hands and her eyes closed, while chewing on her lip. Harper just stared off with his hands clasped in front of him on the table.

"I think we have checked everything I can think of," she said. "What are we missing?"

Harper sat there stoically, not even acknowledging that she was speaking. She gave him his space, knowing that he was working with some kind of train of thought. Then he got up and methodically started opening and closing cupboards. Harper lifted the phonebook out and started rummaging through the pages.

Kate closed her eyes again, trying to get the same level of focus. As she felt the vibration of the phonebook hit the table, she started thinking about the page torn out of the phonebook in the restaurant. Just as she thought about picking the phone up out of the cradle, she heard the beep of the phone as Harper beat her to it.

She looked up and continued biting her lip as she watched Harper carefully walk the cordless phone to the table, carrying it by the tip of the antenna. He then motioned for someone to dust the phone for fingerprints. The silence was deafening as they all watched in anticipation.

After a few minutes of checking and double-checking for fingerprints, the tech looked up and shook his head in disappointment. She felt her heartbeat speeding up from the excitement of coming up with a clue. She reached over and picked up the phone to put it back.

"Hey, Kate, try hitting redial," Harper said in a burst of inspiration.

She slowly turned the phone over so she could see the numbers; first she hit speakerphone, and then hit redial. She looked back up at Harper as they waited.

"Have you used the phone since her disappearance?" Harper asked.

"I don't think so."

After a few rings, voicemail picked up and they continued looking at each other in anticipation of the recording.

"You have reached Bakers Delight, and we are sorry to have missed your call. We are probably making fresh pastries just for you. Please leave a message at the beep and we promise to get back with you as soon as possible. Thanks, and have a great day!" The message ended with a beep and they looked at each other in bewilderment. She hung up the phone without leaving a message.

"Kate, your lip is bleeding," Harper headed for the bathroom and came back with a handful of toilet paper. He handed it to her and she held it tightly to her lip.

"A bakery," she said after a few seconds of silence. "I know that I wouldn't have called a bakery, especially one I have never heard of. This was not a number listed when they dumped the records right after her disappearance."

Harper began pacing the floor.

"We need to send someone to the bakery right away, and we need to find out when this call was made." Harper picked up his radio and called dispatch.

Without hesitation, she called in a dump of the phone records, asking for an immediate response. "He is messing with us Harper, he is taunting us. Oh my God, Harper do you think this could be a clue about the next victim? We need to find out everything about that bakery." She started making other calls to find out who the owner was, so they could get a listing of all employees at the bakery.

They grabbed their things and headed for the door. "Make sure you secure the door and lock it up," she told an officer on her way out.

"I'll drive," Harper said.

Harper weaved in and out of traffic as they drove to the bakery. She received a call back with the owner's name and number. After writing it down, she hung up and immediately started dialing the first number.

The phone rang and rang, but nobody picked up. Frustrated, she hung up and dialed the second number. Within a couple rings, a woman answered.

"Hello," the voice on the other line said.

"Hi, this is Detective Kingsley with the Topeka Police Department. Is this the owner of Bakers Delight?" she said with clear urgency.

"Yeah, me and my sister own it, why?" a woman replied. "Has someone broken into it?"

"And what is your name?" Kate said.

"Cindy Thompson."

"And your sister's name?"

"Marilyn Morris. Has the bakery been broken into? What's happened? Can I please get some answers?"

"I am not sure, but where are you right now?"

"I am home with my husband. Why, is everything okay? What the hell is going on here? Is this a joke? You're scaring me."

"No, this is not a joke. I am sending a car to your house, and someone will explain everything to you. Do you have a phone number for your sister? I only have one number for her, but there was no answer. Do you know how I can reach her?"

"Why? Is she okay?"

"I don't know. I tried her number, but there was no answer and no machine. What time does she leave work?"

"Well, we close at seven, but she often stays late to prepare for the next day. She doesn't have a husband or a life. The bakery is all she has."

Kate was about to continue with more questions, but Harper's radio sounded with the officers on the scene. Apparently the bakery was secure. They found nothing out of place, and it was completely empty.

"Hold on, Cindy, just a sec," she said, as she cupped her hand over her phone and mouthed the words *skip the bakery*. "Cindy, can I confirm your sister's address, and any cell phone number she may have?"

Kate hung up with the sister and they headed over to the home of Marilyn Morris. She felt panic rising in her stomach, knowing deep down that they would find a shell of a home — empty, cold, and forever deserted.

Chapter 62

He couldn't help but to have a wry smile as he looked at his Cinderella sitting there next to him, so completely under his spell. He believed he really did have a way with women, and that they just couldn't resist his charm and dominance. The beast within started to stir, and he felt the tightness in his pants as he envisioned what was soon to happen. He was careful not to drive too quickly, enjoying the foreplay before the release. She looked so sweet with her hands clasped in her lap.

Stan reached over and took her hand in his. "Almost there, sweetness, you really do look beautiful right now."

"Thank you, Steve. It is a little strange being blindfolded. Where are we going?" she said.

Stan tried to be as sweet as he could, but it was starting to wear on him. He could see the finish line and didn't feel like being as nice anymore. It was a struggle for him to stay attentive to her insecurity of being blindfolded. He really was surprised that she was still single, she seemed too sweet and nice. Breaking her spirit would be most rewarding.

"Well, if you won't tell me where we are going, Steve, maybe you could tell me about yourself," she said.

She was starting to annoy him with her nosiness, just like Ruth and Morten. He wanted to tell her that she was downright irritating now. He had to work hard at keeping it together, and he was relieved that they were almost there. He drove through the parking lot and scanned it for any cars. Once he felt satisfied that he was alone, he pulled inside the garage and closed the automatic door behind him. Now it was time to have some fun. He couldn't wait to see the surprise on her face when she woke up tied to a table. She started to squirm a bit.

"Steve, are we there yet?" she said. There was a distinct edge of uneasiness now, and he could feel the beast within stirring.

Without responding, he just sat there and looked at her. He enjoyed watching her discomfort as she struggled not to take the blindfold off. She came close raising her hand.

"Tsk, tsk, tsk," Stan said softly. "Don't spoil the fun."

"I am not having as much fun now. Please remove the blindfold," she said, unsure whether she should take it off or not.

"No. Just sit quietly. No more talking," he said in a much more stern voice.

He could see her chest start to heave as she tried to understand what was happening. Her hands started to fidget in her lap.

"Ok Steve, now you are scaring me. This isn't fun anymore. I don't want to play. Please just take the blindfold off."

It was time to subdue her before she became difficult and things got messy. He slowly and quietly reached behind her, and grabbed the chloroform. Using the same strategy he did with his Ariel, he transferred the chloroform from his right hand to his left, and gently grabbed the back of the seat with his right hand. He leaned close to her ear and gently rubbed his lips along the scarf partially covering her ear. Her body started to respond in uncertainty.

"Take a trip with me?" he whispered in her ear. "To a distant land with castles and kings, a land where dreams come true and life begins anew. Will you be my princess? I will be your king and we can live in infamy together. We will never be forgotten," he said with his eyes closed, not caring whether she responded or not.

"My king, silly, you mean my prince, right?"

He could tell she was engaged in what he was saying, and he was pleased that he could take her from one extreme to the other. She had gone from happy and excited, to scared and uneasy, and now back into the arms of hope. She really was his puppet now. He laughed inside and thought how wrong she really was in her response. He was no prince.

"No, I am your king," he said softly. "I will own you, dominate you, and have you all to myself. You will feed the beast, and I will rape you of your life." Stan put the chloroform on her face as he said it. It took a second to sink in, but by the time she realized what was happening, she was already going and she couldn't stop it.

"I will see you soon, my princess, very soon. Sleep well."

Chapter 63

The ride to Marilyn's home was a somber one. Both Harper and Kate knew the inevitable outcome, and she started thinking of what the next book would be.

"Kate, let's talk this through like we always do. No stone unturned, right?"

After she heard Harper, she realized that she couldn't write Marilyn off. Not yet.

"Right, no stone unturned. Let's talk about this, where the hell is she?" she said, as she started a brainstorming session. "Ok, back to basics. Why her? How does she fit his profile? We have to find the common link."

Kate closed her eyes and started to think back to all the previous victims. What did they have in common?

She started speaking out loud, needing to get it out rather than try to figure it all out in her head. "All women, between twenty-two and thirty-seven, not mothers," she continued trying to keep the thought process going. "All fairy tale references, Sleeping Beauty…" She wrenched in pain as she continued. "Rapunzel, Ariel, Belle…"

It was impossible to find her when they had no idea where he was taking these women or what he was doing with them.

"Harper, he has to be local; he couldn't take these women too far. Not this many times without taking huge chances with getting caught. Where are all these women in proximity to the others?"

"Well, they are all somewhere in the city. The only location a little further out was the grocery store where Sharon worked."

Harper pulled up to Marilyn's house. They both got out and greeted the officers waiting for their arrival.

"Not much to see here, Detective. Seems quiet and undisturbed," one of the officers informed them. "We have made a sweep of the place and, initially, we haven't seen anything that would cause any kind of alarm."

"Thanks, Officer Johnson," she responded after looking at the officer's nametag. "Thanks for getting here so quickly and securing the perimeter."

"Detective, do you think she is the next victim?" he asked.

"Why do you ask? I mean, what makes you think she is a victim?" It was very clear that she was missing something, and she hoped he had an idea.

"Well, to be honest, we get this urgent call to go to a woman's home, where no one is home, and secure it until you get here. That seems somewhat out of the ordinary."

"To be honest, we just don't know. We are following —" her cell phone interrupted her. She answered and was bombarded with questions from the chief.

"Please, Detective, please tell me you are getting somewhere with this. You and I both know it is only a matter of time before the news crew shows up."

Just as she was about to answer, she saw the first news truck pull up. "Too late, chief, they're here."

"We will talk later, but take care of this. Get this girl's name out there, and try to find anyone who may know anything to help find her. See if the news can get her name out, and maybe get us a lead."

"Got it, Chief, on my way," she said, as she saw a cameraman walking up.

"Oh, and Detective, walk a fine line. We don't want panic and pandemonium setting in."

Without waiting for her response, he hung up the phone. Walking up to the news crew, she politely asked them to remain behind the crime-scene tape. As soon as she did, she heard a swarm of questions coming her way.

"Detective, is this a crime scene now?"

"What can you tell us?"

"Is this another fairy tale case?"

"Are you any closer to finding this monster?"

Kate heard the soft-spoken reporter from the Blue Whale before she could even see her. "Detective, should women be scared? What can we do to protect ourselves?"

Kate looked for her in the crowd, and she slowly emerged from the back to await her answer. Tuning all the other reporters out, Kate looked directly at her and started to speak.

"Yes, women should be very cautious right now. Don't be gullible with strangers offering more than they can deliver. Don't go anywhere with anyone you don't know or someone you just met."

She continued on with a plea to the press, "I can answer all your questions shortly, but for now, I need to ask the public for help. Please, anyone who can give us any information on the whereabouts of Marilyn Morris, call immediately. She is the owner of Bakers Delight, and we need to find her. If you have any information or have talked with her recently, we really need to speak with you." After making her statement, Kate motioned to the media that she was finished and looked for Harper.

As she scanned the area, she grabbed her shoulder and neck with her hand. The spasms could be attributed both to the exhaustion of such a long workday and to the emotional drama. Harper and Kate caught each other's eyes across the lawn, and he motioned for her to head to the car. She could tell by his body language that he came up empty handed.

Without saying anything, they both fastened their seatbelts and Harper drove. Before long, they were at the drive through at Starbucks, ordering coffees for the long night ahead.

"Thanks," she said after he handed her coffee. "I didn't realize how much I needed this."

"No problem, I figured it would be a long night of waiting." He laid his head back on the headrest and continued driving.

"Well, you really should give Megan a call. I know you won't listen to me and just go home to her, but you really need to call her."

He picked up his phone and made the call. She took this as an opportunity to review her messages. The only call that provided any hope was from the precinct, letting her know that the artist finished the composite for Matt, the kid at the library. Listening to Harper talk to his wife with such love made her a little jealous that the only person she had to call was missing.

Chapter 64

Lisa felt loneliness and despair controlling her every moment. The only peace she felt was when she took medication to put her out of her misery. She had thought of many different ways to end this non-existence. Her state of mind from day to day determined what method she would use to end this state of hell. Today, she felt tired. Tired of not finding out what happened to her Lauren. She was tired of sitting and doing nothing to help find her, tired of hiding from family, creditors, and herself. Mostly, she was just tired of living, and she had made a decision. She knew deep inside that her Lauren was not coming home. She couldn't bear to deal with this realization, and the only relief she felt from the pain was when she started coming up with ways to kill herself. Her home would be auctioned off in the morning, and she had made no attempt to pack anything or move. She never thought she would live long enough to see her home auctioned off. All her memories of her Lauren were entombed in this home. They both grew up together in this home. She was a young single mother, and Lauren was a smart, ambitious child. Sometimes, Lisa thought Lauren raised her more than she raised Lauren. She always felt such pride in the fact that Lauren was going to make something of her life. She loved nothing more than bragging about how great she was doing in school.

She really didn't feel any obligation to her family. Her sister had made feeble attempts at checking on her, but she knew that their wounds went too deep to ever really heal. Lauren didn't know that her father had always lived much closer than she could ever have imagined. Her sister and Phil got together within two weeks of Lisa telling Phil she was pregnant. Lisa and Phil were high-school sweethearts who never thought that a pregnancy could really happen. The reality of raising a child and growing up was too much for him to handle. Instead, he ran away, too close to home. He and her sister were still married, but Lisa's relationship with them was severed. When the news reported on Lauren's disappearance, that's when they spoke again for the first time in more than twenty years. Lisa was still not sure if her sister called for her, or if Phil had her call because of his guilt at abandoning his only offspring. Later, after they were married for a few years and had sown their oats, they found out that her sister was not capable of having children. She heard that they tried for years with alternative fertility experts, but were never successful. Lisa almost felt bad for them… almost.

Her parents were not alive, and she had no real friends who hadn't run away from this horrible situation. Oh sure, they made the calls and left messages saying, "If there is anything I could do, please don't hesitate to call." However, Lisa knew that in the back of their head, they were just praying that she didn't call. After all, who wanted to deal with the sadness of this situation?

Lisa had decided to write a letter before ending her life, because it was very important to her to make it clear that no foul play had happened. She didn't want the police department to waste manpower or resources on her, instead of finding whoever did this to her Lauren. She had decided to send an e-mail to Kate, knowing that she would get it on her Blackberry. She wanted to make sure her body was disposed of quickly. Tomorrow was a very significant day. It was both Lauren's birthday and the day her home would be sold at auction. She wanted tomorrow to be the day that she passed and was finally put to rest. She knew that Kate would make this happen.

Lisa made a place on the couch for all the items she would need and wanted around her. She opened her laptop and started a blank e-mail. She then walked around the house and gathered some of her most precious items. She took a picture of Lauren and her at their favorite restaurant last year. A time when they never had time to spend together, but they always made it a point to meet up every couple weeks no matter what. Lauren had taken a picture of them and blown it up. She called it her belated birthday present. She also found other odds and ends lying around the house. Chew toys, old candy, pictures, and anything else within tangible reach. After assembling all her favorite items around her, she sat down and started to write.

Kate:

I didn't want to end our friendship this way, just as I am sure you didn't want to become friends in the way we did. I have contemplated this decision for some time now, and I have not made it without much deliberation. I cannot continue living without Lauren and, once the house is taken from me tomorrow there will be only the memories in my head. Please understand that, as much as I treasure the memories, they are just not enough. I can't survive on them alone. The pain keeps mounting and I feel tired, so very tired. The only time I feel relief is when I think of ending the misery. I really don't have anyone right now who I feel close enough with to send this letter to, and I know in my gut that sending it to you is the right decision. I know that you can make my final few wishes happen. Listed below, you will see what I am asking you, and I pray that you will oblige.

1. *Do not resuscitate me in any way.*
2. *Please make my final arrangements for today at Country Haven Mortuary. I will provide you with the list of contacts on my behalf. It is short, but I don't want to deny anyone closure the way it has been denied to me. You can have the mortuary call and explain my wishes to those on the list, and they can decide if they*

want to come to the viewing. It will be short notice coming to a viewing on the same day as my death, but I think it is possible, right?

3.   *After the viewing, please have me cremated with all these special items around me and dispose of my ashes in the following way. Kate, I want to end my life on the day that my baby was born, but I want you to hold my ashes until my birthday. When June 15 comes, I want you to wait until dusk, when the sun is on the horizon and just falling into its nightly slumber. When you see your first firefly, I want you to throw my ashes as high into the air as you can and let the magic of the firefly take me to a new land of wonder. (I know this is dramatic, but doesn't it sound so beautiful?)*

4.   *The last thing I ask of you is to find my Lauren's killer. When you find him, I want you to look him in the eye and tell him that I hope the gates of Hell burn his soul for eternity. I know you will find him, Kate. You are smarter than him; you just haven't figured things out yet.*

I know that this is a lot to ask of you, and I am sorry to do this. These things are so important to me and I know that you will make sure they are done. I wish you the best in life. I will be watching over you and waiting for him to fall into your trap this time. Please don't give up! Find him Kate, find him!

Lisa

After reviewing and revising her letter a few different times, she finally finished. Then she reached over and picked up her injection of potassium chloride. It was much easier to get than one could ever think.

Before she quit working, she took it home with her from the hospital. At the time, she was not sure why she did it, but somewhere in her dark recesses, she must have known it would come to this. She started going over it in her mind and formed a strategy. Once she felt comfortable, she sent her e-mail and made the injection.

Chapter 65

Frustrated at how quickly the night was getting away, Kate looked at the clock on the radio and saw it was just after midnight.

"I just can't figure out what I am missing, Harper. I know there is something right in front of me, but I just can't see it. I wish I could go to one of those mind readers, you know, the psychics who can tell you things?"

Harper's mind was preoccupied with his guilt of knowing his wife was in labor and the urgency of trying to find Marilyn. He kept his phone nearby expecting the call that it was time to come to the hospital and this emotion filled him with excitement and panic at the same time. The excitement of his child being born was like no other but the panic of having to leave Kate alone to find Marilyn weighed heavy on him. After coming back to reality Kate's question registered bringing him out of his zone.

"Ah, you mean the quack jobs?" Harper said, looking at her out the corner of his eye.

"Hey, I would take just about anything right about now."

"Yeah, me too, I hear ya, Kate. I would take anything right now, too." Harper continued, "No stone unturned, right? Do you want to go over everything again?"

As they talked, her phone vibrated, and she saw an e-mail from Lisa. Before long, she only heard Harper as a quiet murmur in the background. She felt her breath escaping as a cold sensation ran through her body.

"Earth to Kate, please…"

"Turn around, Harper, and drive to Lauren's house. Put the lights on, we don't have much time."

"Can you please tell me what is going on, Kate?"

"We're going to be too late. Lisa was a nurse, and she will know the best way to kill herself."

"Whoa, kill her…what the hell do you mean?"

"I just received a suicide letter, and not a typical one. This one is very specific. Listen to this."

Harper got on the phone and dispatched an ambulance to meet them there.

Kate had almost finished reading the letter when they pulled up to her house; she heard the sirens in the distance. The house was very dark, except for a hint of light coming from the front window.

Kate made a mad dash to the house. Turning the handle of the door, she was not surprised to find that it was unlocked. She called out for Lisa.

"Lisa, hey, it is Kate! I am here because I received your e-mail, and I really want to talk to you."

In deafening silence, she walked inside and saw Lisa lying on the couch. Her body was twisted in what seemed like agony, but her face looked serene and free from pain. She knew when she looked at her that she was in a better place. She looked back at Harper, and motioned for him to hold back for a bit. Without saying a word, he nodded his head, and took a seat on the porch steps.

Rather than surveying the room like a crime scene, she could only look at Lisa and what she surrounded herself with at her last moment. She sat next to her and took her hand. She felt the cold setting in, even though she was sure she hadn't been gone for too long. She picked up her laptop and read her instructions once again. She was even thoughtful enough to place a small box close to the couch, which she assumed was for her to gather her belongings. She could feel a lump in her throat as she held back the tears. She felt tears for Lisa, tears from frustration, tears for Kristen and all the other missing girls, and tears from fatigue.

She wanted to catch him more than anything in her life, but it felt like all she could come across was obstacle after obstacle.

Knowing that she still had the pressing problem of Marilyn's whereabouts, she forced herself up and headed for the door. She handed the box of belongings to Harper and explained that she needed to get the phone number for the mortuary out of the car.

"I know we can't stay long, but I need to make sure I grant her this one wish."

Nodding his head, Harper followed her to the SUV and stood outside the door as she fumbled through the car for the phone number. Dialing the mortuary, she awaited the answering machine. After a lengthy message, she finally got the after-hours emergency number. She dialed it, and waited for someone to pick up.

"Country Haven after-hours emergency. Can I help you?"

"Yes, this is Kate Kingsley with the Topeka Police Department. I need to get a hold of Stan."

"Well, Stan is not actually available this late. However, I can take your number and have him call you in the morning."

"No, that is not acceptable. I need you to get him right now and have him call me back."

"I will try to call him, but he may not answer at this hour."

"Call Stan, I will wait to hear back from him."

Once Kate hung up, she placed her head on the headrest, listening to Harper talk with the EMTs.

Closing her eyes, she tried to regroup and come up with a new plan. She held back from looking in the back seat, where Harper put the box of Lisa's belongings. She knew if she did, she would take the chance of losing what little control she had left.

Harper came up to her, placing a hand on her shoulder. "How you doing, kiddo?"

She shrugged.

"We're going to get the bastard," he said.

After a few minutes with no new revelation, she watched the EMTs roll Lisa out to the ambulance. Kate got out of the car and met them as they lifted Lisa into the ambulance.

"Please take good care of her," she said. "She's important to me, and she has been through so much hell. Did you call ahead to the hospital?"

"Yes," one of the EMTs answered. "Everything is just as you requested. We are just taking her to the hospital..."

"Morgue, it's okay, I can handle it. You are taking her to the morgue."

"Okay, the morgue. It shouldn't take long to process her. Then she can be transported to the funeral home. "Perfect, I should be hearing back from the funeral home soon. I want to thank you guys for going above and beyond like this. It really means a lot to me."

"It is our pleasure, Detective —" he said.

"Kate, please call me Kate."

"Just catch him, Kate. We all know you can," the EMT said.

The EMT closed himself inside the ambulance and, within seconds, it was pulling away from the street. She turned and noticed Harper was finishing up talking to the uniformed officers who arrived on the scene. After a moment, they were back in the car; back where they were heading before the e-mail came.

"Do we need another coffee for the road?" Harper said.

"No, I am just anxious to get back to the precinct. We might as well drink the coffee there."

"Let's just get back and go over this again, and again and..."

"Again," she said.

Kate started thinking, why hadn't Stan gotten back to her? She had half a mind to just show up at his house and pound on his door. It had been almost thirty minutes. If she didn't have such pressing matters to attend to, she would have given him a piece of her mind.

Chapter 66

tan felt like he was trying to put a square peg in a round hole. Ever since his princess went into her slumber of darkness, Stan had been plagued with one problem after another.

After getting out of the car, he heard a hissing sound from underneath. He realized that the tire was rapidly losing air, and he felt extremely annoyed that this was happening now, of all times. Without pondering for too long, he decided to get Cinderella inside and secure before he came back out to change the tire. He could not and would not have something as stupid as a flat tire linger over him while he was trying to release the beast within. He started to reformulate a plan to make this work again.

Running inside, he grabbed the rolling trashcan that had been so helpful in the past. Plus, it could be closed, just in case he was interrupted while in the process of transporting. He then realized his next obstacle. One wheel was broken on the can, and he would have to change that out as well — and quite quickly, before she started to wake up.

He ran down, grabbed his tools, and started to work on reattaching the wheel on the container. After all, he couldn't change the ritual. He would not improvise something that he had taken so much time to perfect.

He looked up at the clock. It was getting late, and he needed to get her secured quickly. After finishing the repair, he pushed the trashcan back to the garage. When he opened the door, he realized that there was something really off. She was missing!

"Oh Cinderella, where art thou?" His blood was boiling as fear and panic quickly took over. He stopped everything, waiting for her to make a move. He knew she was in here somewhere, because he could smell her fear.

He tried to listen for her breathing as he slowly walked around and scanned his surroundings. He saw her car door was left open, and a stiletto sitting on the floor nearby. He continued walking toward the car. He reached into the back seat, and refreshed the chloroform on the rag.

It wasn't long before he heard her heavy breathing in one of the corners. He didn't know why people thought that they could be quieter by holding their breath. Eventually, you did have to breathe and, at that point you make more noise than if you were just breathing evenly and calmly. Then again, how often do people have someone trying to catch and kill them?

Having figured out her location, he cautiously approached her.

"Let's not do this the hard way," he said. "If you attack me, then I have to retaliate and, believe me, you don't want the beast to be released. Now do you?"

After a few moments, he heard her say, "What do you want from me, Steve?" Immediately she jumped out of hiding and came after him with what looked like a broom handle. Before he even had to do anything, the poor girl fell down.

Stan hovered over her and said, "Tsk, tsk, tsk. Now you shouldn't have done that. And look, you broke the heel of your shoe." He pointed to the other stiletto on the floor. "You will pay for this, I promise." He reached down, pulled her up by her hair with one hand, and put the chloroform over her face with the other. He hadn't even started, and he had already won. He could feel the beast start rumbling deep within, as he loaded her into the container and took her to his special place.

After securing her, he went back to the garage and changed the tire on the car. He had to have complete clarity before he released the beast; he couldn't cheat himself out of any glory. He opened the car, hearing the soft beep of his phone, notifying him that he had a message. He could still hear the beeping of the phone as he started raising the car with the jack. It didn't take long before he couldn't take the constant reminder that he had a message. He started wondering why he was being called. Morten was on call, and he would never accept an intake before five the next morning.

Before he even had the car jacked up halfway, his curiosity about the call got the best of him. He called his voicemail and got the message from his answering service.

Blown away, he felt like he was going to throw up. He was not sure whether to continue changing the tire, or call the detective back. Neither was his first choice.

Feeling anxious, he decided to go check on Cinderella before doing anything else.

Chapter 67

After arriving at the precinct, Kate left another message for Stan. She once again contemplated driving to his house and giving him a piece of her mind. The only reason she didn't was because Harper was already starting to go through the cycle of information, which they would go over and over until they finally received some clarity.

She decided to go back to the beginning, the basics, and trace back to Kristen. As painful as it was, she could almost feel a calm come over her, and she knew that she was on the right track. She decided to stay focused on all the things that Kristen told her and all the things that had transpired since her death.

Harper's phone rang, and she realized something urgent was happening when she heard him say he was on his way. He hung up and just looked at her.

"Is it the baby?" Kate asked. "If you have to go, go."

"Yes, I told her to call the ambulance, since they can get there before me. I will meet her at the hospital. I am so sorry to do this to you, Kate, but I have to go."

"Yes, you have to go right now. I got this. Maybe I can focus better by myself," she said. They both knew that was an all-out lie.

"No stone unturned, Kate," he said, as he grabbed his things and headed out.

Chapter 68

Marilyn heard silence all around her. As she came in and out of awareness, she began to wonder if she was dead. She tried to force her eyes open, and realized that she couldn't move her arms or legs. She was bound tightly to some kind of cold table. Her circulation was being cut off to all her extremities. She felt a numbing sensation in some areas, and a tingling in others.

Just as she got her eyes opened and noticed her surroundings, she heard a door opening. She immediately began to shallow her breathing instead of holding her breath, since that didn't work so well last time. She smelled his breath hovering over her as he got down checking on her. At first, she was not sure what she smelled, but, after a few moments, she knew it was perspiration. He was sweating, which meant he was scared. Mr. Calm-and-Cool was scared, and that meant she had a chance. She lay as still as she could, until she heard him leave the room.

Chapter 69

S tan immediately felt calmer after checking on her, knowing that she was still subdued. He formulated his next plan of action. First, he finished the car, in case he needed to go somewhere.

He continued to calm himself by going over the Cinderella fairy tale in his head. He could picture his mother reading him the story and now he thought she wished that she could be a part of something so big. He remembered one time in particular, when he really thought they might move out and run away from his father. She always understood him, even when his father would berate him. One time, she stuck up for him and told his father, "Stan is a smart boy. He could be a doctor someday. You should have more faith in him."

"Our Stan?" his father would say. "Oh come on, honey, you know better than that. Look at him. How old is he, and he can't even tie his shoes."

"Well, you can't cook your own dinner, or wash your clothes, or many other things, and you are a grown man," she said as the fury inside her rose.

"It doesn't help that you coddle him and read him girly books. How is he ever going to grow up to be a man, when you teach him to be a sissy?" he said as he looked at Stan and said, "Sissy boy."

"Be quiet right this instant," she said, "He is not a sissy boy, and you are not even a man. You need to leave us alone right now, or we will leave you for good." She stared him down as he left the room.

After a few moments of silence, she picked up the book and started to finish reading.

"Mom, why can't we just move away?" Stan asked.

"I can't son," she said with sadness in her eyes. "There are things you don't understand, but someday you will."

It wasn't long after that conversation that he realized that something was wrong. She was staying in bed longer every morning. She wasn't making breakfast, and some days she couldn't muster the energy to actually make dinner. She started losing weight and looking different.

Then, one morning, she called him in to talk with her while she lay in bed.

"Stan, my sweet boy, I have to talk with you about something."

He knew in the pit of his stomach that she was dying. "Are you going to die?" he asked.

She looked at him with the softest eyes, and nodded. It was like she couldn't even say it for herself.

"Can't you take me with you? Please don't leave me here with him," Stan said, the tears welling in his eyes. "I can't live with him. I will die, Mom. You know that, I will die."

"Just live your life, Stan. Stay out of his way and he will stay out of yours. Be your own man someday. I know you can do it. Find your princess, Stan, and live the fairy tale. Take it all in and grow from all your experiences. Be a doctor, and take what you deserve in life. Don't settle for anything less than what you wish. Live the fairy tale, Stan, live it for me. I love you, son, and I will be watching over you and guiding you in the right direction. Follow my lead, and I will be at your side all the way. I am your biggest fan."

It wasn't long after that when she passed away. He knew now that she would have understood the beast within him, the same beast she never was able to release. He was living the fairy tale that she desperately wanted him to live. Although his mom would never approve of killing princesses, his father would surely have made fun of him for liking them. Calling him names and teasing him. This only fueled his hatred towards his father more and made him want to kill the princesses as much for himself but to show his father how powerful he was.

After lowering the jack on the car, he tightened the bolts on the tire. He was almost to a point where he could let the beast free. The last thing he needed to do was call back that pain-in-the-ass Detective Kingsley. Irritated that she had once again bothered him, but curious about the nature of her call, he picked up his phone and dialed her number.

"Detective Kingsley speaking," she said with an anxious tone to her voice.

"This is Stan with Country Haven," he said. "Please tell me, what the hell is so important to call me in the middle of the night?"

"Sorry to bother you so late," she said, though he got the feeling she wasn't sorry at all. "But I need to talk to you about someone who will be delivered to the mortuary soon."

"What do you mean 'soon'?" We don't take intakes until five. This will just have to wait." He felt panic rising in his stomach, and the beast stirring as it became more and more restless.

"Well, it is a long story. I apologize for waking you up, Stan. Were you sleeping?"

"What the hell does that have to do with anything?" he said, wondering if she already knew what he was up to, but was trying to trick him.

"You're right, Stan, it doesn't matter. I need you to be available for this intake. This is really important to me, and I made a promise that she would have a viewing and a burial tomorrow."

"Who are you to make such a promise?" he said, worried about where this could lead.

"I need you to do this, Stan. If I have to, I will drive to the mortuary and wait with her until you arrive. She will be coming tonight, Stan. Will you please help me?" she said with determination in her voice.

Stan needed a quick change of plans. "Where are you now?" he said.

"I am at the precinct now, but I can meet you there anytime. I can be on my way right now, if you like. They're just waiting for me to call to transport her to you."

"No, just give me a few minutes to get over there, and I will meet them. You don't need to come. I will take care of things. Just have them call the answering service when they are ready to transport, and they will forward it on to me." He tried to sound as helpful as possible.

"Thanks, Stan, I appreciate it," she said. After a moment of hesitation, she added, "I will come by in the morning and meet up with you."

"If you must," he said, and hung up the phone.

Chapter 70

After Kate hung up with Stan, she had that uneasy feeling again, where something was off but she couldn't place her finger on it. She looked over Kristen's file again, thinking there was something she was missing.

Her phone rang and she saw that it was Harper.

"Hey, Harper how is she?"

"I think she's going to be fine, false labor pains. Thank God her mom has been staying with us. Otherwise, I don't know what we would've done. This job really does stink, doesn't it?"

"You really should get some rest, Harper. You really need to be there for her."

"Well, I did get the green light to come back and meet you."

"No, absolutely not, your family has to be your priority."

"Well, you are my family, too."

"You know what I mean. We are both exhausted, and I think we are just not going to get anywhere in this state. I think it will be best for us both to get some rest."

"I will, if you will," he said.

"You know, I am at a roadblock here. I am going home, and I suggest you get some sleep too," she said.

"Promise, Kate?" he said.

"Promise, Harper. Good night. I will talk with you in the morning."

If Kate wasn't so damn tired, she would have lied to him and kept on working. She just couldn't continue at this pace and get anything done. She decided to go home and get a couple hours of sleep in the hopes of being able to see things clearer in the morning. She called the transport team, giving them the information to contact Stan. She also wondered why he didn't just give her his cell number instead of making her go through the answering service.

After thanking the transport team for their hard work and unorthodox hours, she packed up to head home. Then she felt guilty about not being there for Lisa's transport, and realized that she was unconsciously heading for the mortuary.

Sitting at the stoplight, she fought the urge to go to the mortuary. She really didn't want to deal with Stan, and she figured it would tick him off if she showed up after he said he would take care of it. Why the hell did Lisa have to pick this mortuary? Kate thought it must be some sort of test of her tolerance.

Arriving at home, she changed into an old t-shirt and stepped out of her shoes, socks, and work pants. She started falling into a deep sleep before she even hit the pillow.

She could see herself flying again through the air and, as she looked down, she could see the twinkle of lightning bugs going on and off. She closed her eyes as she felt the cool evening air rushing against her face. The crispness of the air exhilarated her, and she took big breaths, taking it all it. She opened her eyes and saw Kristen flying next to her. She had her arm extended out to her, as if she was trying to take her hand. Kate reached for her, but the harder she stretched, the farther she floated away.

"Stop trying so hard, Kate. You always make things more difficult than they really are."

"I just miss you, Kristen. Please come back to me. I will catch you this time. Just don't leave." Sadness came upon her as Kristen floated farther away.

"Stop trying so hard, Kate. Listen to me, listen to everything around you. Answers are everywhere, if you open up and accept them. I will always be right next to you. Find him, Kate. You are so close, just open your mind and find him."

"No, please don't go, Kristen. Stay with me, I need you." Kate could barely hear a whisper come back to her from far away.

"Trust yourself, Kate. I love you."

All she could see was blackness, and everything went silent.

Chapter 71

After hanging up on Kate, Stan made decisions quickly. He put his phone in his pocket, and headed for the special room. There would have to be a huge change of plans. He walked in the room and saw that Cinderella was still sleeping, which was a good thing.

He sat down next to her and came up with his backup plan. After sitting in silence for a while, he decided to transport her to his house. It would be risky, but he didn't have any other choice. He couldn't leave her here, and he couldn't cremate her yet. He had to feed the beast first.

Stan decided that he needed to get her to his basement as quickly as possible. He carefully undid her ankles from the sides of the table, knowing she could wake up at any minute. Once he untied her legs, he bound them together securely in a couple different places. Only then did he feel secure enough to untie her hands from the table quickly, so he could secure them again.

The instant he unbound her second hand, she immediately sat up and started clawing at him. He saw his blood on her hands before he even felt the scratch on his face. He felt the stinging as she clawed at him, over and over.

"You need to settle down, my dear, or I will really hurt you this time."

There was rage in her eyes, and he knew she wasn't going quietly. He decided to take drastic measures and, with one swift punch to the face, he knocked her out cold.

"Now, my princess, you are going to be hurting in the morning." *If you make it that long*, he thought to himself.

He took duct tape and placed it, not so gently, across her mouth. Then he bound her hands securely as he prepped her for transport. Lifting her up and over his shoulder, he carried her a couple feet to the rigged trashcan with the bum wheel.

After securing her, he headed for the elevator. He decided to roll her across the parking lot in the container, rather than load her in the car only to drive across the parking lot. It was much more difficult getting her in and out of the car than it was to just roll her. He kept his fingers crossed that the wheel stayed intact.

About halfway across the parking lot, he got the call that the transport team would be there in about thirty minutes. Beads of sweat ran down his body; he hung up and practically started running to get across the parking lot.

Getting her into the house was a whole different story. He decided to take her down the steep flight of steps that led to the side entrance of the basement. The steps were difficult, and the sound of the container going down was much louder than he would have liked. However, he thought the alternative was much worse. He could see it now: A neighbor getting up for a glass of water in the middle of the night sees the man next door carrying a limp body into his house.

He continued with his plan. As quick as he thought he was going, he realized that the transport team would be arriving within the next few minutes. Once they arrived, he would need a few hours to prep the arrival so he didn't set off any red flags with the detective when she arrived in the morning. Not only would he not get any sleep tonight, but he would also not be able to release the beast until the following night. He would have to keep subduing Cinderella until he could have his time with her.

Once he had her in his basement, he decided to secure her temporarily so that he could greet the transport team. Once they left, he would come back and secure her more thoroughly.

He practically ran across the parking lot to meet the transport team. They were waiting at the back of the mortuary, ringing the bell. "I am coming, I'm right here!" he yelled across the parking lot.

"No problem," one of them said. "We just got here."

As he got closer to them, he saw two men looking intently at him. "Are you okay?" one of them asked. "You have blood all over your face."

Trying to think quickly, he immediately went into a long, boring Ruth-like story about how he came across a mother cat hiding near his garage and how she fought him when he tried to pick her up.

"... then I realized she had a whole litter of kittens, and I knew why she was fighting me. She was scared for her little ones, and I guess I can appreciate that. Hey, do you guys want to see the kittens?"

"No, I really just want to call it a night and get home to bed," one of them said.

"I understand. They are just so damn cute —"

"I would like to see them," the second man said.

Stan thought he was going to pee himself, but said, "Sure, do you want to come right now?"

"Tom, come back on your own time," his partner cut in. "I want to get this done and get home. I hate doing favors."

Feeling relieved, Stan said, "Well, they will be here anytime if you want to come back and see them."

"Thanks," Tom said.

After he finished up and signed their paperwork, they said good-bye and went on their way. Not, of course, before reminding Stan to get himself cleaned up. He couldn't help but stress about meeting with the detective in the morning.

He got the transport down to his special room and wondered if the beast would want to come out and play with her. It didn't take long before he realized that the beast was not going to be coming out until Cinderella came to the ball.

After moving the body to the table, he laid her down and removed her from the bag. It didn't take long for him to recognize the deceased. He watched television, and he had seen the pleas of this mother looking for her daughter. This was so poetic, and so perfect. He felt almost giddy, if not for the fact that he needed to get back home and find a more secure way to subdue Cinderella.

He turned out the lights and left the room, deciding to call Morten in for an early job. After he was done, he could resume getting her prepped for the viewing. That would give him a couple hours to catch some shut-eye — and time to secure Cinderella.

Chapter 72

Kate awoke suddenly from the sound of the trash truck. She squinted to see the time. It was 7:45 in the morning. Muttering to herself, she jumped out of bed and ran to the kitchen to start a pot of coffee, before remembering that she was once again out of coffee, creamer, and every other staple she could think of. She turned back toward her bedroom, picked out some clothes and took a quick shower, followed by what Kristen would call a "five-minute hairdo."

Feeling refreshed and clean, she put her clothes on and pulled her hair back in a ponytail.

She then called Harper.

"Did you get any sleep, Kate?" he said. "Remember, you promised me."

"How is she, Harper? Did you get any rest at all?" Kate said, heading out the door to her car.

"The doctor said she should be fine, but they'll be keeping her for a couple days for observation."

"You know that everyone will understand if you need to take a short leave to take care of your family," Kate said, connecting the phone to her blue tooth and pulling out onto the street.

"She'll be on bed rest for the rest of the pregnancy. Doc said she's under too much stress for the baby and she needs to be calm."

"Hold on a sec, Harper." She pulled up to the Starbucks drive-through window and ordered her usual. After she said, "Okay, so what do you think about taking some time off?"

"Megan doesn't want me to take leave. She wants me to get this guy caught and behind bars. Anyway, I would probably cause her more stress pacing the floors at home, trying to figure out what to do. Regardless, I will stay here until the doc gives us the green light to go home. Once she's home, I will feel more confident to come back, hopefully, tomorrow."

Taking her coffee from the lady at the window, she continued driving towards the mortuary. "I think that is a very good idea, Harper. Try to catch up on some sleep for both of us."

"Will do, where you going now? Any new leads?"

"Not that I know of, I haven't even had a voicemail or a call in quite some time. I'm on my way to the mortuary to make sure they're making all the arrangements for Lisa. I just hope that I can deal with Ruth now, rather than creepy Stan. I am just not in the mood for his BS right now."

"So, I assume she was transported there last night?"

"Yeah, I finally received a call back from Stan. Funny thing is, he was actually pretty accommodating. He was more irritated when I was asking him personal questions than when I asked him to do me this favor, strange, huh?"

"Well, it is his job. Just call me when you get back to the office. I'm going to hang out here until we hear from the doctor."

"Okay," she said and hung up. She looked at the clock on her radio and saw that it was now almost nine. Irritated with herself for oversleeping, she began worrying that Lisa's arrangements were not getting taken care of. She pulled into the mortuary parking lot and jumped out of the car.

Opening the door, she could hear the familiar ding of the bell. The sound gave her a weird feeling, and she found herself at a standstill contemplating it. Sometimes, she would get this feeling, but too often she was too busy to really deal with it. That was not the case today. Right now, she had to figure it out.

"Hi, Detective, how are you today?" Ruth interrupted her train of thought. "I was expecting you earlier, but I can give you a quick update. I have contacted everyone on the list. The only person who I actually was able to get a hold of was her sister, and she was not sure she could even make the viewing at four. I think she was more stunned than anything. Are you okay, Detective? You don't look too good."

Gathering herself without losing her concentration, Kate looked at Ruth and simply said, "I am fine, Ruth. Can I just have a quick minute? I will come find you in your office, if it is okay with you."

"Sure, can I get you any coffee? You know, I start my day off with coffee every morning and my poor husband goes on and on about how it's not good for you, and how it really has some bad things in it. However, for me I think..." Ruth continued on as Kate walked away through the corridor, looking for a bathroom.

Once inside the bathroom, with the door securely locked, she watched her reflection in the mirror, not really looking at herself but looking inside herself. She started pondering all the things she had been going through on this case, in the hopes of coming to some kind of conclusion.

After giving herself a headache, she realized that it was just not going to come to her right at this time. She headed out of the bathroom and found Ruth in her office. "Sorry about that, Ruth, I just needed a minute," she said. Sitting down in front of her desk, she realized that the weird feeling was still there. She knew she was onto something, and she couldn't leave it right now.

"Oh, don't worry about it, Detective. I need minutes all the time. That's what happens when you get older. You start forgetting little things. Like, why did I just get up and go to the kitchen? What the heck did I want to get?" Just as she started to speak again, Kate gently interrupted her.

"I hate to be rude, but can we just get through this? I really need to get back to the office. Better yet, is Stan around? I really would like to get back to the precinct. I have a ton of work."

"Oh, I know, dear, I heard about the girl from the bakery. Did you ever hear any more about her? This is just a crying shame, and scary. Sometimes I just sit and worry about all those women out there who don't even know the danger they are in. I pray for them every night."

"And Stan…" Kate said, waiting for her to answer the question.

"Hmm, Stan, let me think. I know he came in early, right after Morten got done. Morten came in very early to get everything done so that Stan could get her ready for a viewing this afternoon. I know he was trying to get her done before you got here."

"Could you please find him for me?" Kate asked again, as she felt her patience grow thin.

Ruth picked up the phone and dialed him. When he didn't answer, she tried another number. "Hi Stan, I have Detective Kingsley here. She wants to see you. Should I send her down? Oh, I didn't realize you ran home. No problem. I will let her know."

"Stan had to run home real quick," Ruth said, turning back to her. "He said to just have a seat and he'll be right in."

"I don't have time to wait. Can I just see her now?" Kate said, as she looked at her watch.

"Oh, no worry, Detective, Stan lives just across the parking lot. He sold the beautiful home that had been in his family from one generation…"

Kate interrupted her rambling, saying she needed to go to bathroom. Without even waiting for a response, she walked away.

Going on a hunch, she decided to head to the basement. She was not sure if she was doing this because she really wanted to see Lisa, or if she just needed to get to the basement. Finding the door with the wooden stairs, she started going slowly down each step, one at a time.

Chapter 73

The night was long, but he was successful in securing Cinderella. He decided to keep her in the container, just to be practical, and drill some small holes on the top of it for ventilation. He could still hear her sobbing from inside the container, switching from fury to begging repeatedly. The beast within him was rumbling so loud that he couldn't even concentrate on his own thoughts, let alone anything she might be saying.

He already had quite the day, and it had been very productive considering how everything became crazy difficult the night before. He kept telling himself that it was the hard part that made it good. The beast was going to be so happy tonight when he could be released again. He went over all the things that would happen later.

Rapunzel's mom did look the best she could under the circumstances. He was amazed at how good he was at making the dead look so perfect. He remembered back to Sleeping Beauty's mom and how much his princess hated it when he said her mom looked beautiful. He started thinking about how much pleasure he felt when he took her life and made it his own.

His thoughts were interrupted by the ringing of his cell phone. "Hi Ruth," he said.

"Hi Stan, I have Detective Kingsley here. She wants to see you. Should I send her down?"

He told Ruth to tell her that he ran home for a minute, and that he would be back soon. He made sure she understood that the detective needed to wait.

"Oh, I didn't realize you ran home," Ruth said. "No problem. I will let her know."

He hung up and ran for the door. He knew where she would be heading. He ran across the parking lot, feeling the fury within him rise.

He went in the side door of the bay and found the service elevator. Anxiously waiting for it to open, he noticed that Morten was gone, and that Ruth and Detective Kingsley were the only ones in the building. He smiled, knowing that Detective Kingsley was down there alone, and his patience with her was running thin.

Chapter 74

Kate took each step down with a feeling of uncertainty. The fog lifted from her head with each step she took. She knew how much Stan would hate seeing her there, and she had to admit, she kind of relished the thought of irritating him.

She entered the room, noticing Lisa lying on the table. She was fully dressed, and made up to the nines. She had to admit that Stan really did a great job of getting her ready. She placed her hand on Lisa's shoulder and started talking to her.

"I know you are in a better place now, and everything will finally make sense to you. I can only hope that I find the same kind of clarity on this side, so I can avenge your daughter. I promise to never stop trying. No stone will be left unturned. " Just then, she heard the cranking of the old elevator settling on the floor, and the creaking doors open. Feeling a little nervous, she waited for Stan to come barreling in.

"Well, good morning, Detective. You know, I have asked you before to stay out of my personal space."

"I just wanted to see Lisa. I have an obligation to follow this through. Looks like the cat got your face rather than your tongue," Kate said.

"How did you guess?" He gave a wry smile. "I was just telling the transport team about the mama cat by my garage. Do you want to see her?"

"No, I would like to just get on with this."

"Very well, Officer. Let's get on with it."

"Very well, I will do that," she said, irritated that he repeatedly failed to give her respect by calling her Officer. Feeling grumpy she was ready to go head to head with him, however right now she realized her focus was Lisa rather than playing games with Stan. She leaned over and looked at Lisa again. Kate could see him walking up beside her out of the corner of her eye. She instinctively found herself wanting to wrap her hand around her gun, but she restrained herself. She tried to remember that she was cranky and tired.

"You did a really nice job on her, Stan," she admitted, trying to give him some respect. "Yes, I do have a gift, don't I?"

"Not too humble, are you? But, yes, she really does look at peace, finally." Kate tried to keep the conversation light, feeling uneasy that he was in her personal space. As he came closer to her, she could smell perspiration and a dirty-rubber smell coming from him. She backed away.

Stan took this opportunity to lean in close to Lisa. He whispered, barely audibly, "She does look like Sleeping Beauty, doesn't she?"

Kate knew this was like that moment she always heard about, when you are at the doors of death and you see your whole life flash by you. Kate saw all the clues coming together, like a puzzle with missing pieces. She remembered Kristen telling her how much she hated it when the funeral guy told her that her mother looked like Sleeping Beauty. It meant nothing then, but now she felt different, the fog seemed to be lifting. She looked at Stan, remembering the one consistent clue: the blue eyes. Those piercing blue eyes had been haunting this whole investigation. And the incinerator! Not only did she see it, but she remembered Ruth complaining about the gas bills. She took a deep breath, knowing she was in danger.

She took another step back and tried to grab her gun in one swift motion. She was not sure whether it was the quick step back or the gasp that gave her away, but by the time she realized the imminent danger, he was turning toward her. She felt the sharp edge of his elbow hit her smack in the nose. All she could see was a white light and then blackness.

Chapter 75

He had been close to losing it with the detective, and had hoped that he would have enough willpower to keep her at bay a little longer. Now he was going to have to move on, gather his saved money, and start over. It was always the one slip up that got everyone caught. His was the simple use of the words "Sleeping Beauty."

He felt proud of himself, and how he was able to act so quickly under pressure and knock the detective out cold. He first ripped the phone in the room from the wall. He wasn't really sure why, but it seemed important to do. He then grabbed his keys out of his pocket, ran up the rickety stairs, and used the key to lock the deadbolt from the inside.

He ran back down the stairs to his special room and took the detective's gun and put it in his waistband. He took her phone, and put it in his pocket. He then dragged her body over to the incinerator. After much laboring, he got her inside, closing the door and latching it. The igniter would not fire up, though. Now of all times, he thought to himself! The frustration mounted as the sweat started dripping down his sides. He searched for a match to light it manually, but realized he was wasting valuable time. He decided to just let the gas run; it wouldn't take long for that to do the trick. He just hoped that she stayed out long enough.

He took off towards the elevator and stepped inside. Formulating his next moves in his head, he came up with a plan. First, he would take his princess and feed the beast. It would have to be quick and short, but Miss Detective was not going anywhere very quickly. He decided to send Ruth on an errand to buy some time, just in case she could hear the detective's screams for help. He pulled out his phone, careful not to confuse it with the detective's, and dialed Ruth.

"Hi Ruth, I need a favor. Can you please go to the pharmacy at Costco and pick up a prescription for migraine medicine for me?" He tried to sound calm. "If you do this, you can go home early today. I really need it."

"Sure, Stan, are you okay? Costco is quite a drive from here."

"I'm fine. I just have a really long day ahead, and I can't get through it without my medication."

"I will get right on it. What do I do about the detective? She hasn't left yet."

"Don't worry, I am with her downstairs. I will show her out." He cupped his hand over the mouthpiece, hoping she couldn't hear any traffic as he walked across the parking lot.

"Stan, if you're downstairs, how is your cell phone working so well? I know that mine and my husband's don't work half the time inside. Do you know what I mean? Who is your carrier? They have really good reception —"

"Ruth, are you going to do it or not?" He felt like he was going to explode as he opened the back door and stepped inside. "I'm busy with the detective, and I can't sit and chat with you."

"You don't have to get nasty, Stan. I am leaving now," she said.

Before she hung up, he was careful to reel her back in. "Ruth. I'm sorry to be so rude, I just have a lot of pressure, and I have this headache from hell. I just called my doctor and he said he would call it in shortly. I really need it."

He stood at his kitchen window and watched Ruth pull out of the parking lot.

He placed the detective's gun and phone in the kitchen drawer. He didn't want to have anything that Cinderella could grab and turn on him. He then ran downstairs and looked at the loose bricks away from the wall, and looked back at the trash can. He was tempted to make a run for it, but he could hear a soft murmur coming from the container, and he knew that he had to have her before he left. He couldn't upset the beast, or terrible things could happen. He walked over to the container, and started to cut the duct tape that bound it closed. Before finishing he realized that he may need the chloroform to subdue her again; he remembered how feisty she had become before. He ran upstairs to get it when he heard someone walking on to the front porch. He quickly hid inside the broom closet next to the stairs that went down to the basement, and waited.

Chapter 76

Kate could taste the fresh blood in her mouth, as it dripped into the back of her throat. The metallic taste was unsettling, and she licked her lips, trying to get some fresh air. She could hear what sounded like someone letting the air out of a tire, and realized that she was on a hard surface. She forced her eyes open and saw nothing but darkness at first. Then she turned her head and looked all around. She couldn't see anything, but she could now smell the hissing sound. She knew it was gas.

Everything flooded back to her, as she tried to sit up, and realized that she was in a very cramped space. Reaching into the small pocket of her work pants, she pulled out a tiny flashlight and turned it on. She started to figure out her surroundings. After a few seconds, she realized where she was.

She immediately started screaming and thrashing about, in pure hysteria and panic. She started running out of air, and she realized that this was where she was going to die. She closed her eyes, and the first thing she saw was Kristen. She immediately started to gain control again and forced herself to take small breaths as she tried to come up with a plan. She opened her eyes again, and shone the light all around the chamber. She could see remnants of ashes all about her — and she realized where all the victims had ended up. She felt a lump in her throat and tears started forming as she thought of Kristen. She now knew she would never come back. None of them would.

She found the door opening, and tried pushing it with her hand, but it didn't budge. She started pounding on it until her hands bled. After regrouping once again, she maneuvered her body so she had her feet at the door, and start a methodical pounding, as she slammed her legs in unison into the door.

After what seemed like an eternity of slamming, her back started having spasms, and the gas started making her feel light headed. She knew that she was either going to get this door open in the next couple minutes, or she would share the same fate as all of Stan's victims. She raised her legs as close to her chest as possible, and pushed out one last time. She fell to the ground from the momentum of breaking the door open.

Looking around, she realized she was alone in the basement of the mortuary, and Lisa was still lying peacefully on the table. She inhaled life back into her lungs, and caught her breath before she forced herself to her feet and headed for the door. She realized that her gun and phone were missing. Going up the stairs was difficult, but she found it getting easier the higher she went. When she tried to open the door, she realized it was locked with a key lock. Muttering to herself and not having the strength to knock it down from her angle on the stairs, she started banging on the door and yelling for help.

After a few minutes with no answer, she wondered if Ruth was in on everything or, if Stan had killed her as well.

She headed down the stairs much quicker than she had gone up. Once she reached the service elevator she pushed the button. While waiting, she took her backup gun from her ankle holster.

The elevator finally showed up, and she was not sure if she was relieved or disappointed that Stan wasn't there to greet her. All she could think of was getting out. She got on the elevator and crouched down in the corner while it took her up. This was when she realized that Marilyn must be alive. She had to be. He hadn't had a chance to kill her yet, and that must have been why he was so desperate to subdue her.

She knew what she had to do. She was going to Stan's house to save the princess. After exiting the elevator, she found a phone on the wall in the garage. She started to dial Harper's number, before she realized she didn't know it, without using the speed dial in her phone. She hung the phone up, picked it back up, and dialed 911.

"This is Detective Kingsley. Send all units to the yellow farmhouse across the parking lot from Country Haven Mortuary. Come fast and come with caution. Please contact Detective Harper and give him this information immediately." She left the phone dangling as she went through the side door and headed for the yellow farmhouse across the parking lot.

Arriving with speed and caution, she walked up the stairs and onto the wooden front porch. As she walked across the floor she could hear the wood creaking below her. She tried to quiet it as much as possible, but it was just impossible to be quiet. Standing next to the door, she tried to listen for anything that would give her a clue as to where he was, or if he was gone. All she heard was silence as she turned the handle of the front door. No luck; it was locked.

Carefully, she tapped a pane of glass on the front door with her elbow. She then put her cut-up, bloody hand through the door and unlocked it. Before opening the door, she took the same hand and scraped the dried blood from her eyes. She could feel the pain of a broken nose, and she could feel her face was swollen all around her eyes.

Walking through the home, she knew that Stan was there. She could still smell the perspiration and rubber she smelled from earlier. She knew that he had the advantage on his home turf, and that she needed to be a lot more careful than she was back at the mortuary.

Going through the house room by room, she came across a table with a box of fairy tale books on it, and the reality of the situation hit home even more. She should have known all along that it was Stan; there was always something not right with him. She knew she would regret the lives that had been lost because of her lack of clarity.

Winding through the kitchen, she picked up the wall phone and dialed 911 again, just to be certain. Without saying a word, she laid the phone on the counter, knowing the precinct would trace it back to this house. She walked across the kitchen to a door that leading to a steep flight of stairs. She tried to flip a light switch, but nothing happened. All she could see at the bottom of the stairs were faint traces of light around the small windows of the basement. Turning on her flashlight, she headed down the stairs to find Stan. If the broken glass or opening of the basement door didn't give her away, she felt confident that the creaking of the stairs would for sure. Counting the stairs to calm herself, she started the descent into the basement. One…two…it was on three that she heard something behind her, and knew that Stan was not down the stairs, he was upstairs. Just before she could turn around she felt the swift kick of a foot in her back. She went spiraling down the stairs, hitting at least every other wooden step on the way down. She felt her gun fly out of her hand, as she hit the cold and hard floor.

Before she could assess any physical damage she felt herself overcome by Stan immediately. She could feel something over her mouth, and she now knew how he subdued them. She tried calling out in a muffled voice, but before she knew it, blackness was upon her.

Chapter 77

Marilyn realized that help was there; she knew that they were trying to find this crazy lunatic, who had her captive. After hearing the struggle, she wasn't sure if she should be relieved or scared, especially after she heard someone falling down the wooden stairs, and another set of footsteps following behind. All she could hear now was silence. She wanted so badly to call out, but was afraid that she would not get a response from the right person. So she just sat, bound tightly and tried to look out the holes of the container. All she saw was darkness and her limbs felt useless. She didn't even have enough strength to stand up or rock the container on its side.

After an eternity of silence, she heard a muffled voice, followed by a labored walk back up the wooden stairs. She heard the footsteps above her as they faded and she knew she was alone again. The silence was deafening.

After anxiously waiting, she heard sirens in the distance. Even though they were getting closer, they were not coming fast enough.

Chapter 78

After Stan overcame the detective, for the second time, he quickly improvised his next move. He was infuriated that the beast would not get his princess. The police were undoubtedly on their way. Luckily, he had the chloroform and was able to subdue her quickly. After she was out cold, he dug in her pockets, and took her car keys. He didn't have time to tie her up, so he grabbed the duct tape, put it in his mouth and heaved her over his shoulder. Walking up the stairs was difficult, but not impossible, he only needed a quick second at the top to catch his breath. Once up, he rushed out the door and disarmed the alarm on the key chain to find her car.

He thought to himself as he opened the back end, that she drove quite a nice car for such a small salary. He threw her in the back with the duct tape, ran around, jumped in the driver seat, and sped away. He only drove a very short distance before turning down an alley, into what looked like an abandoned driveway.

Jumping back out towards the hatch, the sweat poured off him, as he heard sirens in the distance. He was angered once again at the thought of never seeing the mortuary again. He had things he needed there, things that couldn't be replaced , things that were souveniers of trophies earned.

The more he thought, the more angry he became, and he started taping her feet and hands together. Lastly, he taped her mouth, closed the hatch and started driving.

He muttered unintelligibly, unsure where to go, other than outside of town. He hoped that some kind of inspiration would overtake him, giving him insight. He tried to calm himself as he drove, farther and farther away, from his old life.

Chapter 79

She then heard lots of noise, as what sounded like a herd, descending on the house. People shouted and called out to each other, and she knew the police had arrived. Once she heard multiple footsteps coming down the stairs, she tried calling out through the tape.

"Help, I'm in here," she said in a muffled tone, using all her strength to move the trash can to help them locate her. Finally, she heard someone working on the outside of her prison, and then the darkness suddenly became light. She couldn't see well, but she heard perfectly.

"Marilyn, you are safe," the officer said, as he and another officer reached in, picked her up, and carried her upstairs. Once upstairs, the brightness blinded her, but she didn't mind; she was free again, and that was all that mattered.

They laid her on the kitchen floor and carefully removed the tape from her mouth. The pain was worth it and she tried to be tough as they pulled it away. By then the paramedics arrived, put her on the stretcher, and wheeled her towards the ambulance.

A man came running up. "I'm Detective Harper. My partner was the one that saved your life. She's missing. I need you to tell me everything you know. Time is very crucial right now."

Slowly at first, she tried speaking, but she had a hard time getting words out. The pain from the tape was horrible, and her throat was dry. She pushed onward and tried her hardest to communicate with the detective.

He leaned in close, and listened intently.

"First I heard him. Steve, that horrible man, starting to open the container he had me in. Then he stopped, and went back up the stairs. From then, I only heard some movement upstairs and then a door close. I think I heard glass breaking, but I'm not sure. After that I heard someone start walking down the stairs and then it sounded like they were rolling down. After that it sounded like someone was rushing down after. I could hear Steve talking incoherently while he was walking heavily back up the stairs." As she tried to continue talking the tears were rolling down her face and she was shaking uncontrollably, then she finished with "after a few moments I heard the sirens."

"That is very helpful," he said.

"What is the name of the detective?" Marilyn asked still trying to control her emotions of a near death experience. The relief of being saved was overcome by the concern for the Detective that saved her life and her sobbing continued.

"Detective Kingsley, not only is she my partner but she's also a dear friend," he said.

"I know you'll find her, and when you do, please tell her I want to thank her in person for saving my life," Marilyn said.

"If I know her, I am sure she will want to see you as well, I will let her know." He squeezed her hand before dashing off.

Chapter 80

An officer, standing with a woman he didn't recognize, called over to Harper waving him back.

"What's going on here?" he said.

"This is Ruth," the officer said. "She's the receptionist at the mortuary—"

"Yes," Ruth interrupted, "there is a problem. I can't get into my office. No one will tell me anything. Last time I saw something like this, I think it was on CSI and there was a bomb. However, you all are not wearing bomb suits and —"

"Please calm down," Harper said, motioning her under the crime tape and off to the side.

"No, I won't calm down and who is that in that stretcher there. Oh my, is she dead? Oh jeez I don't like seeing dead people. Well, I mean dead people that I am not expecting to see. I see lots of dead people, but not like that little boy in the movie, in a different way. Why are they putting her into the ambulance? She must be dead if the sirens aren't on. She's dead, isn't she?" Ruth said without taking much of a breath.

"She's not dead."

"I need to talk to Stan. Oh he is going to be so mad. He doesn't like dealing with things like this and he doesn't have his medication and he isn't answering his phone —"

Harper abruptly interrupted her. "Ruth, shut up and listen, I don't have time to deal with you right now and I need answers fast."

Ruth seemed taken aback, but shut her mouth.

"I'm looking for my partner, Detective Kingsley. Have you seen her?"

"Well yes, earlier. She was in the basement with Stan when he called and asked me to pick up his medication. I drove all the way to Costco. All that wasted gas for what? Nothing, I tell you. There was no prescription — "

"Ruth, just answer the question. Please, my partner is missing and I need to find her," Harper said exasperated.

"Stan was going to let her out. I don't know where she is. Now, my turn, who is that woman over there, what happened to her?" Ruth said.

"She was the next victim of the Fairy Tale Murderer. I'm sure you have heard of him, right?" Harper said.

"Why is she here? I don't understand."

"Stan is the Fairy Tale Murderer. He has taken my partner and I have to find her. I think it would be a good idea for you to go home for the day. This is going to take a while."

Ruth stood there in silence. It took a few seconds of contemplation before she really put it all together. Once the light bulb went off in her head she said, "Oh my, Stan is the bad man? I don't understand. He was such a quiet boy. I wouldn't think he had it in him. You don't think he is coming after me, do you? I hope he doesn't think it's my fault that he got caught. Do you think I need police protection? I need to call my husband. He is not going to be happy if we have to go into hiding. He never liked me working for this family. He always thought that they were weird, but I needed the job and..." Ruth looked up to see the Detective was walking away talking on his phone.

Chapter 81

Kate first felt the throbbing in her head as she tried to open her eyes. Her sense of smell was greatly weakened, between the blow to the face, the gas in the incinerator and the fall down the stairs. However, she could smell something familiar that she couldn't quite place. As all the pieces started falling into place, her recollection came back to her; she slowly opened her eyes. She immediately knew why the smell was familiar — she was in her own car.

She felt around to see how she was going to get out of this. Stan was driving her car while senselessly muttering. The minute Harper knew she was gone, he would put out a Bolo on her SUV, and track her car through the LoJack she reluctantly had installed. He would remember the conversation they had about how expensive it was, and how she thought it was silly. It was Harper that convinced her to do it, even though her argument was that Mexico was too far away.

She tried to calculate how long they were in the car, even though she had no idea where they were because she'd been knocked out in the beginning of the ride. She tried her best to loosen the tape. She was pretty sure her shoulder was dislocated, and she knew her nose was broken and her hands were cut up really bad.

She scrambled around as quietly as she could, trying to get to a tiny pocket knife she kept in the same ankle holster as her spare gun. With her hands tied behind her back, having her shoulder dislocated was almost a good thing, if it wasn't for the pain. It allowed her to stretch further towards her ankle.

She was almost there, feeling the bumpiness of the gravel road they just turned on. She knew her time was limited, so she scrambled even more so in an attempt to not have him overtake her a third time. She finally was able to reach the pocket knife, but before she could use it, the car came to a halt. She concealed it in her palm as she waited for Stan to open the hatch. She only hoped she would have an opportunity to use it to cut the tape, or better yet, Stan.

Chapter 82

Stan decided that he needed this to end quickly. He needed to move on and go underground, until this whole thing blew over. He also needed to get back to the house for his escape plan money, and then get out of town. Since he didn't have a backup plan for this situation he had decided to drive to the lake, dump her in the water and take off on foot.

By the time they found her car she would be dead, and he would be gone. No one would anticipate him having the audacity to go back to the house. However, that is exactly what he needed to execute his plan of action. The other hiding places would suffice but the longer he waited to get the money from the basement of his home the less likely he would be to actually get to it. With everyone looking for the Detective he figured he could slip in quickly and be off into the wind.

The beast within was enraged. He had to find another victim to feed it, even if he couldn't take his time to do it properly. He reached the lake and backed in close to the water. He took a big breath, headed to the back of the car and opened the hatch.

He looked down on her and smiled. "Now look at you, what a weak little girl you are. You can't even defend yourself, and you call yourself a police officer. Oh, right, I mean detective. But, not a very good one, good grief all those clues and you still couldn't save those women. You really should be ashamed!"

He felt relieved for her inability to talk back. However, her eyes were black as night and they cut through him, making him feel uneasy.

"Enough of that, I have places to be and people to see. I really have to be going before the Calvary comes for you. It is a pity that Cinderella never made it into my fairytale. She really was quite the princess," he said.

Her eyes were like daggers, and he had to force himself to not look away. He reached in, pulling her out by her feet. She fell to the ground and made a guttural sound, the air expelling from her lungs.

"Oh, sorry, did that hurt? It's the least I can do for all the pain and disappointment you have given me."

He pulled her to the water, waded in up to his chest and pushed her out in front of him into the lake. She was bound so well that she really couldn't move much in her attempt to free herself. He watched her struggle to keep her head above water, until finally, she went under. He was surprised that her eyes never changed. He never saw fear in them, only hatred, and he was happy to see her slip under out of sight.

He walked out of the water, knelt down, and intently watched, before he turned, and walked away towards the cover of the forest. He felt vindicated to have beaten her again, but he was almost sad to lose her as a rival. In the end though, he realized that she was just not worthy of him.

Once hitting the cover of the forest, he started running, looking for an escape route. Finally, after running for what felt like miles, he came to a camp site with the campers packing up their pickup truck. With the truck almost loaded, Stan was able to crawl into a small space and cover himself up. He didn't know where they were headed, but anywhere was better than where he was.

As Stan hid in the truck, he started formulating his next plan. He needed to sneak back into the house and retrieve his money. The question was more of when he could get in. He had to lay low until the next day; by then the place wouldn't be swarming with police.

So, he patiently waited and felt complete relief when he heard the motor start on the truck; he was heading out.

Chapter 83

Kate could feel herself going under water; once she was completely submersed she started cutting the tape with the knife. She was grateful for those days when she was on the swim team, and how she had a room full of medals. She prided herself on her ability to hold her breath under water. After swim practice, she would sit on the bottom of the pool cross legged with her eyes closed, relaxing. Some of her best clarity came at those times.

However, now her lungs burned as she held her breath and worked at the tape. The water was murky around her, as she felt herself once again becoming light headed. She tried working faster, but the longer she went without air, the more her lungs burned and the slower she worked.

Finally, with one last cut, her hands were free; she used all her strength despite her dislocated shoulder, to swim towards the light of the surface. She felt like a cat with 9 lives, as she refused to be overtaken and drown.

Just when she hit the surface enough to gasp some air, she heard splashing, coming towards her, expecting to see Stan. Instead, it was Harper.

"I got you, Kate! Hang in there, I am coming. You will be ok." Harper lifted her and carried her out of the water. Putting her on the ground, he hugged her tightly. "I told you to get LoJack. Good think you listened for once."

Kate was trembling from the cold water, the thought of the incinerator, Stan touching her and getting the best of her. Tears ran down her face from all the emotions of what has happened and she couldn't help but to still feel the pain of losing Kristen.

"This is the second time you have saved my life. How much am I going to owe you?" Kate sputtered.

"Bunches, Kate, bunches and bunches."

"Did they get him?" Kate said.

"Not yet. The good news is he is on the run and without resources. We will catch him Kate. It's just a matter of time." Harper pointed to the ambulance pulling up. "Your chariot waits."

Rather than arguing incessantly, she realized that she was not getting out of going to the hospital and went willingly. It wasn't until she got there that she discovered how bad off she was. It took a few hours of stitches, CAT scans, and an arm sling before she was settled in her room dozing off into some much needed sleep.

It wasn't long before she could feel someone take her hand and squeeze gently. She knew without opening her eyes that it was Harper. Fearful to lose control she kept her eyes closed and squeezed his hand back and muttered, "no stone unturned" as she raised a corner of her mouth with the best smile she could muster.

"Do you need anything?" Harper said.

Opening her eyes Kate looked at Harper and said "just to catch that bastard".

"We will, I promise Kate, we will". Harper said, "but first things first, you need to get some rest."

Kate remembered Marilyn and hoped that her injuries were minor. "How is Marilyn, is she here? I want to see her."

"Yes, she is here, when you are up to it she would love to meet you."

Without hesitation, Kate was grimacing as she sat up and started to get out of bed. Harper moved around next to her and took the IV bag and guided it along her side as she started walking out the room.

"I suppose you wouldn't listen if I told you this can wait?" He said.

Kate wasn't sure what she wanted to say to her, but it was comforting to see her alive. At least she was able to save one of the victims.

After seeing Marilyn, Harper said "Well, you have come this far, there is someone I would like you to meet as they headed for the elevator."

The elevator doors opened to the pediatric floor and Kate looked at Harper and smiled, she knew that there was a new addition to his family. Walking in the hospital room Harper took his free hand and put it on Kate's shoulder. She could see Megan laying there with a baby swaddled in her arms.

"I would like you to meet, Kristen," he said, beaming with all the pride a father should have. "She was born this morning, I hope you don't mind that we named her Kristen."

"Are you kidding? I am honored. This has been one hell of a day," Kate said as she covered her mouth, aware of her language. She pulled her hand away, and mouthed an apology followed by a big smile.

"I wouldn't expect anything else from Aunt Kate," he said, laughing.

"Harper, she is so beautiful. Just like Kristen. Thank you."

"Megan extended her free arm out to Kate and beckoned her over. After sitting on the bed Kate leaned down and kissed little Kristen on the forehead as she held back the tears of happiness.

Harper walked Kate back to her room while his wife and new baby daughter rested, he assumed she was too wounded for him to worry about her working for a couple days. She would most likely be released from the hospital the next day but for now Harper felt like she was safe and he started back to see Megan.

"Thank you Harper, for everything." Kate said as he started walking out the door. "One more thing, real quick, where are my guns?"

"You won't need them right now, remember? Rest Kate," Harper said and then pointed to the closet in the room. "They are in there, but I trust you will be good, for now, right? I have made arrangements for one of the officers to drop your car off to the hospital, they should deliver your keys to you as well. Abbey will be coming by and bringing you some fresh clothes in the morning. See, I have it all under control, all you have to do is rest and take care of yourself."

Kate replied with heavy eyes "Of course, you can trust me".

"I have heard that before, I mean it Kate, be good and get some rest. I will check in later." Harper walked through the door and down the hall.

Chapter 84

Kate slept hard for a good fifteen hours. By the time she awoke it was already late afternoon the next day. She couldn't believe she had lost so much time in the manhunt for Stan.   Even with all the bandages on her face, sling on her arm, and band aids on various parts of her body, she felt relatively good. She hadn't even noticed the nurses or the sounds of the hospital around her, they must have given her a sedative to knock her out.

Once she got herself up and out of bed, she could feel the aches in her body, and headed to the closet to get dressed. She knew she needed to get back to work and she was happy to see that Harper had left some clean clothes and her car keys for her with a note saying "come find me before you are released". Kate didn't want to bother Harper and his family, but more importantly she wanted to get back to work. She knew Stan was out there and she needed to find him.

After dressing she quietly snuck out of the hospital and used her car remote to find her SUV. Feeling guilty she drove out of the parking lot and straight for the nearest place to get coffee. After driving through for coffee and taking some aspirin from her glove compartment she starting feeling herself again. She headed home and took a quick shower while she tried to think where Stan would go. Taking the shower proved much more difficult with her dislocated shoulder, but the feeling of the hot steamy water was so relaxing. She let herself soak until the hot water started running out.

Getting dressed and heading back to her car, she knew exactly where she was headed. She needed to look through the yellow farmhouse for any clues as to where he may have gone.

The drive over to Stan's home felt like eternity and she could still smell the faint aroma of perspiration and rubber in her car. She hated that he was in her personal space, and she now understood why he hated her in his all those times.

Once arriving to the house she could see the sun was still up, and wouldn't descend for another hour or two. She really didn't want to be in that creepy house once it got dark. She also knew that Harper would have her head, if he knew what she was doing behind his back. She felt guilty about it, but it was something that she needed to do. She had to figure out a way of finding Stan and she didn't want to pull Harper away from his family.

Walking up to the porch for a second time, she ducked under the crime scene tape, and broke in. It didn't take long before she was inside and looking for clues.

Most everything was barren; there were many boxes that hadn't been unpacked and most of the furniture was old and outdated. The kitchen cabinets only had a few necessities and there was no paper trail of anything. She figured that he most likely had all those kinds of things at his office since he recently had moved in. She would check his office next if she couldn't find any clues here.

As she stood at the top of the wooden basement stairs she felt anxious and remembered her tumble before. She could still feel the pain of each step on various parts of her body. She moved down the creaking stairs, with her gun in her good hand, and the flashlight in the hand in the sling. It was hard to maneuver the flashlight, but she wasn't taking any chances, until she was positive she was alone.

Once down the steps, she surveyed the whole basement, and only then did she feel comfortable holstering her gun. It was a relief to use the good hand to hold the flashlight. She looked around at a basement as barren as the rest of the house. It was almost completely empty other than what she imagined was old boxes left by the previous people who lived there.

Kate just about gave up and headed for the mortuary when her flashlight caught a glimpse of something that looked off. It was very subtle, but suspicious enough for her to need a closer look. As she neared, she saw that there was a brick that was just a little different than the others. The true clue was the scattered mortar pieces on the floor. Putting the flashlight in her mouth to get a closer look, she pulled on the brick to find a little opening behind it. In the opening she saw a dusty bag. She moved a couple bricks surrounding the bag and pulled the bag out, careful not to disturb the mortar around the opening. Her heart raced as she opened the bag and saw lots of money, credit cards, identification and many other odds and ends. She knew she was looking at Stan's getaway bag, and she also knew that he would be coming back for it.

She carefully put the bag back in place, replaced the brick, and used her foot to move the fallen mortar away from the area. She then found herself running up the stairs, without pain due to the adrenaline, and out to her car. She grabbed for her phone to call Harper a couple times, but decided against it. This was her fight and she needed to end it herself for complete closure. She didn't want to take the chance of anyone making a scene and scaring Stan off. She was worried that she may have already scared him, but her gut told her he would be back, probably that very night.

Parking her car down an alley a few blocks away, she backtracked the least conspicuous way she could. She figured Stan was around or on his way and she didn't want him to catch her off guard. This was her turn and she wanted to be completely ready and in control of him this time.

Once back in the house, she went to a basement corner where she could see the stairs and the getaway bag, and waited. She pulled her phone out, turned it to vibrate, grabbed her gun, and rested her arm on her raised knees. She didn't mind waiting because she knew he would have to come; he needed the money to start a new life. He wouldn't just walk away.

The shadows of night set in and before long she sat in complete darkness waiting for Stan.

Chapter 85

Stan rode in the back of the pickup for a good hour before they made a stop. He could hear people talking as one started pumping gas. He waited until he heard them talking again before he attempted to peek out. He didn't want to get caught, not now when he was so close to being free again.

Looking out, he couldn't see anyone. He was pretty sure the campers were talking inside the cab of the truck. He cautiously climbed out the side and started walking away. Soon, he found himself in a residential neighborhood and looked at the street signs to figure out his location. He was relieved to still be in Topeka, but he knew he had a long way to go to get to the house. The sun had not set yet and he really wanted to be in the dark to move as quickly as he needed. As he walked through the neighborhood, he spotted a couple bikes in a yard, and quietly rolled one away and jumped on it. He rode quickly through the streets searching for a jacket or hat left out for him to grab.

After only a couple streets, he came across a house with laundry on a clothesline in the backyard. He jumped the fence and grabbed a hooded sweatshirt from the line. He was disappointed that it was royal blue with KU on it, since he really wanted something less noticeable. However, this was the best he could do, so he pulled the hood up and started riding for a place to safely spend the night. He figured the police would still be in and out this evening and he couldn't take the chance of being caught. After riding the bike for what seemed like hours, he had a brilliant idea.

He would sleep in Rapunzel's abandoned house. They would not suspect him to show up there, and it would be safe for him to sleep and wait until the next evening.

When he arrived at the house he found the same window open as before and he crawled inside. He didn't have to search long to find Rapunzel's bed. When he opened the door to her room, he could still smell her. He lay in her bed and rubbed his face into her pillow. He found himself falling asleep and reminiscing of his time with her.

Morning came quicker than he expected. Lucky for him, the house was still completely full. He rummaged through the cupboards in the kitchen looking for any type of food. Without much to pick from, he settled for a jar of peanut butter, a spoon, and stale saltines. It would do for now as he waited for the streetlights to come on and darkness to fall again.

Within seconds of the street lights coming on, he was back on the bike heading for the house. The closer he got, the darker the sky became. Stan kept riding even though his legs were burning from fatigue. He figured it was well after his neighbor's bed time, since she was old and not well. He parked the bike on the side of her garage and crept toward the side door to the kitchen. After looking around, he felt safe to get the hidden key under the rock, and open the back door. He walked in, quietly closed the door behind him, and headed for the wooden stairs to the basement. Starting his decent, he remembered how he kicked the detective down the stairs. It was killing him not to watch the news or read the paper and couldn't wait to read about the detective's fate.

The stairs creaked as he rushed down the steps and headed towards the wall with the loose bricks.

Chapter 86

Kate was settling in for a long night, when she heard a door open. Within a few seconds, she heard the creaking of the wooden stairs, she quietly stood up in the corner and waited for Stan to come to the wall. She couldn't wait to see the look on his face when he saw her pointing her gun at him.

Waiting until the right moment, she stepped forward and forced her bad arm to shine the flashlight, just as she had rehearsed over and over earlier. She knew exactly where the money was from her location and the second she heard the brick move she shined her flashlight on him and called out. "Put your hands up, Stan, or I will shoot you without hesitation. I think you know that I would rather have you dead than in jail. One way or another, you are mine," Kate said with fierce conviction.

With his back to her, Stan called out, "You wouldn't shoot an unarmed man, would you? Where is the sport in that, officer?" He laughed, before saying, "I guess I should have killed you myself when I had you in my grasp."

Kate inched toward him. "You are too much of a coward to kill me yourself, and you threw me in the lake because you're scared of me. You should be Stan because on even ground I will kick your ass."

"You have such big words for such a little lady. Oh, how confident you are with a gun in your hand. I have never needed a gun to get my princesses. They willing gave in to the beast, they wanted to be famous and I wanted to oblige them."

"Enough talk, I want you to turn around slowly and keep your hands in the air," Kate said, as she inched towards him.

"You should have seen how Kristen begged for her life, it was quite pathetic. At least the others were fighters. Kristen was weak. She cried like a baby as she begged for her life. She kept saying over and over, 'Help me Kate, please help me'. I had to kill her just to shut her up." Stan turned around and smiled.

It took everything she had not to shoot him, but she didn't want to take any chances of messing up the investigation. He was either going in with a good arrest, or he was going in a body bag. She tried not to let him get under her skin, but the words he said made her feel sick.

"Enough talk, Stan. Now I want you to get on the ground, on your stomach, arms out." She wasn't taking any chances. She was within a few feet of him and she raised her voice and repeated her previous statement with even more authority.

At that moment Stan jumped into the dark shadows. Kate searched for him with the flashlight and caught a glimpse of him, as he was headed right for her. She was able to get a round off before he tackled her, and she could hear him scream as the bullet made contact.

This time when he tackled her she didn't let go of her gun, despite the fact he was on top of her and trying to pin her down. She could feel her shoulder dislocate again as she heard a loud pop. It didn't stop Kate from striking him in the head repeatedly with the gun. She fired another round through his lower back, and felt the bullet come into her gut, as it went though him. This was enough to subdue him, and as he went limp on top of her, she heard him moaning. She wasn't sure where the first bullet struck, but she knew that he had been hit with two.

She struggled to roll him off of her. As she worked at it, he started laughing. Eventually, he was on his back and she was on her knees above him. She placed her gun squarely on his forehead and pressed down into his skin.

"I should just kill you right now. Why waste tax payer's money keeping scum like you alive. You make me sick. As Lauren's mom, Lisa, said,

I hope the gates of hell burn your soul for eternity." Kate could barely keep herself up.

"You mean Rapunzel? Oh, my sweet princess. Now she was a fighter, unlike your Kristen. Go ahead, detective, pull the trigger. I don't believe you have it in you. I win again." Stan started laughing again, as if he didn't feel the pain of the gunshot wounds.

For the first time in Kate's professional career, she knew she was going to break protocol and pull the trigger. She didn't even care if it meant the end of her career, or if she would go to jail. All she wanted was him dead.

She started to pull the trigger when she heard someone calling her name. It was Harper at the top of the stairs. She thought to herself, *damn you, Harper.*

"Kate, are you down here?"

Kate waited a few long seconds, the tears welling in her eyes.

Harper appeared with the beam of his flashlight filling up the room. The moment he spotted Kate with her gun on Stan's forehead, he stopped walking.

"Kate, you know he's not worth it. You can't shoot him, not like this. Please, just pull the gun away from his head. Let's just start with that." Harper slowly started walking towards her.

"Seriously, Harper, you show up here? Why did you have to come? I had this all under control," Kate said,

"Yes, officer, listen to the man. Pull the gun away. You don't have the guts to follow through," Stan said.

"Kate, don't listen to him. You have been trained not to be manipulated into doing things you will regret later." Harper crouched down next to her and reached out for her gun. He kept his gun on Stan, as he disarmed Kate.

"I told you I would win. See, you are too weak, just like Kristen," Stan said, just before Harper clocked him with his gun and knocked him out cold.

Once Harper called it in, he looked to Kate and smiled. "I should have known you couldn't be trusted."

"I should have known you would find me just in the nick of time, once again." Kate said while resting her head on Harper's arm as they silently waited for the police and paramedics to arrive.

This time her hospital visit and recovery was a little longer. However, she didn't mind, knowing that Stan was in custody and couldn't hurt anyone again. She was relieved that they took him to a different hospital and wondered if that wasn't Harper's doing. Maybe he was worried she would sneak out at night and finish what she started earlier.

She looked over at Harper sleeping in the chair next to her bed and she whispered, "Thanks again, what I owe you now?"

"Bunches and bunches, Kate, bunches and bunches. Glad to have you back." Without opening his eyes, Harper smiled.

Kate smiled back and closed her eyes again, for much needed sleep.

✦✦✦

June 15 came around so much sooner than she had expected. All Kate's physical injuries had healed, but the emotional ones had left deep scars. She still missed her Kristen, even though she had the peace of knowing her killer would serve a life sentence for his crimes. There was not enough time for him to serve, and she thought he deserved to have the same fate that his victims had. Kate wanted him to feel the same fear.

She drove to one of her favorite places in the country, where there were two ponds close to each other in a cow pasture. She knew this place well, because she had gone fishing there since she was young, and she remembered when night came, it would be far enough away from the city lights to see the fireflies.

She pulled up to the pond, and saw the sun just hovering over the horizon. She got out of the car and sat on a rock near the edge of the pond. Fish were making swirls in the water, frogs bellowing, and crickets singing in the distance. She closed her eyes and took it all in. The air was clean, and the world seemed clear again.

She opened her eyes and saw the sun inching below the horizon, and noticed the first firefly blinking in the distance. She walked deep into the trees, where darkness showed itself first, and waited. She opened the urn with Lisa's ashes while the fireflies lit up the darkness. She held the urn out sideways, away from her body with her arms extended, and started spinning. The fireflies continued blinking, and she continued twirling, until she felt like she was going to fall down from dizziness. She looked into the urn, saw that it was empty, and whispered into the wind, "No stone unturned."

288

www.ingramcontent.com/pod-product-compliance
Lightning Source LLC
Chambersburg PA
CBHW060542180626
46817CB00002B/686